A SUSPICIOUSLY SIMPLE HISTORY OF SCIENCE AND INVENTION

(without the boring bits)

John Farman is British and lives in South West London. He has an MA (Design) from the Royal College of Art and the lowest mark ever recorded in Maths O-level.

D0111631

A Suspiciously Simple History of Science & Invention

WITHOUT THE BORING BITS

....

JOHN FARMAN

(and drawn by him too)

PAN

First published 1991 by Piccadilly Press

This new edition published 1994 by Pan Macmillan Children's Books
a division of Pan Macmillan Publishers Limited
Cavaye Place London SW10 9PG
and Basingstoke

Associated companies throughout the world

ISBN 0–330–32807–7

1 3 5 7 9 8 6 4 2

A CIP catalogue record for this book is available from
the British Library

Phototypeset by Intype, London
Printed by Cox & Wyman Ltd, Reading, Berkshire

Contents

Introduction

Hands up all those who think science is boring. When I first started this book, I might have agreed with you. Come to that, if I was to go back to the chemistry and physics classes of my old school, I most certainly would. Subjects, however, are only as boring as their presentation, and so saying I've attempted to show you the history of science and invention in a way that would make most academics cringe.

Why did our ancestors discover and invent things in the first place? There are many reasons, but the foremost must be because they were fed up with what they already had. Most inventions and discoveries are just improvements on what already exists – a sort of fine-tuning. Sometimes, but this is rare, they are just plucked out of thin air. Often it is just a case of being in the right place at the right time (with the right brain).

As you read through the book you will notice that many periods are really buzzing science-wise (chapter 7 for instance), whereas others, like the Middle Ages, were so held back by mythical and religious mumbo-jumbo that the poor old scientists spent most of their time watching their backs, rather than getting on with the business in hand.

Sorry if you were hoping to find the history of mathematics within these pages, but, quite honestly, I couldn't find a single joke so I left it out.

I'm certain that my selection of what's important or not is open to criticism. All I can say is that I chose on the basis of what seemed relevant to our lives in the late twentieth century – so there!

Primarily this book is to be enjoyed. If, while you're having a giggle (hopefully), you happen to learn something, don't (as I often say) blame me.

CHAPTER I

Once Upon a Time Before There Were Scientists

Although the Greeks were probably the first to sit down and try to apply scientific and philosophical thought to the world around them, early man made some important discoveries. These were inventions that he tripped over by accident or as the need popped up.

Early Homos

Mr and Mrs H Habilis at some stage gave birth to a young Homo who became erectus, a much improved model. He was to fiddle around with his new stone tools for the next million and a half years. Progress was excruciatingly slow in those days. He hadn't abandoned wood and bone, however, and evidence from those dreadful early cave paintings showed that he was terrorizing his animal near-brothers and sisters with comparatively sophisticated weapons like slings, bows, spears, fish-hooks and the bolo (the stone with the hole).

Trial and Error

Notches and funny, man-made grooves on lumps of old rock and bone apparently tell us that these early chaps were using rudimentary mathematics. There are some amongst us, I must confess, that never got much further, but we can't blame them for that.

Homo erectus was now able to hunt and gather further afield, trudging his way through Asia and Europe. One finds travelling so much easier when one's not on one's hands and knees doesn't one?

Then an even newer model, Homo sapiens (like what we are), having been part-exchanged himself, promptly part-exchanged his old stone tool-kit, for a nice, new, shiny metal one. He also hunted and gathered further and wider, but must have been a pretty good swimmer, as he reached Australia 45,000 years ago.

Life must have been a bit haphazard for those early travellers. Maps and tourist guides, showing public conveniences, campsites and restaurants were not easily available. Often the plants and shrubs that they were forced to graze on looked quite scrummy but, one false mouthful, and they'd be pushing up daisies (if there were any). Having said that, it was only by fouling things up every five minutes that the poor devils learned anything anyway.

Pets

The next major advance came 10,000 years ago when man decided to stop chasing beasts every time he was hungry and start befriending them. Animals, being rather stupid, were well taken in and allowed themselves to be domesticated. They still ended up being eaten but it's always so much nicer to be consumed by someone you like and trust. Historians now reckon that our ancestors had known how to keep animals, and even raise crops, much earlier, but waited until the rapid rise in population forced them to do something about their ever-reducing supply of grub. Even modern hunter-gatherers know quite a bit about agriculture but they generally think it's too much like hard work.

Civilization Starts Here

After what we now call the agricultural revolution, small communities grew into societies and then became civilizations, with all the advantages that they bring (we won't mention the disadvantages). In Egypt, for instance, they were so fed up with the floods messing up their lives every year that a central state was necessary to get things straight. Although we know lots about the major civilizations like Egypt and Mesopotamia, little is known about how, why or when things got going over in places like China and India, but we can be fairly safe in assuming, however, that they were all up and running by 3000BC. We learned about the Egyptians from the clever Greeks, and the mighty Mesopotamians through the dear old Bible. Unfortunately, no one in the Western world knew a thing about life over in the Americas until they got themselves discovered in the fifteenth century. Without any help from 'abroad' they'd domesticated their own plants and animals and used quite sophisticated medical skills for mummification and trephining, which was drilling holes in heads to cure headaches. (Gives me a headache just thinking about it.) The Mayas of South America developed numerical skills that we're only just beginning to understand now.

ASTRONOMY

Even the most primitive of our ancestors must have noticed the stars moving about quite a bit – so, having not much else to look at of an evening, they probably sat around theorizing. Much later, after the agricultural revolution, there were some real advancements in astronomy. Stonehenge is now reckoned by some people to have been some kind of observatory (albeit draughty), though it's clear they could have really done with a nice telescope or two. The great pyramids were built dead accurately on north to south lines which proves that someone must have known something about the sun, moon and stars. Planting crops had always been a bit haphazard, to say the least, so they had to develop a 365 day calendar to know where they were, planting-wise (it takes the Earth 365 days to make a full turn on its axis). Eventually eclipses were predicted, sundials constructed, and the stars catalogued for the use of astrologers. This probably meant that they had to suffer the likes of Russell Grant even in those days. Some things never evolve.

GREAT, BUT COULD YOU MOVE IT ROUND A BIT?

PYRAMID SALES INC.

Some Great Breakthroughs in Astronomy

9000–8000BC: A bone, found in what is now Zaire, and marked with what looked like a crude record of months and lunar phases, probably dated back to this time.

5000–4000BC: The Egyptian calendar, based on 365 days, and starting with the day that Sirius (the Dog Star) rose in line with the sun was instituted as early as 4241BC. This told them when to put their macs on, as it coincided with the annual flood.

2600–2500BC: A Chinese person stuck a straight stick in the ground and worked out that the sun's shadow got to roughly the same place every day. It was the first sundial. Unfortunately, it was not velly good at night.

1800–1750BC: Star catalogues (no! they weren't for sale), planetary records were started in Babylonia.

1500–1451BC: Thutmosis III erected Cleopatra's Needle in Heliopolis as a huge sundial. It now stands on the north bank of the Thames in London, very close to Big Ben (which is a jolly sight easier to tell the time by).

800–750BC: The sun got turned off in Babylonia and they recorded the first solar eclipse.

MEDICINE AND LIFE SCIENCE

Little seems to be said about biological and medical knowledge at this time, but it's safe to say that if mummification was going on in South America and Egypt, they at least must have known a fair bit. It stands to reason that if you're continually whipping out the internal organs of your fellow stiffs, you're going to get to know what these bits look like and even what some of them do. There was no National Health or BUPA but I don't think the deal was that bad. A fair price for successful surgery seemed to range from between 2 to 10 shekels. If it went wrong the doctor responsible would have his hands cut off – and the patient presumably got his money back (if he was still around to collect it). I'm sure if that was still going on, there'd be quite a lot fewer practising surgeons around (particularly on the piano). Ancient manuals show that their surgical practices were quite sensible and their knowledge of drugs could teach us a few things today.

They might have been getting quite sharp at cutting ex-people up, but their treatment of disease was a bit on the hit-and-miss side. This wasn't helped by the involvement of religion. It was thought that each part of the body had its own god (the god of noses?), and every god had its own priest. I suppose if you got sick in those days, you might expect loads of priests at your bedside. I don't know which is worse.

At the Doctor's

Though we suppose that many early cultures knew quite a lot about herbal cures and primitive surgery, the Egyptians were the first to think of writing it down. Egyptian healers became the best in the world, and sick people turned up in their waiting-rooms from all over the Middle East and later the Mediterranean, providing they had the cash to pay for it. Like America now (and England soon) medicine became easily available – at a price.

Injuries were treated a little more intelligently. They often put mouldy bread on open wounds making use of the penicillin that hadn't been discovered yet. Castor oil was taken to help them sh ... shake off constipation, and poppy juice to relieve pain. Radishes, onions and loads of garlic were given to the thousands of poor devils that built the pyramids, as the priests believed their antibiotic properties would ward off disease. I think it's more likely that it kept them from getting too close to each other, hindering any chance of rebellion. Although modern doctors and herbalists agree there might have been something in these practices, nobody sees a lot of point in their other habit of giving the poor devils Nile mud, dung and urine. It certainly wouldn't go down a storm with today's stroppy building workers. They seem to prefer six pints of lager and a meat pie. Come to that, they might now have gone for the Egyptian doctors' other habit of mixing medicines with beer or wine. It might not cure you, but if you're going to die you might as well die happy.

Egyptian medicine went into decline around 1200BC (are you surprised) but its influence carried on until well after Egypt became Roman in 30BC.

Some Great Breakthroughs in Medicine and Life Science

10,000–9000BC: The dog was made to behave itself for the first time, being domesticated in Mesopotamia (Iraq) and Canaan (Israel). Sad really; one minute it was running around with its mates, willy nilly, having a good time, and the next it's one walk a day to the end of the street and back.

9000–8000BC: Goats and sheep were domesticated in Persia and Afghanistan. Attacks by flocks of ferocious sheep were severely curtailed.

8000–7000BC: It was around this time that a lot of the vegetables that we can find every day in the corner shop, were domesticated. Potatoes were finally captured and eaten in Peru, followed by beans (not baked) and rice in Indonesia. Farmers in the Nile valley, instead of pulling their hair out every time their land flooded, put it to good use and invented flood irrigation.

7000–6000BC: The Chinese discovered that, although a bit smelly on the outside, pigs tasted pretty good. There seems to be no record, however, of the first sausage. Nobody seems to know whether the chicken or its egg were discovered first, but either way, they were domesticated in southern Asia. The cow was shortly to follow them into captivity. He (or should I say she) had, for the first time, to suffer the indignity of being milked every five minutes. Still, it was nice to know that you had one other function apart from being eaten or, even worse, worn.

Fab things like sugar cane, bananas, coconuts and yams were grown in New Guinea and Indonesia. They now had all the ingredients for banana splits and milk shakes.

Then one of the great dates in the history of science and invention. A watershed in human development. The Turks discovered – wait for it – macaroni. Shame they weren't mates with the Jordanians who'd just invented woven baskets. They could have put their macaroni in them.

Funny-looking pears called avocados were grown in Mexico while an enterprising Indian (up India way) finally climbed up a local palm tree to see what the strange, sticky fruit tasted like. Sorry, I don't know the exact date.

Meanwhile, back in the Ukraine, some guy decided to find out whether horses minded if you sat on their backs or, even better, would let you tie them to that unused cart (waiting for wheels) in the garage. His personal horse, being a bit on the gullible side, allowed this to happen and so sentenced all his species to a lifetime of drudgery serving the human race. Mind you, there was worse to come, indignity-wise, as anyone who's seen a dressage competition or circus must agree.

4000–3000BC: The juice from squashed grapes was left hanging around for a while in Turkestan. When they finally got round to drinking this old fermented grape juice (wine), they found that it made them giggle and eventually fall over. Meanwhile, over in Mesopotamia, the first lager louts were created, owing to the invention of beer.

The poor old Cretans, not to be outdone, were squeezing their olives. Though the oil was pretty disgusting to drink, they found it rather pleasant to cook with, and sprinkle on their salads.

Apparently you could get a nice cup of tea in China around this time. It seems the Emperor Shang Yeng was sitting in his backyard drinking his afternoon cup of hot water (he and his poor subjects weren't allowed anything else), when some leaves fell off a branch above and landed in his cup. The Emperor was delighted with the new aromatic drink. I dread to think what we might be drinking if a bird had been sitting up there.

The first records of domestic cats start here with the soppy old ancient Egyptians. It was only, believe it or not, a hundred years ago that specific breeds developed.

2000–1800BC: Paddy culture of rice occurred in south-east Asia. Paddy fields were constantly flooded, and the poor rice collectors had to (and still do) spend all their days up to their knees in muddy water, paddy paddling.

Physicians formed a proper medical group in Babylon and Syria, but their practice was based largely on astrology and a belief in demons.

The strange practice of sticking needles into people to make them feel better (acupuncture) was invented by the Chinese. The theory goes like this. Disease is caused by a disruption to the flow of energy. This can be remedied by action taken on one or more points along the meridians, or pathways, along which energy shoots round the body by vibration. The action turns out to be a sharp needle inserted into one of these points, which apparently does the trick.

1550–1500BC: A papyrus was found from this date describing 700 medications and loads of diets and fasts. They also seemed to have the first massage parlours and knew a bit about hypnotism.

1000–950BC: The dreaded porridge looms. Oats were domesticated in Central Europe.

TECHNOLOGY

When agriculture had its revolution, technology began to develop fast. It was found that metal could be melted down and made into other forms. The wheel was used, at first, flat, for throwing pottery; and on its side, for sticking under carts to make them go faster. The Egyptians, desperate to tell everyone how clever they were, wrote anything and everything down on whatever they could find. First it was clay bricks, then reeds (papyrus) and finally cows – or should I say cow-skin (parchment).

Building techniques improved no end, especially after practising on those weird, triangular-shaped stone heaps, called pyramids. The Egyptians then went on to knock up some rather nifty palaces and temples. Standard weights and measures made life a lot easier, as did money, which replaced animal, corn (and sometimes wife) swapping. The need to know what time it was led to the development of sundials and water clocks.

Early Measures

Before tape measures, rulers or scales, the ancients managed to measure short lengths, area, volume and weight moderately accurately. Long distances, on the other hand, seemed to be calculated by how long it took someone to get somewhere. One can only presume that a fast walker would say that somewhere was much closer than someone with a bad leg. An acre was described as the area that you could plough in a day. Small measures were based on parts of the body (no lewd comments please!). For instance, an inch was reckoned to be the equivalent of the last joint of the thumb; and the yard, the distance between the end of the nose and the tip of the fingers with the right arm outstretched (why the right arm?). One would imagine that an Egyptian yard would be slightly shorter than a Chinese yard, as Egyptians have much longer noses. When it eventually occurred to

← (yard →

the ancients that people differ in size, they took the measurements off a favoured monarch. These early standard measures were always getting lost in wars, which were all the rage in those days.

Some Great Breakthroughs in Technology

100,000BC: An amorous Hungarian whipped off the front tooth of a passing mammoth, and carved a bracelet for his girlfriend. I doubt that she was that impressed as it was the first jewellery ever seen.

79,000BC: For the last few thousand years, our ancestors had just sat around till dark and then grudgingly gone to bed (not that they had any). Then someone invented a lamp, fuelled by animal fat with a wick made of moss. Sophisticated cave life was taking shape.

30,000BC: Early man was beginning to find it necessary to count all his possessions (tools, lamps, bracelets, wives etc.). The first record of counting, as such, was found on a wolf's leg-bone in France. It had fifty-five cuts, arranged in groups of five. No one knows exactly what they represented. Maybe it was the number of three-legged wolves around.

25,000–20,000BC: Being a mammoth must have been a bit 'iffy'

to say the least in those days. Someone in Poland threw away an unwanted tusk and found that it flew in a circle and came back. He had inadvertently invented the boomerang. He and his chums kept it secret for 13,000 years when an enterprising Polish boomerang salesman probably flogged the idea to some aborigines in Australia.

A French caveperson, bored with walking around in filthy old animal skins draped over his or her shoulders, developed a bone needle. French fashion was born, and soon they were able to knock up chic little outfits for family and friends. Believe it or not, the first tailored garments were made by the Russians, not generally regarded as leaders in haute couture.

10,000–9000BC: Time to brighten up the living room again. In Lascaux (South of France) paintings of animals were found on cave walls. Imagine having to live with them year in and year out. At least we've learned to put those awful modern pictures of galloping horses and cross elephants in frames – so that we can chuck them away when sick of the sight of them. It's also interesting to note that these ancient paintings showed use of the first proper paint ever recorded. Pigments like manganese oxides were mixed with animal fats or urine and put on the walls by use of frayed sticks, fur or blowpipes (the first aerosol?). I must admit, the idea of blowing urine-based paint on the walls doesn't really thrill me that much.

The first ever map was found in Russia, carved on a bit of bone and, conveniently, bang in the middle of the area it described. People were beginning to wander further afield in those days, so they probably made maps as they went along (to help them get back?).

In a place called Jericho (a town in Israeli-occupied Jordan), builders started using sun-dried bricks to build houses. Unfortunately, they couldn't wait for mortar to be invented so the buildings had a nasty tendency to fall over. This could account for the line in the old hymn in which Joshua fought the battle of Jericho – 'and the walls came tumbling down'.

6000–5000BC: Chinchorro Indians, from Chile, found a way of preserving their parents by embalming them and then wrapping them up in cloth. They were then called mummies (why not daddies?).

5000–4000BC: Those clever old Mesopotamians worked out that if you tie a bit of cloth onto a tall stick and shove it in the middle of your boat, it moves along quite nicely without you having to do a thing.

4000–3000BC: In China the first plough, called an 'ard', was invented. It wasn't very good so the cattle found it quite 'ard to pull.

The Chinese concocted ink out of smoke, glue and 'aromatic substances'. Smelly ink?

After working with this ink, the scribes probably needed to wash their hands. Good news – soap had just been invented. Bad news – it was in Mesopotamia.

The Egyptians who'd started using copper a thousand or so years before, started smelting (melting) silver and gold which they liked much better.

The earliest shoes to be found were Egyptian and made of papyrus. No one distinguished between the left and the right foot until the 11th century AD.

Mirrors of polished metal were first used in Egypt. Just to make sure they could use them at night, they also invented candles.

The Sumerians developed a way of filling teeth instead of yanking them out. Most history books credit the Muslim physician (dentists weren't invented yet) Abu Zakariya with the invention in the eighth century. But now you know better.

2900–2800BC: In Egypt they built the Great Pyramid of Cheops at Giza for Pharaoh Cheops (see daft names for pharaohs), while in England, several years later, all we could manage was a boring old pile of rocks called Stonehenge.

The Great Pyramid was a bit labour intensive, as it took 200,000 men thirty years to knock up. It's interesting to note that rope with equally spaced knots was used as the first accurate measuring device.

2700–2600BC: While Huang-ti was busying himself being Emperor of China, Mrs Huang-ti spent much of her time undressing silkworms (strange woman) and in so doing, inventing silk.

2100–2000BC: The oldest known standard of length was based on the foot (yes, I said foot) of the statue of the ruler Gudea of Lagash. It was 10.41ins long (size 7?) and divided into sixteen parts.

Some of the very first buttons were found in Scotland. It beats me what they had to button up in those pre-kilt days.

2000–1800BC: There is a lot of support for evidence that the very first brassieres were worn by female gymnasts in ancient Rome (and who can blame them).

Most people think that the Romans were the first to sort out their ablutions. Wrong! The Cretan Palace of Minos not only had bathrooms, but the first internal water supply. Both Greek and Roman baths, however, were made of silver or marble. Funny, when you think that so much later, in the Middle Ages, they had to put up with rotten old wooden tubs.

Mathematicians worked out a theorem which, later, jammy old Pythagoras got the credit for. This, as you well know, goes like this: The squaw on the hippopotamus is equal to the sum of the squaws on the other two hides. Or . . . the square on the hypotenuse of a right-angled triangle equals the sum of the squares on the other two sides.

1000–950BC: Don't go thinking that the game of poker was invented by American gangsters. It was developed in Persia at this time and was called 'AS'. It was brought back to Europe by the Crusaders along with a lemon.

Lemons, in fact, were grown first by the Chinese, but were popularized by the Romans who called them the 'Apples of the Mede'. They were used extensively for medicinal purposes, as an antidote to poisons and as an insect repellent.

Babylonian Queen Semiramis, with a little help from her slave friends, built the first tunnel under a river (the Euphrates) in order to get to the Temple of Jupiter from her palace on Sundays without having to wet her feet.

....

CHAPTER 2

New Thoughts in Old Heads – 600–529BC

Mention Greek civilization to most people, and they instantly think of kebabs, Demis Roussos, and foul coffee that you can stand your spoon up in. It might interest you to know that back in the sixth century BC, a civilization began that was to transform the development of what we call science. Up to this time, science had gone hand in hand with myth and religion, especially in Egypt and Babylonia. The Greeks, bless them, never did go a bundle on the religious version of Creation and, being dead practical, attempted to unlock the Earth's many secrets by reasoning and observation.

So, what got your average Greek philosopher out of bed in the morning? It was the need to know, understand and, therefore, try to come up with better theories than what he'd been fed before. This was OK at first but, after a while, the leaders of the established religions started getting their togas in a twist. Even some of the big names had to tread carefully to avoid being exiled (or worse).

Their life got a bit easier by the fourth century BC – remember the centuries go backwards as we get towards the birth of Christ – but now the Greeks were beginning to argue amongst themselves (typical) about fundamental issues. Atomists like Leucippus and Democritus had always believed reality to be only a matter of matter, whereas the Pythagoreans thought the universe should be viewed in form and number. Many of the famous philosophers of the time are still renowned today. Men like:

Hippocrates 460–377BC

Hippocrates is generally regarded as the 'father of medicine'. He hit the headlines (except there weren't any) by being the first physician to ease medicine away from the clutches of the gods and, much more to the point, from magic. He thought it not a bad idea actually to examine the patient, instead of just praying for him or, worse, casting spells. The significance of this was enormous. Let's face it, if it wasn't for old Hippocrates and his chums we could have the likes of The Great Presto heading our hospitals.

Hippocrates was always going on about the human body's ability to heal itself without help from above, and refused to believe that nasty diseases like epilepsy were sent by some grumpy god. Remarkably, he recorded all his failures as well as successes, which became the backbone of proper scientific research. His idea that patients should be studied in their whole environment is something that has relatively recently come back into fashion.

His greatest hit, the 'Hippocratic oath', is now believed only to have been attributed to him. Never mind, it goes as follows:

'Whatsoever house I enter, there will I go for the benefit of the sick [suppose that rules out dinner with friends], refraining from all wrong-doing and corruption, especially from any act of seduction, male or female [?], of bond or free. Whatever things I see or hear concerning the life of men, in my attendance of the sick or even part therefore, which ought not to be noised abroad, I will keep silence thereon, counting such things to be as sacred texts.'

This means, roughly, that if you're a doctor you mustn't fiddle around with your patients (outside the job that is) and if you find out any juicy gossip, keep it to yourself.

Aristotle 384–322BC

Athens, by this time, had become the centre of learning and all the boffins had moved there. One of the stars was a chap called Aristotle who many think was the father of science, instead of Galileo who came along centuries later. Mind you I don't suppose science gave a damn who its father was.

Most scientists would argue old Aristotle was mega-important in the development of Western civilization. He wrote on every known field of knowledge and was probably the first to study pure science in a modern investigative way. The son of a doctor, Aristotle was born in northern Greece. Having always been on the bright side he was, at seventeen, taught by Plato, who'd in turn been taught by Socrates, who'd started the ball rolling with his Socratic method. The gist of this method when you boiled it right down, was: realize how important you are; don't take anything at face value; get to the truth by asking your own questions.

When in his early forties, Aristotle landed a fab job teaching a lad called Alexander (son of Philip II) who was later to become 'Great'. It was Alexander the Great who spread Greek scientific ideas from Greece to India. This might not seem that impressive to you, but at the time it was the only bit of the world they knew about.

C'MON ALEX YOU'RE NOT GREAT YET.

Unfortunately, it would take another book to go through everything Aristotle achieved, but it is fair to say he founded the sciences of logic, physics, biology and humanities. After lunch he gathered facts about phenomena in an orderly and systematic way, so inventing the encyclopedia.

His main belief was that everything in nature has its place. Why do fish swim in water? Why do stones fall to the ground? Why are some men born rich and others skint? He answered all questions with the same phrase — 'because it's their nature'. Sounds like he'd have made a good Tory politician.

Aristotle, however, didn't approve of atoms. If matter was composed of atoms, he said, then they must have space between them. These spaces must be vacuums and he didn't believe in vacuums. Because he was taken so seriously by the rest of his philosopher mates, atoms went completely out of fashion.

Archimedes 287–212BC

Now some people are bright and others, like Archimedes, make everyone else look plain stupid. He lived practically all his life in Syracuse, a Greek colony on the island of Sicily, where he was best mates with its ruler called Hiero II. Archimedes, then a mathematician, was often asked by his friend to help him out with various problems. One day Hiero told him that he doubted his goldsmith's honesty and wondered whether Archie could fathom a way of finding out whether his flash new crown was pure gold or not. Poor Archimedes pondered to no avail for several days until one day while stepping into a long-needed bath he realized that for every bit (yes, every bit) of his body that went in, an equal amount of water went out. He then invented streaking by dashing into the street wearing nothing but a grin from ear to ear, yelling 'Eureka!' (I've discovered it).

EUREKA!

Back indoors he put Hiero's crown in the bath and measured the water it displaced. Then he weighed the crown and put an equal amount of pure gold in the water which should have displaced the same amount of water as the crown. However, the crown had displaced more water proving that other metals, less dense than gold, had been added. Everyone was delighted with the discovery except perhaps the goldsmith who soon didn't have a head to put anything on – never mind a crown.

Archimedes went on to apply his new principle to all other kinds of water displacement – very useful when designing ships. Then he invented levers and catapults.

Dodgy Times For Science

When the Roman Empire fell in AD 407, Aristotle's ideas went with it, not to be re-introduced until the twelfth century. From 146BC, Rome dominated most of the Mediterranean including Greece itself. Although the Romans didn't specifically have a go at the scientists, they didn't help them much either. Greek science continued to flourish mostly in Egypt, which Rome hadn't managed to get its hands on. After the Roman Empire most of the Greek world got absorbed into the Byzantine Empire, and things went from bad to worse for the poor old philosophers and scientists. The rise of the Christian Church didn't exactly help either. For starters a Church that was always threatening the end of the world as punishment for a naughty population, as it did then, is hardly likely to encourage investigation into how the universe really worked. Also they reckoned that all this new-fangled scientific knowledge would be of little use when you got to heaven (and even less in the other place!).

It even reached the point where secular knowledge and science became associated with heathenism, leading to incidents like the burning of the famous library of the Temple of Serapis in Alexandria in 415. This, would you believe, was instigated by St Cyril, the Bishop of Alexandria. Mind you, how could you ever trust a saint called Cyril.

ASTRONOMY

Unlike the Babylonians who'd got it into their heads that the planets were gods, the Greeks, as you might now suspect, weren't having any of it. Mind you, in some ways their ideas were almost as whacky, as they believed that the celestial bodies were something to do with the weather. Their weather forecasts must have been a hoot (Michael Fish take note). They weren't that interested in accurate observations so their calendar was a right mess. Much worse, every Greek city kept its time differently. Just imagine how many times they must have had to change their watches and the clocks in their cars.

They were fascinated with the universe and how it was ordered, but all the great philosophers had different (and weird) ideas. Thales for instance assumed Earth was floating in a huge sea. Anaximander believed that the Earth was a circular disc suspended in space and that the stars were attached to the inside of a sphere which rotated around it. The Pythagoreans believed we rotated round a huge fire, but didn't connect it with the sun.

Aristotle, clever as he might have been, reckoned that the Earth was the centre of the universe, while Aristarchus was laughed out of court for suggesting that the sun was the centre of the universe, and that all the planets including Earth, revolved around it.

Aristotle's version won and was firmly believed until the Renaissance and Copernicus.

Some Great Breakthroughs in Astronomy 600BC–AD529

590–580BC: The first known date in history can be pinpointed as May 28, 585BC. The event was a battle between the Medes and the Lydians. What's so special about a boring old battle? I hear you ask. Well, this one was different. One of the first recorded eclipses of the sun occurred. It so frightened the wits out of both sides, that they forgot to carry on fighting.

440–430BC: Meton (of Athens) developed the Metonic cycle. This wasn't a new means of transport, but a nineteen-year period in which the sun and moon seemed to come together when viewed from the Earth. This can be used to predict eclipses and also forms the basis for the Jewish and Greek calendars.

410–400BC: The first horoscopes, based on the positions of the planets at the time of birth, were available in Chaldea.

380–370BC: Greek philosopher Democritus, pointed out that the Milky Way consisted of loads of teeny weeny stars, that the moon was like the Earth and, incredibly, that matter (including yours truly) is composed of atoms.

360–350BC: Those clever Chinese reported the first supernova, though they didn't know what it was. (See p.00 when we found out).

300–290BC: Chinese astronomers Shih Shen, Gan De and Wu Xien compiled star maps that would be used for hundreds of years. They were all put together in AD305.

Conon, the Greek mathematician (not destroyer), is remembered for convincing his boss, Berenice, Queen of Egypt, that her hair, which had been cut off and dedicated to the gods, had not  been stolen but had become the constellation Coma Berenices. If she believed that, she'd believe anything.

270–260BC: It was at this time that Aristarchus of Samos first challenged Aristotle by saying that the dear old sun was in the middle of our solar system.

240–230BC: Halley's Comet was spotted for the first time over China. It will pop up again and again in this book.

Eratosthenes of Cyrene ever so cleverly measures the world's circumference. He doesn't do half badly either with a figure of 28,500 miles (it's really 24,822 miles).

140–130BC: Poseidonius, a Greek philosopher, calculated the Earth's circumference wrongly. This rather irritated Chris Columbus 1500 years later who believed Asia to be much closer to Europe than it really was. This, of course, is crucial in the exploring business if you're trying to work out how much grub to take on a trip.

130–120BC: Hipparchus now waited for a total eclipse of the sun to work out the size of the moon. I'd have thought it would have been too dark to work out anything.

AD140–150: Ptolemy wrote a manuscript which was to become the most important text on astronomy throughout the Middle Ages. It's safe to say that we can blame this document for scientists continuing to believe that the planets revolved round the Earth.

AD490–500:   Aryabhata, an Indian, has another go at the Greek measurements of the solar system. Although he put forward the idea that the Earth rotates, he never doubted Ptolemy's daft theories.

LIFE SCIENCES

Aristotle was the undisputed father of life sciences. He made it his job to classify all the plants and beasts he could get his hands on. He divided his animals into those with blood systems and those without. Those in the first group he further divided into fish, amphibians, reptiles, birds and mammals. It's not inconceivable that he'd have supported Darwin's theory of evolution had he been around at the time.

Before Aristotle, the Greeks believed that women's role in birth was much the same as the relationship of earth to a seed. Man supplied the seed and she was just a convenient receptacle to put it in. (I bet Greek feminists loved this.) Aristotle discovered the embryo and realized that in procreation the contribution of the mum, who actually carried the egg, was just as great, if not much greater, than that of the dad, who only has to fertilize it. I'm sure a woman who'd been pregnant for eight and a half months might just agree.

Alcmaeon vied with Hippocrates as the founder of medicine – I suppose because he was the first to suggest that the brain is top organ in the human body. He also discovered the optical nerve (what a nerve). It was later in Rome that another 'great' called Galen, was to make his mark. He wasn't that popular with animals, as he was always cutting them up. This was because he wasn't allowed to use human beings. His often wrong theories were not disputed for over 1500 years.

Some Great Breakthroughs in Life Science 600BC–AD529

570–561BC: Xenophanes, a Greek philosopher, was understandably a bit puzzled when he found seashells on the top of a mountain. Unlike his mates, who thought the clever crustaceans must have either walked or slithered there, he speculated that the surface of the Earth must have risen and fallen in the past. Nice thinking, Xenophanes!

I CAN EVEN HEAR THE SEA

520–510BC: A chap named Anaximander, writing about nature, suggested that all life began grovelling about in slime, eventually crawling out to drier places. This, of course, is the rather unscientific beginning of the theory of evolution, but I bet Charles Darwin would have something to say about that. Anaximander, unfortunately, flushed with the success of his theory, went on to say that humans originated from the sea and that the first ones must have looked fish-like. Come to that, my old biology teacher looked a bit fishy. I wonder . . .

500–490BC: Greek physician and philosopher, Alcmaeon of Croton, is the first person ever to dissect his fellow man (for non-criminal purposes).

500–491BC: Navigator Hanno of Carthage, rushed home, after having seen something big, hairy and extremely unpleasant down Africa way. It was probably the first sighting of a gorilla. All suggestions of what else it might have been will be carefully considered. Come to that, it was probably the gorilla's first sighting of a navigator.

450–440BC: Now here is something that really has got a lot to answer for. Greek philosopher Empedocles gets a few Brownie points for recognizing that the heart is the centre of the blood system, but then goes on to say that it is the centre of the emotions.

25

Centuries later we're still having to endure stupid love songs about hearts flying, breaking, crying and heaven knows what-ing. I don't ♥ Empedocles.

Poor old Empedocles, fed up with the gods not asking him to join them, jumped down the mouth of the volcano Mount Etna and was never seen again. Talk about delusions of grandeur.

430–404BC: A very nasty plague broke out during the Peloponnesian War between Athens and Sparta. Try as they might, scientists failed to work out what it was. And they still don't know.

350–340BC: Aristotle puts 500 animals in eight classes (sounds like my old school).

340–330BC: Praxagoras, another Greek physician, realized that there was a difference between veins and arteries but believed that arteries were just hollow tubes carrying air. Back to the surgery, doc.

300–290BC: Epicurus announced that organs develop through exercise and weaken when not used. There are a lot of us who are living proof of this theory.

The great Greek act Herophilus of Chalcedon performed public dissections of the liver, spleen and retina and lots of other bits and pieces. Could be a nice little earner for the National Health Service!

130–120BC: Greek physician Asclepiades treated disease with diets, baths and, would you believe – exercise. His success rate was rather poor.

100–90BC: The Chinese finally got blood circulation right, at least righter than anyone before William Harvey in 1628.

AD10–20: Thaddeus wrote a book on the virtues of alcohol in medicine. What a wonderful excuse for a drink.

AD 50–60: Pliny the Elder (elder than whom?) wrote 37 volumes summarizing all that was known about astronomy, geography, and zoology (including daft legendary monsters), cribbed from other sources. I wonder what he did with the rest of the week. Pliny died rather tragically aged 77 when he sniffed too much of the erupting volcano Vesuvius, which he was studying.

AD 170–180: Galen of Pergamum, the famous Greek physician, took the first pulses as a diagnostic aid.

PHYSICAL SCIENCE

Greek natural philosophers found progress very slow at first. To find out what was the matter, they had to find out what matter was. Some believed that water was the main constituent, while others thought it was fire or air. Nobody really rated old Democritus's whacky idea that matter was composed of atoms, although in retrospect they'd have kicked themselves.

The main trouble was that those early Greeks would sit around yapping about all these ideas instead of getting out to observe and experiment. Strange as it might seem, however, many of their uninformed speculations were much later proved to be not far off the mark.

Their theories about motion were all a bit off the wall, however, mostly following Aristotle's daft notion that motion is caused by each object striving to reach its natural place. If you take that premise to its logical conclusion, it means that if you get something nicked it will eventually make its own way home. Nice one, Aristotle!

Some Great Breakthroughs in Physical Science 600BC–AD529

480–471BC: Protagoras believed that sensory perceptions were all that exist, which meant that reality must be different from one person to another. Brilliant! I'll just get into my chicken and go for a drive.

450–440BC: Empedocles got the idea of elements nearly right, and his choice of fire, air, earth and water as the four elements was to bedevil science for 2,000 years (and isn't quite dead yet). He also said (rather hilariously) that they can only be changed by love or strife.

430–421BC: The optical telegraph was invented. It sounds pretty flash, but don't get too excited. It was just a series of bonfires used to signal from hilltop to hilltop. It seems so obvious, but again, someone had to think of it first.

270–260BC: Zou Yan, a Chinese philosopher, stated that there were five elements – water, metal, wood, fire and earth. What about noodles?

10BC–BIRTH OF CHRIST: A Roman geographer had a great theory that the zone around the equator was so hot that people couldn't cross it to reach the southern side where a whole load of nasty strangers lived. Mind you . . .

AD100–109: Hero of Alexandria discovered that air expanded with heat. He also wrote about simple machines which he'd invented, like the very first coin-operated slot machine for dishing out holy water.

TECHNOLOGY

Who needs technology when you've got slaves? This had been the attitude up to this period. The Greeks managed to get to grips with smelting of iron, because they needed it to make weapons, and in Alexandria there was generally a bit more interest in technology probably because of the Egyptian influence. Ctesibius probably started their school of engineering (a sort of Greek tech.) and was responsible for such wonders as the force pump, a water organ (water music?) and mechanical water clocks. Hero of Alexandria was fiddling around with steam engines and Archimedes, who was brill at applying science to technology, was busy with his screw – a device for lifting water in irrigation systems.

The best bit about slaves was that they were terrific if you wanted to build big things like aqueducts and bridges. Although the Romans are usually remembered for this sort of thing, it must be said that it was the Greeks who managed to build the first water-carrying tunnel through a mountain.

Some Great Breakthroughs in Technology 600BC–AD529
600–591BC: The Chinese found a way of fumigating houses to get rid of bugs. Aerosols were to come a bit later.

The first dictionary came from Mesopotamia, and was written in Akkadian, the language of the Assyrians and Babylonians. We didn't manage an English dictionary until 1480 when William Caxton published a bilingual dictionary in English and French for tourists. It only had 36 pages so I really doubt whether the two nations got much closer in understanding one another.

29

Anacharsis the Scythian sailor, fed up with never knowing where he and his boat were in the morning, invented the anchor.

580–571BC: Thales, a terribly talented Greek, was the first to prove general geometric propositions. If you hate geometry – blame him.

c. 550BC: Theodorus of Samos (a Greek island near Turkey) was said to have invented ore smelting (getting metal out of stone), although most historians say it was practised since the Bronze Age. He also gave us the bubble level, locks and keys, the carpenter's square, and the lathe.

It is now thought, however, that the ancient Egyptians had huge wooden locks years earlier. Trouble was that these locks were usually bigger than what they were locking up.

530–500BC: A Greek architect called Eupalinus built his first aqueduct – a bridge that carried water.

420–400BC: Archytas, an Italian toymaker, developed the theory of the pulley and invented – wait for it – the very first steam-powered toy pigeon. At last!

410–400BC: Dionysius the Elder, ruler of Syracuse, invented the forerunner of the catapult. I can't imagine what the forerunner of something as simple as a catapult would look like. He also developed the quadrireme, a crazy-looking boat with four banks of rowers. I doubt if it really went any faster. Seems to me a bit like putting four engines in your car.

400–390BC: Another Chinese person, called Lu Pan, described as semi-legendary (how can one be 'semi'-legendary), made the first kite (or maybe the first semi-legendary kite!).

380–370BC: Plato is said to have invented a water clock with an alarm. Perhaps this first alarm clock used water to wake you up. He also worked out (heaven knows how) that there must be a continent on the other side of the Earth which he called the antipodes. If you could ever get there, he thought you'd find Atlantis.

310–300BC: The clever Chinese invented the piston bellows, producing a continuous stream of air. Again, us thickos in the West didn't catch on until the sixteenth century.

300–290BC: Flushed with the success of the bellows, the Chinese went on to develop a harness that is pushed by a horse's chest rather than its neck. In Chinese horse circles, this was a red-letter day.

Euclid, a well-known clever person, wrote *Elements* which organized mathematical thinking in Greece. It included information on plane and solid geometry, and the theory of numbers. It became a basic textbook in maths for 2,000 years. I hope he had a good deal with his publisher.

283BC: First lighthouse was built in Alexandria – last boat runs aground?

260–240BC: Archimedes (of screw fame) developed the lever, and pulled a large ship onto land. Shouldn't it have been the other way round?

Philo of Byzantium designed the first chain drive so that he could reload his catapult quicker.

200–190BC: The development of gears led to the ox-powered water wheel for irrigation. Oxen were no doubt pleased, as they didn't have to push so flipping hard.

Proper concrete was used to build the Roman town of Palestrina, while in Rome they laid the first paved roads. Greece, by the way, was now occupied by the Romans, and poor old Carthage was destroyed.

140–130BC: The Chinese made the first paper; it was used for packing, clothing(?), and as the reference books state rather coyly – personal hygiene. The Chinese had, in fact, at last invented the toilet roll. I don't even want to think what they used before. Maybe old kites!

In Illyria the Yugoslavians at last had a first. They developed a water mill for grinding corn.

90–80BC: Sauma Ch'ien's *Historical Records* included the first known information on parachutes. It puzzles me what they could have jumped out of.

46BC: Julius Caesar, that Roman geezer, acting on the advice of the Greek astronomer Sosigenes, introduced the Julian calendar of three 365-day years, followed by one of 366 days. In order to get all the seasons straightened out, they had to give the year 46BC an extra 67 days. This was the longest year ever.

40BC: Andronicus of Cyrrhus built the Tower of Winds in Athens. Not only was it a water clock, but also a solar clock. It became the most famous of all timekeepers for the Greeks. A bit like Big Ben in London.

Syrians learned how to blow glass.

10–1BC: Herod the Great (the one who tried to zap Jesus) had the first large harbour constructed in the open sea (now at present-day Haifa). It was made of giant blocks of concrete.

The Chinese (again) managed to drill deep wells to get salt water and natural gas. Would you believe they got down to 1,460m? I wonder what they wanted salt water for?

CHAPTER 3

....

Medieval Science — AD 530–1452

When in AD529, Emperor Justinian closed the Academy and Lyceum in Athens, and the Arabs destroyed the Museum of Alexandria, scientific activity practically ground to a halt in Europe. Church scholars started a revival in the twelfth century, but that nasty old Black Death in 1347 soon put a stop to that.

The revival was to come in the mid fifteenth century when the terrible Turks overran Constantinople and a lot of Greek manuscripts were nicked and brought back to Europe in 1453. Obviously the introduction of printing was to help a lot as it gave many more people access to ideas.

Europe Goes Down

If you're looking for reasons for the decline of science in Europe between 530 and 1000 you might have to put the blame at the feet of the Romans. The trouble with those Romans was that they had absolutely no interest in theoretical science. It seems they were having too much fun inventing things to enhance their lifestyle. And when their own empire became a bit dodgy, the cities, roads and aqueducts fell to pieces and trade became very limited. Science couldn't possibly flourish under these conditions.

Medicine, although very much a science, survived the Dark Ages mainly because the Christians thought they'd better look after their sick at least, so studied the works of Hippocrates and Galen in their many monasteries. In fact it was the high level of medical teaching at Salerno in Italy during the ninth century that had heralded the revival of the rest of science at the back end of the Middle Ages.

Meanwhile, the Arabs ...

Islamic culture luckily stepped in to bridge the gap while science was in the doldrums in Europe, and the Islamic Empire became top of the civilization charts. I should imagine the main reason was that Arabs, being such incredible wheeler-dealers, traded all over the known world, and were able

REMEMBER, A LOT OF KNOWLEDGE IS ALSO A DANGEROUS THING

to bring the best bits of the foreigner's hard-earned knowledge home with them. Many other cultures threw their lot in with them bringing even more new ideas, especially when translated into Arabic. The Arabs even got hold of loads of Greek manuscripts when they turned over Syria in the sixth century.

But they didn't just pinch everyone else's ideas, they had quite a few of their own. For instance, they practically revived astronomy with al-Zaerkali compiling the Toledan tables, a record of planetary positions, which was to stay in use for three centuries.

Arab Sums

Arab mathematicians managed to take the very best from the Greeks and Indians (turbans not feathers) and became extremely handy with equations, trigonometry and numeric calculation. They invented the symbol for 0 (zero) which the Romans didn't have, and also separate symbols for each number. The term 'algebra' comes from Mohammed ibn Musa Al-Khowarizmi's book *Al jabra w'al muqabalah* (glad they shortened it).

At the Doctor's

To give some idea of the development of medicine and health care just consider that in Baghdad alone there were over a thousand government-licensed doctors. Although they had hospitals, and even mental homes, their knowledge of anatomy was a bit lacking, not surprising as body-chopping was still not permitted by Islamic Law.

Carry on China

Up till about the fifteenth century the Chinese had always been a lot better than the western Europeans at making science work for them. They were fiddling around with printing, paper, magnets, clocks, water wheels and rockets – to name but a few – long before we were. But it wasn't just in technology that they were racing ahead. In fact a lot of the stuff that boffins like Newton came up with had been sorted out a couple of thousand years ago by the clever, but rather inscrutable, Chinese. The Chinese attitude to nature became very different to that of the Europeans back in the Renaissance. They just refused to separate the material from the sacred world and didn't believe that man could influence (let alone dominate) nature.

Come Back Science, All Is Forgiven

You can thank the Emperor Charlemagne for the gradual return of science to Europe. Being a bit of a dumbo himself (he could never master writing) he saw the need for education and made sure that all his monasteries had a  little school attached from 787. When these cathedral-schools grew up they became the first universities. The Christians were also to learn lots about Islamic culture when those war-weary Crusaders came home from fighting Saladin and his not-so-merry men.

Unfortunately, religion was still getting in the way of free scientific research, but Thomas Aquinas (who later got sainted), saw no problem in the thirteenth century, with science and religion being in the same bed. The trouble had been with Aristotle, who'd caused a lot of fuss as a few of his words were thought by some to imply that God didn't actually create the world, that miracles didn't happen, and that the soul doesn't carry on after we die. By 1274 the Pope had had enough of all this and issued a condemnation of 219 scientific propositions. Poor Thomas Aquinas had the back of his hand slapped too, for having been tainted by that naughty old Aristotle.

Scholars being scholars, however, they soon dumped Aristotle, but carried on saying basically what he'd been saying all along in a more palatable way (Popewise).

MIDDLE-AGED ASTRONOMY

Ptolemy's *Almagest* became the best astronomy book throughout the back half of the Middle Ages, but was still based on Plato's principle that the motions of planets had to be explained in terms of uniform circular motion. Thomas Aquinas calmed the Church down by saying that the 'Prime Mover' was God. The Arabs grudgingly accepted these ideas but greatly improved the techniques of viewing the stars.

Some Great Breakthroughs in Astronomy 530–1452

630–650: The Chinese made a clear statement that the tail of a comet always points away from the sun.

660–680: The first English sundial was built in Newcastle. Shame they don't get much sun there.

1000–1010: A calendar of 365 days divided into twelve months of 27 or 28 days was introduced in India. As this fell short of a complete year, they chucked in an extra month every now and again. The Chinese had been working a ten day week, but they must have been getting a bit knackered by the weekend as they shortened it to seven.

A supernova or 'guest star' was visible from China, Japan, Europe and the Arab Lands for several years. They still didn't know what it was.

1066: A large comet, known as Halley's Comet, was seen over England. I wonder if it was that same old comet that our Harold was squinting at, when he got that froggie arrow in his eye.

1250: Alfonso X (sounds like a black rap singer) ordered the Alphonsine Astronomical Tables. They only got the printed version in 1483 (we all know how unreliable printers are), but the tables were used, however, for three centuries.

1270–1280: Chinese astronomer Zhou Kung set up a huge 40ft gnomon (pole) for measuring the sun's shadow. He set it in a vast field (gnomon the range?).

BRUDDY CROUD

1430–1439: Ulugh Beg, a Mongol astronomer, published a new table of star positions and a new star map. It was a great improvement on Ptolemy's – though his son, Master Beg, begged to differ and assassinated him a couple of years later.

1440–1450: Nicholas of Cusa wrote a book containing the idea of a continuous universe (shock, horror) and reckoned that all heavenly bodies were alike ... and, would you believe, that the Earth revolved round the sun. Obviously a nutter.

LIFE SCIENCES

Medieval biology was heavily influenced by Aristotle's method of investigation, which tried to find out the function and purpose of organic structures. Botany and zoology fell out and became different sciences. Both included weird tales and fables, describing incredible animals and monsters that were completely believed by the *hoi polloi*. Monasteries generally looked after the medical knowledge of the ancient Greeks, and medicine went on a storm in the Middle Ages, but it was in Italy and France that the great medical centres were set up.

Although there was extensive use of herbs and drugs doctors still believed in astrological influences. The main drugs were based on arsenic, sulphur and mercury (specially for skin complaints). Opium was used as an anaesthetic as they obviously thought it better to be out of it during an operation. Arab physicians became especially good at ophthalmology and even became skilful at removing cataracts.

Some Great Breakthroughs in Life Science 530–1452

640–650: Well done to the Chinese physician Chen Chuaan for noting the symptoms of diabetes mellitus including terrible thirst and sweet urine. (Nobody's that thirsty.)

1000–1010:
A ginormous five volume treatment of Greek and Arabic medicine by Avicenna, called the *Canon of Medicine*, was

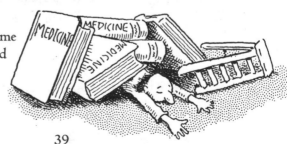

released. It would dominate the teaching of the subject until well into the seventeenth century.

1140–1150: The Norman King Roger II (sounds a bit unlikely) decreed that you could only be a doctor if you'd got a government licence. About time too.

1250–1260: Albertus Magnus wrote *On Animals* in which he tells about all the insects and animals that he'd cut to shreds. St Francis he most certainly was not!

1300–1310: Girolamo Savonarola, an Italian surgeon, rather cleverly made his victims – sorry, patients – chew weeny little sachets filled with henbane (a narcotic poison), poppy seeds (opium?) and mandrake (another narcotic poison). It apparently deadened the mouth. I'm surprised it didn't deaden the blooming patient.

1310–1319: Humans get the knife this time. Mondino de'Luzzi's *Anatomia* was the first book on human dissection ever written. At least they were corpses before he started. Either way, it doesn't sound like my kind of bedtime reading.

1370–1380: The first quarantine station was set up in the Port of Ragusa (now Dubrovnik). Those suspected of having the plague had to stay for 40 days. Hope they got luncheon vouchers.

1410–1440: Benedetto Rinio described and illustrated 440 plants that had medical uses. He should have got together with old Girolamo. One could see if he could poison people, and the other could have tried to make them better.

The dreaded influenza was spotted in Paris for the very first time in 1414.

1450–1452: The first proper association of midwives was founded in Regensburg (Germany).

Physical scientists (chemists and physicists) were always looking over their shoulders at the ancients, especially old-timers like Aristotle. They couldn't get away from Thomas Aquinas's dumb idea that all the heavenly bodies were being continually pushed by someone (God?).

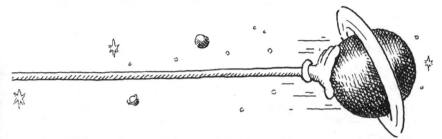

They played about with magnetism, but it was not till much later that scientists knew what it was, let alone did anything with it. Chemistry, on the other hand, was totally dominated by alchemy which sounded lots of fun.

ALCHEMY

Most people tend to think of alchemy as chemistry gone wrong. Although it was a magical and mystical way of looking at the world, it did make some real contributions to proper chemistry.

It started in China, where they were trying to find the Elixir of Life to give themselves immortality. It's a jolly good job they didn't – they've got a bad enough population problem as it is. The nearest they got was when they managed to embalm the Lady of Tai, using a nasty brown liquid containing mercuric sulphide and pressurized methane. She was exhumed 2,000 years later and was unfortunately still very dead, but in perfect condition (Nancy Reagan?).

While the search for this elusive 'elixir' grew, alchemists also became obsessed with the 'Philosopher's Stone' which if discovered could turn all metals in its proximity into gold. A chap called Paracelsus, a very well-respected Renaissance physician and scientist, reckoned he'd found it, but died in a fall when drunk before he could prove it (he obviously hadn't been drinking the Elixir of Life either). Isaac Newton is supposed to have gone round the bend trying to find 'The Stone', but it's more likely to have been the effects of all those nasty chemicals he'd been playing around with.

Lavoisier finally put the lid on the 2,000-year-old study of alchemy with his scientific view of chemistry released in the eighteenth century.

Some Great Breakthroughs in Physical Science 530–1452

880–910: Arab chemists celebrated the distillation of alcohol from wine. I bet that was a good party.

960–970: Roman doctor Scribonius Largus came up with the first toothpaste. It was made of vinegar, honey, salt and glass frit (the stuff you make glass out of). If you think that sounds yucky, you probably wouldn't go for Pliny the Elder's rather popular invention of urine as a mouthwash, which lasted well into the nineteenth century. And if you think THAT sounds bad, how about the practice of Chinese dentists yanking out teeth with their fingers? It's said these weird guys used to pull nails hammered into blocks of wood for up to six hours a day to strengthen their fingers.

1000–1010: The Chinese discovered for the first time that coal burns. That's good. It's not much use for anything else.

Tseng Kung-Liang, another Chinese whizz kid, came up with several recipes for gunpowder (take three eggs . . .), but kept it secret for years and years. I know! How on earth do you keep gunpowder quiet?

1150: Everyone through history has tried to make a machine that will run for ever without any help from wind, water or muscle. The Indian mathematician Bhaskara thought he'd cracked it but, unfortunately, his machine kept stopping. Loads of scientists followed, but in the eighteenth century Gottfried Wilhelm Leibniz blew the gaff and proved that energy couldn't be pulled out of nowhere. But did that stop them? Not a bit of it. Scientists and whacky inventors still try to crack perpetual motion to this day.

1220–1230:   Alchemist Arnold (Arnold?) of Villanova, Spain is in the reference books as nearly having discovered carbon monoxide. How do you nearly discover something I hear you cry! Search me! To save his reputation our Arnold did manage to prepare pure alcohol which, in my humble opinion, makes up for everything.

It could only have been an Irishman who discovered how to farm mussels. Paddy Walton became shipwrecked on the French coast and, failing to find any of those charming little seaside bistros, had to find another source of grub. He decided to catch birds by hanging nets from large wooden stakes planted in the sea. He didn't catch too many birds (even French birds aren't that stupid), but soon found the nets covered in mussels (under the water, silly!). Personally I'd have rather chewed the nets.

1290–1300:   Marco Polo's book of travels describes coal, asbestos (and mints?) for the first time in Europe.

1304:   Theodoric of Freiburg, a Dominican monk, was ordered by his boss to investigate rainbows (funny bloke?). Theo did just that, and his experiments with water drops explained much of how and why they are formed. No pot of gold though, folks.

1310–1320:   Philosopher Raymond Lully of Majorca was rather successful in discovering ammonia. But in 1315 he happened to preach against Islam while in Bougie, Africa, and was, not surprisingly, stoned to death by the natives. You should have stuck to chemistry (and Majorca), Ray.

In 1316 the pope of the day (sounds like a dish) John XXII outlawed alchemy (spoilsport).

1350–1360:   A très brave Frenchperson, Jean Buridan rejected the idea that God and/or his angels pushed the stars round their

43

orbits. He claimed it was initial impetus that did it. He died in the same year (say no more!).

1400–1410: Oil was used as a base for paints. Somebody was taking the urine!

1420–1429: It was known that coffee was drunk in Aden at this time. It was supposed to have been discovered by a Yemeni shepherd who couldn't work out why his silly sheep wouldn't sleep at bedtime. It appears the woolly insomniacs had been chewing the red fruit of the coffee plant.

TECHNOLOGY

If society in the Middle Ages had been based on slavery, technology wouldn't have developed at the pace it did. Why invent a machine to do a job when you've got loads of cheap, 'willing' helpers. Water wheels and windmills, which did loads of different tasks, were big business and in 1086 (according to that nice Mr Conqueror) there were over 5,000 water wheels in England alone. By the end of this period we had spinning wheels and quite sophisticated printing methods, as we'd pinched the Chinese way of making paper off the Arabs.

It seems very simple, but agriculture was speeded up no end by the invention of the iron ploughshare and oddly enough, the horsecollar (or should I say ox-collar?). Up to that time the pressure from pulling heavy loads had been on the poor beast's windpipe instead of his shoulders, which must have hacked him off no end.

Engineering and architecture went through their greatest expansion period since the Romans, and architects found ways of building brill cathedrals, the complexity of which staggered the general public.

Some Great Breakthroughs in Technology 530–1452

577:   Women under siege in Northern Ch'l (China), from cross neighbours, invent the very first matches in order to cook and keep warm.

600–610:   Windmills start turning in Persia (Iran).

650–660:   Callincus, an Egyptian, invented a particularly nasty substance that burned in water. It really speeded up the art of enemy boat-burning.

680–690:   Empress Wu Tse of China had a thing about cast iron. First she built a pagoda 294ft high, then ten years later an iron column which weighed 1,325 tons to commemorate the Zhou Dynasty.

720–730:   A Buddhist monk I-Xing and Chinese engineer Liang Ling-Zan built a water clock with an escapement to make it tick (but not ling).

810–820:   The root of all evil looms. The Chinese government issued paper money drafts; proper paper money arrived 60 years later. Don't you wish they'd stuck at loo paper.

984:   Ch'iao Wei-Yo, fed up with his boats breaking up and being plundered every time he hauled them from one level to another, invented the lock for canals.

1070–1080: Clever Tseng again; he described a magnetized iron 'fish' that floats in the water and always points south. I wonder if he managed to invent one to point north?

HE'S GOT A ONE TRACK MIND.

1190–1200: The Chinese invent the very first fishing reel. Perhaps that metal fish had escaped (south).

1200: Sharks' teeth and sea-shells were proving a bit dodgy to shave with. It seems the first proper razors date from this time.

1220–1230: A window at Chartres cathedral shows the earliest known Western wheelbarrow. That's nothing, the Chinese had been using them for years. They even had some wind-assisted wheelbarrows (with sails).

Those Chinese again. This time they invent a bomb that chucks shrapnel all over the place. It's difficult to work out how it did it, as Henry Shrapnel (who claimed to have invented it) lived in the eighteenth century. Having said all this, however, it was probably the appalling noise of these bombs that scared the enemy away.

1232: During a siege by the mighty Mongols, the crafty Chinese flew kites to send messages behind enemy lines.

1250–1259: Black day in goose circles: the quill was invented for writing.

1280: A Florentine physicist Salvino Degli Armati stuck two bits of curved glass either side of his nose and made a spectacle of – or should I say on – himself.

1288: A small cannon is fired in China (I wonder what he'd done wrong).

1300: If like me you're bored clueless (or cueless) by billiards and snooker, blame Henri de Vigne who built the first table for his boss Louis XI. It might not seem like it, but Steve Davis came centuries later.

1370: The first steel crossbow killed the first unsuspecting soldier in battle.

1420: Sigismund, current Holy Roman Emperor (see well-paid jobs) invaded the brazen Hussites. Their boss Zizka was waiting with some brand new – hot off the drawing board – secret weapons: horse-drawn carts covered with sheets of iron, full of nasty bowmen. They must have done the business, for Zizka's little 25,000 army whipped poor Sigismund's 200,000 army good and proper. Knock off the 't' and you have the first armoured car.

CHAPTER 4

··

Here We Go Again – The Renaissance
– 1453–1659

If those terrible Turks hadn't overrun Constantinople; and if all those Greek-speaking scholars hadn't nipped out of the back door to Europe with all their manuscripts; and if that beastly old Black Death hadn't put paid to half the population – then . . . the Renaissance might never have happened. Renaissance means re-birth and at that time meant the revival of all the classical Greek and Roman studies.

Curiously enough, a hundred or so years after the Black Death, cities and towns started to blossom. There's nothing like having half the population suddenly six feet under, to force those remaining to get their act together. Mechanical devices and heavy trading sure make up for missing people. If it's difficult pin-pointing when the Renaissance actually started, it's even trickier saying when it ended. It does seem, however, that what became known as the scientific revolution started in the later Renaissance. This chapter will drag you through to just before the founding of the Royal Society in England, when science was to become a little better organized.

Leo and Mike

The beginning of the Renaissance was much more arty than sciencey. Top of the bill were guys like Leonardo da Vinci and his chum Michelangelo, while chaps like scientists Paracelsus and Tartaglia, though undeniably clever, hardly got a look in on the lasting-fame stakes. Alchemy and astrology were all the rage at this time, overshadowing chemistry and astronomy. As for physics, it had to struggle to absorb Aristotle's rather trendy ideas before it could even think about a modern approach to physical motion.

Other Influences

Explorers were now turning up every five minutes with weird and wonderful plants and animals which everyone in Europe, fed up with the boring grub they'd had to eat in the Middle Ages, looked at longingly. Biologists John Ray and Carolus Linnaeus were lucky to have had anything left to classify, later in the eighteenth century, as most of this new stuff disappeared straight down the throats of the masses.

Leonardo's incredible brain also helped push the horizons of science ever forward. His studies of anatomy, coupled with pro-digious ability as an engineer and slightly mad inventor, spurred others on to leave their daubings and try different things. It must be said, however, that many of their ideas were mere fantasies, way ahead of their time, and therefore had very little direct influence.

The Renaissance spread from Italy and hit northern Europe in the sixteenth century dovetailing nicely with the Reformation. Trade went barmy and Francis Bacon described the new century as 'the opening of the world by navigation and commerce, and the further discovery of knowledge.'

The Scientific Revolution

This really started in the mid sixteenth century when loads of scientific societies sprung up. Astronomer Copernicus had been top ideas man, but his revolutionary view of the universe got him, and a lot of his fans, into quite a bit of aggro with not only the Catholic Church, but Luther and the Protestants (great band).

Copernicus was the first to dare suggest that the sun was the centre of our solar system instead of the Earth as Ptolemy had stated. Later, the jolly unpleasant Inquisition would even burn a chap if he broadcast these views, and stars like Galileo in 1633 had to tread very carefully.

Maths was made easier by the introduction of all those cute little symbols like + and × that we now know and love, and it helped to make it a universal language (except in my house). New branches of this hideous science were called algebra, analytical geometry, probability (?) and logarithms. By the way, have you heard the old gag about the constipated mathematician who worked it out with logs.

Modern philosophy started when a French guy called René Descartes came up with the mind-shattering statement *Cogito, ergo sum* – 'I think, therefore I am' . . . Don't ask me what he thought he was. He believed it possible to get the truth purely by reason and developed the above statement to eventually prove (he thought) the existence of the world and then God.

Overall it's old Galileo who gets my vote for man of the match. He introduced experimentation which laid the foundations for the sort of science we know today.

ASTRONOMY

Nicholas of Cusa, as mentioned in the last chapter, had refuted Ptolemy much earlier by gingerly suggesting that the Earth moved round the sun. Most Renaissance astrologers thought he was off his trolley so didn't take him that seriously. They were, however, finding the old way of thinking more and more difficult to live with.

When Galileo finally showed off his new telescope it changed astronomy for ever, and later his old rival Kepler went far beyond Copernicus to work out the detailed movements of the planets.

Some Great Breakthroughs in Astronomy 1453–1659

1472: Regiomontanus (born Johann Muller) did the first in-depth study of a comet. It later became known as Halley's Comet (unfair I call it).

1497: Nick Copernicus, the Polish astronomer, described and recorded how a star could be hidden by the moon (seems pretty obvious to me).

1504: Christopher Columbus, explorer-extraordinaire, frightened a group of very angry natives by predicting a total eclipse of the sun – and got himself out of a tight spot to boot.

1540: Peter Apian told the world that the tails of comets always point away from the sun. Old news, Pete, you should have read this book. We could have told you that (see p. 37).

1543: Copernicus's new book on the revolutions of celestial bodies backed up poor old Nicholas of Cusa's theory that the Earth and other planets have a habit of going round the sun.

1572: Tycho Brahe, a Dane, saw a new star which he called 'nova' which (believe it or not) means new.

1574: Tycho, flushed with success, went on to compare parts of the universe with human organs. Slow down, Tycho, I think you might have been overdoing it.

1580: Obviously the King of Denmark was impressed with our Tycho, as he built him a flash new observatory on the island of Hlveen, the first proper observatory since that of the long dead Beg (see p. 38).

1584: Giordano Bruno defended Copernicus's view that the stars form a planetary system, the universe is infinite and the Earth revolves round the sun. Careful, Giordano! Unfortunately he was overheard and in 1600 the powers that be (the Inquisition) had him burned at the stake. I think I'd have kept my opinions to myself.

1598: Tycho was really doing well now and moved in with the Holy Roman Emperor Rudolph II in Prague. The rich life didn't seem to suit him, however, as he died two years later. Johannes Kepler got his job, but not the flat.

1604: Kepler had to justify his existence so reported another couple of nice new novas pretty jolly quick.

1609: Galileo built his first telescope which magnified everything thirty times. With it he proved conclusively that Copernicus was right. He observed 'Earthshine' for the first time, which is when the whole moon glows faintly from the sunlight reflected off the Earth.

1610: Galileo really hit the big time and became famous all over Europe when he published a series of newsletters called *Starry Messengers*. These described his sightings of Jupiter, Saturn, the Milky Way and Venus. He sent this following message to Kepler:– 'SMAISMRMILMEPOETALEUMIBUNENUGTTAUIRAS'. In those days scientists used to send each other impossible anagrams of their discoveries to make sure the recipient didn't ever claim them for themselves. This one when unscrambled and translated said 'I have observed the most distant of planets to have a triple form', which isn't much clearer to me than the first one. What in fact old Galileo had seen were the rings of Saturn. What he thought he'd seen was a large planet with two little bits, one on either side.

1616: Take it easy. Galileo. He got his knuckles rapped by

Cardinal Bellarmine over that old Earth-round-the-sun business. Look what happened to Bruno.

Kepler's *Rudolphine Tables* told the world where to find 1005 stars and calculated the movements of the planets.

1633: You were warned, Galileo. This time he gets summoned by the Inquisition again who accused him of taking the Mickey out of Pope Urban VIII and of failing again to denounce old Copernicus. He recanted, but apparently had his fingers crossed, and was kept under house arrest. The Copernican theory was officially denied by the Catholics until, can you believe, 1922.

1645: Ismael Boulliau calculated that the central force acting on planets must be proportional to the inverse square of the distance. Seems OK by me.

1656: Christian Huygens from Holland discovered that the rather bizarre 'handles' on Saturn observed by Galileo were really rings. For good measure he also discovered Saturn's largest satellite Titan.

1659: Huygens becomes the first to spot the surface features of Mars (no, it didn't look like chocolate).

LIFE SCIENCES

Medicine was to progress more than any other life science during this period, particularly anatomy, which was based on the work of Galen. The more the young Renaissance Italian students peered

I'VE NEVER SEEN ONE OF THOSE BEFORE.

into the dissected corpses, however, the more they saw the flaws in what they'd been told.

Leonardo and his chums were a great help to physicians who were trying to work out how our muscles worked, as was William Harvey when he discovered that our blood whooshes round a whole network of tubes, ducts, and valves.

Paracelsus (sounds like a headache cure) was really an alchemist, but recommended the use of chemical medicines whenever possible.

Biology also showed great improvement with scientists like Otto Brunfels and Leonhard Fuchs beavering away describing and drawing plants much in the way old Aristotle had done. Many of these early biologists still, unfortunately, believed in mythical animals (Mickey Mouse) and plants with magical powers (magic mushrooms?).

Some Great Breakthroughs in Life Science 1453–1659

1490: Christopher Columbus found that native Americans were using tobacco as a medicine. Warning: tobacco can severely improve your health.

1459: Charles VIII's army got infected with syphilis by camp followers of the defending Spaniards when they took Naples. The army thoughtfully brought the disease back home to infect the whole of France, the Italian peninsula, and northern Europe. The Spaniards had probably caught it originally from Columbus's saucy sailors when they came home from America. Syphilis was the name of a rather grubby mythical shepherd who first had the disease . . .

1494: Don't believe that life as a monk was always one of self-denial. John Cor made the first whisky for his Abbey, but being a typical Scot kept its production secret. The first official distillery was in 1823 at Glenlivet.

1500: Jacob Nufer, a Swiss, performed the first recorded Caesarean operation on a live woman.

1520: Alchemist Philippus Paracelsus was heavily into opium (man) and used it as a medicine, naming it laudanum.

1545: In a book on surgery by physician Ambroise Paré, a Frenchman, the use of soothing ointments, instead of boiling oil, for the treatment of wounds was prescribed. I bet his patients were glad they'd gone to him.

1550: A fairly unknown physician called Elshots was the first to inject medical products into human veins, though they'd been doing it to animals for years.

1553: There ain't no justice in this world. Michael Servetus was found to have written a book that reckoned that blood recirculates from the heart to the lungs and back. This idea, and his slightly unorthodox theological views got him burned at the stake by that nasty old John Calvin.

1579: Lost an eye? You're in luck. The first glass ones were in the shops this year.

1580: Prospero Alpini noticed his plants were getting rather fond of each other. He discovered that they, like animals, have two sexes. Farmers apparently had known it for years.

1614: Franciscus Silvius was one of the first physicians to pour scorn on the theory that illness was caused by an imbalance of the four humours – blood, black bile, yellow bile and phlegm. They don't sound that humorous to me.

1624: Physician Thomas Sydenham, nicknamed the English Hippocrates, was the first person to identify measles (it certainly wasn't acne).

He also advocated the use of opium for pain relief, Cinchona bark (quinine) for malaria and iron for anaemia.

1648: Jan Baptisa van Helmont had a strange habit of weighing trees. In a famous experiment using a willow tree, he showed that its increase in weight was not drawn from the soil.

1652: Olaf Rudbeck had an audience with Queen Christiana of Sweden. He took his dog along and, rather unfeelingly, dissected it for her. He was, it seems, demonstrating the lymphatic glands.

PHYSICAL SCIENCE

Much of the development of physical science during the Renaissance was practical rather than theoretical, and discoveries outside this practical field were just isolated instances. Alchemists were doing their bit for chemistry, but they were such weird and secretive guys, that no one knew what they were up to. As far as physics was concerned, it was only really Galileo who made it into an experimental science.

Some Great Breakthroughs in Physical Science 1453–1659

1470: Alum was discovered in Tuscany. Hi, Alum.

1490: Leonardo da Vinci noted that, left to their own devices, liquids in narrow tubes tend to rise and crawl up the sides. The first observation of capillary action (sounds more like caterpillary action).

1500: Hieronymus Brunschwygk in his *Small Book* described furnaces, mines, stills and herb distillations used in medicine. Twelve years later he published another book which was bigger than the *Small Book* which he called – all together now – *The Big Book*.

1517: Girolamo Fracastoro wasn't that wild on the old Noah's flood yarn. He said that because fossils are found in so many strata of rock it disproved that the creatures all died in a flood lasting only 150 days. Elementary my dear Girolamo.

1546: In his strangely titled book *About the Nature of Digging* Georgius Agricola invented the word fossil for anything dug from the ground (I wonder what Giro had called them).

1557: Julius Caesar Scaliger (pretentious or what?) made the first reference to platinum.

1565: Konrad Von Gessner's *On Things Dug Up From The Earth* contained lots of drawings of fossils, though he believed they were just rocks that looked like bones or shells. In that case, wasn't it a bit of a stupid idea for a book?

1581: Galileo, obviously bored stiff during a service at Pisa Cathedral, became fascinated by the hanging lamps above. He declared that the time of the swing of a pendulum had nothing to do with the width of that swing. Brilliant, but wrong. The fact is that it depends on the length of the pendulum. Having said this, Galileo's obsession with pendulums was to lead to accurate clocks.

1586: Simon Stevinus was the first man ever to work out that the speed of a falling body is not connected to its weight. Sorry

Aristotle, that's another one of your theories down the pan. A few years later Galileo did loads of experiments on gravity and motion, proving Simon right.

1591: English mathematician Thomas Harriot thought he was the first to notice that snowflakes are six-sided. Sorry Tom, the Chinese had six-sided snowflakes centuries ago (and knew it).

1592: Galileo developed a thermoscope, a really dodgy thermometer. It might have been horribly inaccurate, but they used it for ten years all the same.

1597: Galileo wrote a letter to Kepler saying (grudgingly) that he'd come to agree with old Nick Copernicus's scheme of the solar system.

1600: William Gilbert described the Earth as a great spherical magnet. His *Concerning Magnetism* is the first book on physical science based entirely on experimentation.

1620: Jan Baptista van Helmont coined the term 'gas' to describe substances that are like air. The word was his own peculiar spelling of the Flemish word for chaos.

1630: Cabaeus noted that electrically charged bodies first attract each other and then repel each other after contact. Sounds like the average soap-opera plot.

1632: Galileo introduced relativity to physics by pointing out that experiments made in a closed cabin couldn't be used to tell whether the ship was moving or not. Silly man, why didn't he just look out of the porthole.

1637: Busy as ever, he then corrected many of Aristotle's theories of motion and friction in a book with a title too long to bother with.

1643: Evangelista Torricelli made a first barometer using a vacuum. The first ever known to science.

1654: The Grand Duke of Tuscany invented the first sealed thermometer. Fahrenheit, 60 years later, used this design to develop the modern thermometer.

TECHNOLOGY

If you had to choose the one great technological advancement of the period, it would have to be movable type. Like most things, the canny Chinese had seen it all before, but it's generally reckoned that Gutenberg (the inventor) didn't get the idea second hand. He did, however, glean the concept of printing and paper from the Chinese. Other innovations like maps, globes, and mechanical clocks were also developments of things seen before, but it was Leonardo's notebooks that, much later, set the world on fire. He was way ahead of his time, and when he wasn't painting his grumpy girl, Mona (Lisa), he'd be scribbling away, in mirror writing, inventing levers, parachutes, helicopters, and motor cars. To be strictly accurate none of them actually worked, but at least he thought of them first. Or did he?

Some Great Breakthroughs in Technology 1453–1659

1457: Nobody seems to know what the word tarot means or what language it comes from. The game was first referred to in this year by St Anthony. Although a bit spooky, it's generally regarded as the father (or mother) of all modern card games.

1460: There's a very strange, and very old, painting of a French Madonna and child in which Jesus is seen playing with what looks like a toy helicopter, worked by pulling a string. OK, it could have been a flying top, but even so, one is tempted to wonder where Leonardo got his idea from years later.

1474: William Caxton printed the first book in English. It was a translation of a popular medieval French romance.

1492: Martin Behaim made the first globe map of Earth. Had the poor chap waited a few years, he'd have been able to put in the Americas and the Pacific Ocean which no one had found yet.

1493: Christopher Columbus, while holidaying in Guadeloupe with his fellow explorers, was the first to taste the nana nana. If that doesn't mean much we now know it as the pineapple.

1500: Chinese scientist Wan Hu tied 47 rockets to the back of his chair in an effort to build the first flying machine. The device exploded, killing Wan who was the 'pilot'. I hope you're not smiling.

1502: The first spring-driven pocket watch was invented by Peter Henlein.

1509: The earliest fragment of wallpaper was from this time. It was thought to be a substitute for embroidery.

1543: Ball-bearings were first made of wood, invented by the sculptor Benvenuto Cellini. He'd just knocked up this statue of Venus and thought it a shame that the punters couldn't see it from all sides. He put four little balls in the base and it turned round a treat.

Proper ball-bearings, made of metal, weren't seen until 1794 when Welshman Philip Vaughan wanted to find a way of making his carriages move more easily.

1552: Yoghurt came on the market, but not for the first time. It was invented by an angel in biblical times. He or she gave some (I don't know what flavour) to Abraham which apparently accounted for his long life. The French are now top consumers, getting through 28lb a year each (but not all at once).

1564: Horse-drawn coaches had been around for years on the continent, but only used by women and invalids. They were introduced into England in 1564 but you only got to go in one if you were really royal or really rich.

1570: The Neapolitan writer on natural magic Giovanni Battista della Porta almost certainly invented the camera obscura, a device for reproducing an image on paper in order to trace it.

1589: The godson of Queen Elizabeth I, Sir John Harington,

became a real hit with his mates when he invented the first water-closet. Lizzie was well impressed and had one put in at her place, but they didn't catch on generally as most homes didn't have running water. So, therefore, you even had to be rich to go to the toilet. The most famous manufacturer much later, in Victorian times, was a certain Thomas Crapper. His products were so well known that people often talked about going for a Tom (is that right?).

1598: Gasparo Tagliacozzi was the first to suggest skin grafts. He tried to replace lost noses (how do you lose your nose?) with the flesh of other people. He blamed his failure on the force and power of human individuality. Sounds like an excuse to me. Actually it's interesting to note that losing your nose through syphilis was the big joke in Elizabethan drama.

Which came first, the screw or the screwdriver? Who cares. They both appeared together (obviously) around 1598.

1602: Fed up with never knowing where their coal carts were going, mine owners in Newcastle developed the first rails. They were made of wood at first, but became cast iron in 1763.

1603: Coke discovered; not in America as a drink, or Colombia as a drug, but in England as a fuel. A chap called Hugh Platt invented coke by burning coal in a confined space at 115 degrees centigrade.

1605: The first newspaper or gazette appeared in Antwerp and was produced by the printer Abraham Verhoeven.

1608: A Dutch spectacle-maker, Hans Lippershey, was looking through bits of glass at his weather-vane one day (as one does), when he put two bits in line and discovered they made it bigger (the weather-vane, stupid). He had just started to invent the tele-scope. Galileo heard about it, improved it and became the first to study the sky. Isaac Newton claimed the credit for inventing the telescope in 1672 (cheeky).

1616: Philip III of Spain held a competition open to anyone, to find the longitude at sea. Galileo, hoping to win the prize (and a pension), came up with this great idea of using the satellites of Jupiter. Philip completely ignored him (rude b . . .), but Galileo's method went on to be used to find the longitude on land. You can't win 'em all.

1624: Cornelius Drebble, a Dutch physicist who was James I's kids' teacher, invented the first submarine. It was a crazy wooden boat that sailed (?) for 5 miles, 16ft under the Thames, rowed by sixteen brave oarsmen. What fascinated scientists, however, was how Drebble produced the oxygen that was pretty essential. He took the secret to his grave.

1640: Nicholas Sauvage, a French coachman, started the first taxi service on the rue Saint Martin in Paris. The first proper metered, motorized cabs were invented by Louis Renault (didn't he do well) in 1904. I hope Louis's drivers were a bit more together than the lunatic cabbies in Paris these days.

A deeply complex and intellectual board game began at this time in Venice. It became known later as 'Snakes and Ladders'.

1642: Blaise Pascal, a brilliant young French inventor, produced the first machine to calculate the money his father, a dreaded tax collector, collected. It was the forerunner of the modern calculator, called the Pascaline and worked on the same principle as the car milometer.

1650: I bet you didn't know that Cyrano de Bergerac (him of big nose fame) suggested seven ways of getting to the moon.

Although six of them were just plain daft, one of them – by rocket – seems to have caught on.

German physicist Otto von Guericke perfected the air pump. In order to prove the theory of vacuums to the sceptical public he used teams of horses, who failed to pull apart spheres only held together by the pressure of air (vacuum).

He went on to prove that when in a vacuum, sound couldn't travel, animals died, flames went out and, best of all, a feather would fall at the same speed as a lump of lead.

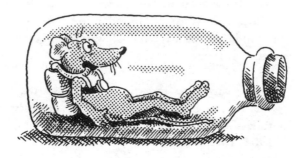

CHAPTER 5

Newton and Co. – 1660–1734

A calculus fit to compute on,
White light, and a head to drop fruit on,
A mind to absorb it,
And soar into orbit –
That's all it takes to be Newton.
Gina Berkeley

The Royal Society and the Académie des Sciences in France kicked off another phase of scientific development mainly because it meant that scientists could at last have somewhere to go and have a good old chinwag about what they'd been working on. Mathematicians, unfortunately, couldn't get it together, so had to stick to letter writing. The result of this was loads of arguments about who thought of what first.

Top of the boffin pile was a guy called Isaac Newton who escaped the plague in 1665 (a resurgence of the Black Death) when he dashed out of Cambridge and went home to Mum in Woolsthorpe.

The following year was to be the most creative in his life. He wrote it all down in this book called *Principia* which was to be the top work on physics for over 200 years. Unlike Descartes, the first modern philosopher, he based his theories on what he saw, rather than what he thought after he'd seen it (?). He called it the method of analysis and synthesis, but you get the general idea. This was OK as far as it went, but it's fair to say that Newton went on to use intuition to deduce and predict things which he later proved by experiment.

He managed to stay on the right side of the Church by telling everyone that natural phenomena could always be explained by maths, which they seemed quite happy with. It must have also helped that he was deeply religious, so they realized that he was hardly likely to cut off his own nose to spite his face, so to speak. He believed in this 'perfect being' (God) who not only created the universe but also gave the laws of nature a direction.

It was during this time that physics and metaphysics (philosophy) decided to go their different ways. Newton was perfectly happy to go by the mathematical rules of, say gravity, without having to wonder about their cause. If he couldn't prove a theory, he just wouldn't have it in the house. So Aristotle was shoved to the back of the cupboard and scientists started again to study the results of their own experiments. They began recording things in terms of values such as weight, volume or temperature.

They unfortunately couldn't get their (by no means small) brains round the concept of energy and tried to grasp qualities like heat, magnetism and chemical energy by describing them in terms of material, or weightless fluids passing through solids. This was all very well but they got in a right pickle, observing things that they didn't really understand. Actually, it didn't matter that much because, as most of these observations were pretty sound, they could act as a basis for advances in physics and chemistry for ages.

All Together Now
When old Newton found out that one law could explain most things on Earth, as well as in space, people started to get it into

their thick skulls that the 'celestial bodies' (stars) weren't of a divine nature. When Edmond Halley predicted the return of his blessed (or should I say unblessed) comet in 1682 and 1758, based on mathematical calculations, it seemed to put the tin lid on it, and proved Newton's theory of gravity.

Newton's Big Ideas

Newton's First Big Idea seems rather obvious. If an object is just sitting around, minding its own business, or even travelling along at a steady pace, nothing will change this state of affairs until something else comes along to change the situation (you don't say?).

His Second Big Idea says that force, as such, is something that causes a body to move. I have actually proved this. Try lying down and see what force it takes to get up again.

The Third Big Idea states that for every action there is an equal and opposite reaction. Therefore, if you kick your dog it will usually bite your ankle; if you get terribly drunk you'll no doubt get a hangover; or to be serious (for once), the power coming out of the back end of a rocket, will make it go the other way.

Having worked all this out, our Newton decided to have a rest from thinking and went to sit in his backyard. Now if you or I had seen that wretched apple falling from a tree, we'd have either ignored it or eaten it. Not our Isaac! He wondered why it had

SCIENCE CAN WAIT

fallen downwards (silly man) and gradually he realized that it must have had something pushing or pulling it and that the moon orbits the Earth held by that same force. From this he deduced that all the bodies (or apples) in the universe are affected by a force varying inversely with the distance between them. He called this force – all together now – gravity, and at a single deft stroke did away once and for all with that old rubbish which declared that the stars were moved by devils or angels.

PHYSICS

Everything that Galileo and Kepler had put forward about planets and a need for a force to keep them in orbit, was made clear by the theories of Isaac Newton. The likes of Descartes, and theories of vortices and such were rapidly kicked into touch. There were also loads of advances in the understanding of light, ranging from the first mathematical look at refraction to the discovery of its actual speed.

Otto von Guericke discovered how to create large amounts of static electricity, but sadly didn't know quite what to do with it once he'd captured it.

Light Switches On

All the old scientists, right up to Descartes and Kepler, had reckoned that there was just no limit to the speed of light. Galileo wouldn't have it, however, and tried an old experiment that had been used for measuring sound. He put his assistant on a faraway hill-top and flashed at him (a light!). He then measured the time it took before seeing the response. Guess what? It didn't work. Galileo soon realized that the largest part of the delay was caused by the time it took for his stupid assistant to react to the first sighting.

A Dutch astronomer, Ole Romer, cracked the problem by using a much greater distance to measure the light beam. Working with the relationship of the Earth, the sun, and eclipses of Jupiter's satellites, he calculated that the speed of light had to be around

150,000 miles per second. Olé! He was almost right. Years later, with dead flash laser equipment, the speed was calculated at 186,282 miles per second. So, what's the odd 36,000 mps when you're shifting that fast?

Some Great Breakthroughs in Physics 1660–1734

1663: Blaise Pascal published a book (unfortunately he was dead by the time it hit the streets) that suggested that, in a fluid, pressure is exerted equally in all directions.

1664: Christiaan Huygens suggested that the length of a pendulum with a period of one second should be used as the standard unit for length.

1665: While Newton was at his mum's he busied himself inventing a calculus (a brand new method of calculation); discovering that white light is a mixture of colours and developing the laws of gravitation. Some people will do anything to get out of washing up.

1667: Men throughout history have never liked the idea of women being as clever as them, and scientists are no exception. Henry Oldenburg, first secretary of the Royal Society, called science a 'masculine philosophy'. Margaret Cavendish, Duchess of Newcastle, wouldn't have it and became known as 'Mad Madge' because of her unladylike interest in science. Despite terrible opposition, she became the first female member of the Royal Society. It's unbelievable to think that no other woman was admitted until 1945. They couldn't have thought a great deal of poor Madge.

1672: Frenchman Jean Richer, while on his travels, found out that the swing of a pendulum of the same size takes a longer time on the equator than at home. The things some people do on their hols. Clever-dick Isaac Newton worked out that it was because there is a bulge in the Earth at the Equator, and a flattening at the poles which obviously (according to him) affected gravity.

1679: Robert Hooke from the Isle of Wight dropped Newton a line suggesting that gravitational attraction varies inversely with the distance from the sun, and wondered whether this might suggest that the planets' orbits might just be elliptical. Grumpy old Isaac didn't reply.

1684: Hooke then showed off to Sir Christopher Wren (top builder) and Edmond Halley (Ed Halley and the Comets?) that he'd sorted out the laws governing the planets' movements. Wren told him where to go and offered a prize to anyone who could crack it. Halley went round to Newton's house to ask what planetary orbits would be like if attracted to the sun. Newton, of course, replied, 'An ellipse, for I have calculated it.'

1702: Guillome Amontons, fed up with Galileo's rotten old thermometer, invented a much better one.

1704: Newton wrote a book on optics called *Optics* which became a standard in experimental physics for the rest of the century. It ended with a load of, now famous, unanswered questions (like, whatever happened to that blinking apple?).

1705: You've heard of 'chicken in a basket', well Francis Hauksbee's speciality was 'clock in a vacuum', which proved that sound (tick-tock?) needs air to travel.

1709: Gabriel Daniel Fahrenheit from Danzig, a German (or should that be Gerperson), discovered that alcohol is good for measuring temperatures and invented the alcohol thermometer.

1714: Fahrenheit had too much of the alcohol and switched to mercury for his thermometer. The scale, as you know, was named after him.

ASTRONOMY

Newton's theory of gravitation finally gave the scientific OK for the Copernican system and Kepler's laws. Telescopes were also much improved so it became much easier to see what everyone was going on about. When they came to realize that the sun was just one of a million stars, it became clear that human beings were no longer the centre of the universe.

The two big names in astronomy were Edmond Halley and Giovanni Cassini, an Italian (as if you hadn't guessed). Halley worked on how often his pet comets appeared and also the proper motion of the stars, while Giovanni explored (not literally) the solar system and found out lots about its planets and moons.

BIOLOGY

Descartes had always told everyone that animals were but simple machines (simple they may be – but machines?). When biologists got microscopes that really worked, they were able to prove just how wrong he was. But still they couldn't grasp how the things that made a cat a cat or a wombat a wombat were passed from mother to baby.

Jan Swammerdam formulated a rather whacky 'pre-existence theory' which went along the lines of – as the seeds of all living creatures were formed during the Creation (that must have been a busy five minutes), each generation is held in the one before.

Anton van Leeuwenhoek persisted in using an old fashioned single lens microscope, but even though it was a bit knackered, he managed to spot that there was a whole world of teeny little animals, scurrying around, invisible to the naked eye, and perfectly happy. Hooke also went into the mini-world and carried on turning up his microscope until he discovered cells for the first time. Physiology became a lot healthier largely due to a dead clever Italian called Marcello Malpighi, who spent his days up to his elbows in lungs, nervous systems and invertebrates.

Some Great Breakthroughs in Biology 1660–1734

1660:   Malpighi showed the world that his beloved lungs were not just large empty balloons, but millions of teeny pockets of air and a complex load of blood vessels. He then circulated his work on circulation (bloodwise).

1665:   You can't keep a good Italian down. Malpighi then discovered that the nervous system consisted of bundles of fibres connected to the brain by the spinal cord.

1667:   Jean-Baptiste Denis astounded his French mates by transferring 12oz of lamb's blood into a sick boy. The boy survived but rumour has it he grew long white curly hair and made strange bleating noises. Later experiments had a nasty habit of killing the patients (and sheep), and poor Jean-B was tried for murder. He got off, but was baa'd from ever doing such operations again.

1668:   Francesco Redi disproved that maggots appear, as if by magic, in rotten meat. It was one of the first controlled experiments known to science.

1671:   This time Francesco was ready for another experiment. He dissected a torpedo fish to study its electric organ. He didn't realize, however, that the shock he got was caused by electricity.

When will people
learn that you must
always unplug electrical
goods (or fish).

1675: Nicholas Steno demonstrated that dogfish (and catfish)

have eggs inside them, but give birth to live offspring. I wonder if they chased each other. He went on to conclude that all mammals must have eggs.

1682: Nehemiah Grew grew lots in his back garden to demonstrate the male and female parts of flowering plants.

1691: John Ray's *The Wisdom of God Manifested in the Works of Creation* (and that's the short title) suggested for the first time that fossils are the remains of long-dead animals. He became head natural history man and was the first person to work out that whales aren't just very big fish.

1711: Luigi Marsigli, on the other hand, made out that corals aren't plants, but animals (well, sort of).

1716: Louis Jean Marie Daubenton, a French biologist, wrote a best-seller in sheep circles called *Advice to Shepherds and Owners of Flocks on the Care and Management of Sheep.* I do like a snappy title! I think one piece of advice to shepherds and sheep might have been, don't go near anyone called Denis (see 1667).

MEDICINE

The great discoveries in biology began to influence medicine as soon as people began to apply their learning. Anatomists continued exploring parts of the human body, especially the brain and the ear. Bernardino Rammazzini was the very first doctor to notice that certain kinds of cancer are affected by where one lives (cigarette factories?). Moreover the practice of inoculating against smallpox spread from Turkey to England, and to the American colonies, while fab new thermometers helped doctors a lot.

Some Great Breakthroughs in Medicine 1660–1734

1664: Tom Willis's *Anatomy of the Brain* was the most complete and accurate description of our grey matter and nervous system so far.

René Descartes, in a book published after his death, described animals as purely mechanical beings. He reckoned that there was no 'vital force' that made them different from other material objects. "Scuse me, René, just got to pop out to take the Hoover for a walk.'

1666: Richard Lower demonstrated a direct blood transfusion between two dogs (bloodhounds?).

1667: Thomas Willis announced the rediscovery of the connection between sugar in urine and diabetes. No great shakes, the ancient Greeks, the Chinese and the Indians had known all about it before.

1691: Clopton Havers (Clopton?) published the very first book about human bones. The hip bone's connected to the leg bone, etc.

1703: Good news, Isaac Newton was elected president of the Royal Society; bad news, it was almost finished owing to lack of interest in the natural sciences. He got the club back on its feet, however, in a couple of years.

1707: Giovanni Maria Lancisi wrote an article with very few jokes called *On Sudden Death* which was mostly about heart attacks.

1717: Giovanni Lancisi reckoned that there might be a connection between that dirty little traveller, the mosquito, and malaria.

Lady Mary Wortley Montagu put her money where her mouth was and, bringing back the practice of inoculation against smallpox from Turkey, had her own kids done.

1718: A German physician Friederick Hoffman wrote nine volumes of a book which related muscle tone to health. Mind you you'd have needed muscles to pick up the ruddy books.

1728: French surgeon/dentist Pierre Fauchard described how to fill teeth with tin (if you were poor), gold (if you were rich), and lead (if you wanted to be poisoned).

1731: John Arbuthnot wrote an essay suggesting that dieting might be good for health. I wonder if he knew what he was starting?

CHEMISTRY

The study of matter up to this time was still caught up almost entirely with alchemy, which was bound up with mystical and spiritualistic notions. It was Robert Boyle, 'the sceptical scientist', who made chemistry a rational and experimental science. He introduced words like elements, acids and alkalis and developed his own pet law of gases discovering at the same time hydrogen and phosphorus. Boyle's law stated that the volume of gas changes in simple inverse proportion to pressure.

During this period not much was done to develop theoretical science but many new substances were discovered. The now infamous phlogiston theory was to hold chemistry back until it was found to be bogus.

The Phlogiston Theory

Since ancient times people had struggled to work out what fire actually was. Those old Greeks assumed it was an element like air and water, so left it alone. Robert Boyle thought he'd finally cracked it when he discovered that fire needs air, and that if air is removed from a vessel combustion cannot exist. He also worked out that animals need air to live (this animal certainly does!) and that it is essential if one wants to provide oxides from metals by heating them (calcination).

The Germans wouldn't have it, however, and preferred to believe that combustible matter contained something called 'oily earth', later called phlogiston, a substance released during burning. Everyone seemed jolly pleased with this until some bright spark noticed that metals had a habit of actually gaining weight during calcination (heating a substance to a temperature below melting point) instead of losing it. The scientists racked their brains and came up with the only possible answer (albeit wrong) that phlogiston weighed less than nothing. A neat way out.

Many years later, our boy, Joseph Priestley was fiddling about with the calx of mercury (what's left after calcination) and found that when heated up it produced a special air in which things burnt brilliantly. He shoved some of this 'new air' in a jar with a nice new mouse and found it lived much longer than all the ones he'd been shutting in jars with 'ordinary air'. Priestley believed in the phlogiston theory, so called this air 'dephlogistonated air'. He wrongly believed that air got extra phlogiston from our breathing and from fire (good for the fire-eating profession I should think).

A French chap called Lavoisier discovered a bit later the real truth. The so-called dephlogistonated air is really a gas (later to be called oxygen) and that fire absorbs air and gives off non life-supporting gases like carbon monoxide. Lavoisier's theory of combustion swept away anything that went before.

TECHNOLOGY

It was at this time that the first steam engines were put to work pumping out mines. The extra coal that was produced paved the way for the Industrial Revolution. Abraham Darby discovered how to make iron using coal which was essential for the new technology. Mind you, a lot of the new inventions, like the 'Spinning Jenny', which spun eight threads at once, and the 'Flying Shuttle', which automatically returned the shuttle, really hacked off the workers who (quite rightly) saw them nicking their jobs.

Some Great Breakthroughs in Technology 1660–1734

1660: It was by this time that the greatest violin-maker of all, Antonio Stradivari, had brought the violin to perfection. He'd be proud to know that half his violins are still in existence, though he'd probably turn in his grave if he learned that the dreadful Nigel Kennedy had got his hands on one.

Britain at this time was mining 2,000,000 tons of coal a year, 80 per cent of the world's total. It's nice to think we could once do something better than foreigners.

Otto von Guericke impressed the world when he showed the power of atmospheric pressure. His machine consisted of a metal cylinder in which a piston moved up and down. Using his pump he created a partial vacuum which made the piston plunge down the cylinder at the same time lifting a weight by ropes and pulleys. This was the first time they'd actually put air pressure to any use.

1662: William Petty, an Englishman, heard about the boats used in the Pacific islands and built two catamarans which licked the pants off the normal single hulled type.

1664: The first postmen were 'invented' by Louis XI of France who set up a postal service not seen since the Roman Empire. Mail was delivered by messengers on horseback, which was probably a jolly sight more efficient than it is now.

1665:   Dud Dudley claimed the secret of making iron from coal instead of charcoal.

1673:   Christiaan Huygens, the brilliant Dutch astronomer, mathematician, physicist and all round clever-dick, reputedly built a motor driven by gunpowder, but surprise surprise, there seem to be none around any more.

1679:   Denis Papin, big man around steam, invented the 'steam digester', a kind of pressure cooker for cooking 'the oldest hardest cow-beef' (yum-yum), rendering it as tender as the freshest and choicest meat. Despite all his wonderful work with steam, and many amazing inventions including the first steamship, poor Den was no good at business, and died skint and forgotten in London in 1712.

1680:   The first minute hands appeared on clocks. I suppose before this you could only be late in hours.

The first evidence of a revolver was a bronze horse pistol (for shooting horses?). It can be seen in the Tower of London and was made by gunsmith J. Dafte (which I'm sure he couldn't have been).

1683:   Most people think that the croissant was invented by the French. It wasn't. It was made first in Vienna by the Polish baker, Kulyeziski. The city had been besieged by the terrible Turks led by Kara Mustafa (Mustafa croissant?). When the Turks were beaten they apparently left lots of coffee behind. Kulyeziski was given permission to open a coffee shop and he produced these funny little sweet rolls to celebrate the victory. They were an instant hit.

1690:   French monk Dom Pierre Perignon might well have invented champagne by accident. It seems like monks spent most of their time inventing alcoholic drinks (and drinking them). Dom was no exception. He blended several white wines together in his monastery in Champagne. Not only was this against all the rules of wine-making, but also he kept the wine in tightly corked bottles which kept the carbon dioxide in and made the wine 'bubbly'.

1698: Thomas Savery's 'Miner's Friend' was the first practical, steam-powered machine. And friend it was, as it pumped out water from mines, saving the poor miners from getting their feet (or even more) wet.

1700: It became fashionable around this time for women to colour their lips with a fairly horrid, slightly scented pomade (oil or ointment for hair) dyed with the juice of black grapes. It wasn't till the twentieth century that lipstick as we now know (and love) it, was produced.

1710: Bartolommeo Cristofori is generally credited with the invention of the piano in 1698. To be precise it was a clavichord with small hammers. The pianoforte, as such, came shortly after, in 1710.

1714: The British Parliament passed a bill setting up a prize of £20,000 to anyone who could develop a good way of finding the longitude at sea (without getting wet).

In 1714 Henry Mill, an Englishman, invented the basic idea of the typewriter, but there isn't a single one surviving (they never built things to last in those days). In 1808 Pellegrine invented another sort for his blind girlfriend Countess Fantoni, but nothing's left of that one either (or the poor Countess, I suspect). The real inventor of the modern typewriter was an American, Christopher Sholes, who sold the idea to the Remington Fire Arms Company who were looking for something else to make after the bottom had dropped out of the gun business when the American Civil War ended. At first he had to practically give them away, as nobody seemed that interested.

1716: Bored with comet hunting, Edmond Halley went completely the other way and developed the first diving bell with its own air refreshment system.

1718: There was a young lawyer named Puckle . . .
James Puckle of London invented the first flintlock machine-gun. It had a rather neat refinement. Apparently it fired round bullets for shooting at Christian enemies and square ones (which hurt more) for killing Turks. Good job there weren't any Christian Turks is all I can say.

1730: Jonathan Hulls borrowed one of Thomas Newcomen's fab

I THINK IT MIGHT HAVE BEEN A BIT TOO HEAVY.

new steam engines and shoved it in his tugboat. It wasn't much cop but it was the first.

Lancashire weaver John Kay built a spinning machine which knocked the spots off anything seen before. Up to then it had taken two people to weave a large width of cloth. Kay's flying shuttle returned back to the operator without any help from the other end. The fabric was improved, costs were cut, and half the poor machine operators had to look for other jobs. I bet they asked our John to shuttle-off.

1734: A German doctor called Fuchs thought it would be a good idea to fill glass balls with salt solution (and we can't blame him for that). He apparently used some of them for throwing at fires, but nobody seems to know what he used the others for. Anyway they didn't work very well, so the world had to wait until 1816 when Captain George Manby invented a proper fire extinguisher.

....

CHAPTER 6

The Industrial Revolution and the Age of Enlightenment – 1735–1819

Any doubts about whether Isaac Newton was a nutter or not, were completely swept away in the first bit of the eighteenth century. The scientific revolution of the seventeenth century was to have a deep effect on philosophy, with scientists scurrying around, trying to apply our Isaac's explanations of natural phenomena to just about everything science wise. Very often, however, they got themselves into a bit of a tangle, probably because they weren't as bright as he was.

In France at this time, there were a bunch of hommes calling themselves materialistic philosophers, who completely chucked out any idea of a spiritual god when explaining natural phenomena, preferring to see it simply as a mechanical system. They included us humans in their system, but reckoned even history itself was just a physical process following the same rules as they'd applied to science.

Empiricism and Rationalism

In the sixteenth century there were two approaches to philosophy. The first, 'empiricism', reckoned that one could not be sure of anything unless one had actually done it or seen it oneself (gutter press take note!). The second, 'rationalism', made out that you can get just as far by reasoning. Philosopher Immanuel Kant in the eighteenth century took the big prize when he invented the term 'enlightenment'. This solved their dilemma by stating that 'empiricism' and 'rationalism' may now be friends as the two go hand in hand, which I'm surprised no one had thought of saying before.

He also introduced the idea of causality, which maintained that one event causes another to happen, which is a bit like what Newton was rattling on about. For example, if you bang someone very hard on the head, he will generally fall over (or hit you back). Kant admitted this general principle, which he called an 'a priori' concept, could not be proved but said there were just some things we must accept even if we haven't experienced them personally . . . so there! Space and time he put in the same drawer, refusing to lose sleep trying to fathom them out. Once these concepts have been accepted, Kant said, our approach to science, especially physics, is, if anything, made easier.

The Great Chain of Being
Another philosophical idea kicking around at that time was a trifle whacky. Some 'enlightenment' scientists like the Comte de Buffoon – sorry, Buffon – saw all lifeforms as being in a continuous chain. This, in effect, meant that at some stage minerals grew into fossils, fossils into plants, plants into animals, and so on. I bet they'd have gone a bundle on the sort of 'science fiction' in which half plant, half animal types (like triffids) chase us around willy nilly.

The Encyclopédie

This was a jolly grand livre in seventeen volumes which enabled 'enlightenment' philosophers and scientists to communicate their knowledge to the public. This *Encyclopédie* became extremely famous, not only because of its size, but because of editorial views that showed two fingers to the Church and State.

The New Romantics

This wasn't a fashion trend, but a back end of the eighteenth-century reaction to the materialism of the 'enlightenment' scientists. This started strangely enough in Germany (romantic Germans?) and spread to France, then England. Instead of using reason, they preferred sentiment (yuk!), saying that all nature should be seen as a single organism, tinged deeply with spirit (gin?).

Industrial Revolution

Nobody seems to know what started the headlong rush to build machines to make work faster and 'efficienter' in England. Coal must have had something to do with it, as wood had long been unsatisfactory for heating or iron-making. Increased trade had lots to do with it; for example, tons of cheap cotton was pouring in from the American Colonies and India which the British had been exploiting like mad. But it was a new breed of 'capitalists' who had

the most to do with it. These were not like the rich landowners who'd always had loads of loot. No; these guys were that dreadful breed – self-made men. You know, those pompous oafs that they're always making TV series about – living in big 'ouses and paying their workers peanuts. They were the ones that took all the cottage industries and squashed them into factories. Soon all the 'civilized' nations jumped on the band-wagon and followed Britain's industrial lead.

This is all relevant, because this leap in technology really affected science. Thermodynamics (the study of the relationship between heat and mechanical energy) was spawned from the newly developed steam engine. Organic processes were dropped in favour of chemical ones, and the chemical industry, as we now know it, commenced. Medicine developed mainly because of the need to keep alive the poor beggers forced to work in t'mills, down t'mines or live in overcrowded substandard hovels.

MEDICINE

During this period there were several important developments. Albrecht von Haller published a flash medical encyclopaedia in 1757. This let modern physiology (the study of life processes) go out on its own, unaccompanied for the first time, and become a new science.

Marie François Xavier Bichat found histology which, as if you didn't know, is the study of the tissues of living things. Disease was finally tackled on a large scale when Edward Jenner introduced vaccination to fight smallpox at the end of the eighteenth century.

Some Great Breakthroughs in Medicine 1735–1819

1748: A charming little book called *Account of the Putrid Sore Throat* (Barbara Cartland watch out!) was penned by a John Fothergill. Amongst all the rest of the fun it gave the first description of diptheria.

1751: The first ever proper mental institution opened in London. Any Londoner could probably hazard a guess as to why.

Robert Watt demonstrated that the contraction of the pupil in response to light is a reflex action. I suppose it could also be said that the contraction of a pupil in response to a smack round the head from teacher, could be seen as a reflex action.

1752: William Smellie (please!) approached obstetrics (the study of childbirth) in a scientific way for the first time.

1753: James Lind, a scurvy expert (someone's got to be), discovered that lemon juice has a curative effect. Later they made limes compulsory as part of the diet of British sailors who became known as 'limeys' which sounds better than 'lemonys'.

HOW TO SPOT A LIMEY

1754: The first female student graduated as a medical doctor from the German University of Halle ('bout time too).

1756: The first false teeth were cast from a model by Phillipe Pfaff. Try saying his name with brand-new false choppers.

1761: You know when doctors tap your chest to see if it sounds OK? Well, the first person to do it was Leopold Auenbrugger, an Austrian who was also a musician (probably a drummer).

1768: Robert Watt's *Observations of the Dropsy of the Brain* (sounds a bit careless) gave the first description of tuberculosis meningitis in children.

1772: Antonio Scarpa discovered the Labyrinth of the Ear. This wasn't a science fiction film for the deaf, but the description given to the semicircular canals, vestibule and cochlea that we've all apparently got in our lug-holes.

1774: Everyone knows that Franz Mesmer used hypnosis to help cure disease. What you probably don't know is that he made a fortune flogging magnets in Paris, to draw out the pain caused by neuralgia. It started that highly profitable trade which one still sees in the form of copper bracelets for pain relief (you can fool some people all of the time).

1775: Sir Percy Pott suggested that chimney sweeps in London develop cancer of the scrotum and/or the nasal cavity from exposure to soot, more proof that cancer can be related to environmental conditions (and clean chimneys).

1785: Wild-flower lover William Withering discovered the use of digitalis (from the foxglove) in the treatment of heart disease (in foxes?).

1786: Benjamin Rush suggested for the first time that some illnesses may be psychosomatic. Which means that physical illness can start from mental origins. Which means if you think you're sick, you'll more than likely get sick. I wonder who invented the first 'sugar-pills' to cure these afflictions.

1790: English physiologist Marshall Hall found out, for the first time, why our knees jump when tapped. He called these movements reflexes. Maybe even more important, he was the first person to denounce bleeding people as a treatment for illnesses. As someone who faints if he pricks his finger, I'm right behind you, Marshall.

1791: If you've heard about the way they treated loonies in the eighteenth century (putting them on show at the asylums for instance), you'll be relieved to know that it was Frenchman Phillipe Pinel who advocated treating them better.

1796: Homoeopathy started when a German called Hahnemann became intrigued by stories of a Countess Chinchona who was the vice-queen (wife to the Viceroy) of Peru (well! it's a job). She apparently was cured of a rather horrid fever by chewing the bark of a local tree which was named after her. Funny thing was, Hahnemann took large amounts of the bark over several days and suffered most of the symptoms of the same fever that Chinchona was supposed to have been cured of. Obviously, its bark was worse than its bite. He then went on to try lots of other weird plants and the same thing happened (funny guy). The result of all this was his theory that medicine produces a very similar condition in healthy persons to that which it relieves in the sick.

1797: The Royal Society made rather a big boo-boo when they rejected out of hand Edward Jenner's inoculation techniques.

1800: Humphry Davy (of miner's lamp fame) discovered nitrous oxide as an anaesthetic. It was good for a laugh as well (laughing gas).

1805: Franz Joseph Gall was the first to suggest that different bits of the brain do different things, but then went on to say that our brains can be studied by feeling the bumps and observing the shape of the skull (phrenology). Sorry, Franz, you've got that bit wrong. In fact his local emperor, Francis I, told him to button his lip on the subject.

1815: Although we'd had thermometers for years, it took Carl August Wunderlich to realize that taking temperatures accurately could be rather useful.

1817: James Parkinson got his own personal disease when he defined a palsy that causes shakes.

1819: A stethoscope was used for the first time by René Théophile Hyacinthe Laennec. It was only a wooden cylinder, but it enabled René to investigate lungs, hearts, livers and things.

Blood pressure was first measured by a doctor Poiseuile (a Frenchman). Up till then the quacks had had to be content with always taking the pulse.

CHEMISTRY

Thank God chemists finally kicked out that poor old phlogiston theory. It had really held any advances back throughout the eighteenth century. The scientific revolution got round to chemistry through the sweat and toil of Lavoisier, Cavendish and Dalton. Having said that, it didn't hit the commercial world till the following century (probably because they couldn't get their heads round how chemical reactions really worked). It was most definitely Lavoisier's correct version of combustion and John Dalton's atomic theory that allowed the rapid development to happen.

Some Great Breakthroughs in Chemistry 1735–1819

1766: Not much to report up to 1766, when the eccentric and extremely absent-minded Henry Cavendish discovered hydrogen. The son of a lord, Cavendish disliked men and was scared stiff by women (doesn't leave much, does it?). He discovered hydrogen (calling it inflammable air) to be the lightest of known gases, and that, surprisingly,

when burnt with oxygen, small drops of water appeared. He therefore worked out that water is made up of the two gases.

1733–1804:   It was around this time that Joseph Priestley met Benjamin Franklin. Priestley was impressed by the American envoy (and boffin) and although not having had much to do with science before, got quite worked up about what Franklin had been doing. He studied all that was so far known about electricity, and in no time at all published a definitive history of electrical science which was to make him famous. He then switched to chemistry. Priestley lived next door to a brewery (lucky bloke) and noticed that strange heavy gas kept pouring out of it. It turned out to be carbon dioxide and Joseph's experiments led to the invention of fire extinguishers and also, by realizing how much it cheered up water when dissolved, to the start of the huge soda water and soft drinks industry. The trouble was, his liberal political views really got up the noses of English society who eventually caused his house to be burned down (hope the brewery was OK). He eventually packed his bags, and soda water, hightailing it off to the States to find even more fame and fortune.

1772:   Antoine Lavoisier began his experiments on combustion by proving (rather rashly, I think) that diamonds will burn, and that when sulphur or phosphorus are burned, they actually GAIN weight.

1772:   Cavendish and Rutherford each (suspiciously) discovered nitrogen. Rutherford, generally, seems to get the credit.

1774:   Priestley discovered oxygen, which annoyed Swedish chemist, Karl Wilhelm Scheele, who'd come across 'fire air' two years earlier. Unfortunately, he'd omitted to publish his findings. Tough bananas, Karl. First come, first famous.

It really wasn't Scheele's year. He discovered chlorine, manganese, and barium but didn't cop the credit for any of them either.

1778: Oh dear, oh dear, Lavoisier announced that air contained two gases — oxygen and nitrogen. It's so unfair, poor old Scheele a few years earlier had said exactly the same thing, but had called oxygen 'fire air' and nitrogen 'foul air'.

1783: Chemist Nicholas Leblanc was also well hacked off. He won a competition set by the French government to find a practical way to get sodium hydroxide and sodium carbonate from salt, but they didn't give him the cash. To make it worse, Leblanc's process made possible the large-scale manufacture of soap. Poor old Nick was forced to wash his hands of it.

Persistent as ever Scheele went on to discover (and be credited for) lactic, hydrocyanic and citric acids.

George Monge liquefied sulphur dioxide. The first person to turn gas into a liquid.

1791: The very last supporter of the phlogiston theory, Richard Kirwan, finally put his hands up and surrendered.

1794: In recognition of his wonderful contribution to the furtherance of scientific knowledge, the father of modern chemistry, Antoine Laurent Lavoisier, had his head chopped off by the guillotine of the radical faction of the French Revolution.

1799: Bleaching powder (Vim, Ajax, etc.) was invented this year by Charles Tennant. He had the cleanest sink in Britain.

1806: Poor old Nicholas Leblanc (see 1783) finally topped himself owing to total poverty. He never made a single franc out of his wonderful discovery. That's the French for you!

1807: Humphry Davy kept himself busy discovering potassium, sodium, and – after a little rest – barium, strontium, calcium and nearly magnesium (not isolated until 1929). The following year, while at the seaside, he managed to discover iodine in seaweed.

1808: Anyone who becomes a teacher at the age of twelve must be a bit on the bright side. John Dalton, a Quaker, was no exception. Although his major work had been studying the weather, he wrote a book in 1808 which was to formulate the modern atomic theory of matter. The three basic ideas were as follows:

1. All matter is made up of very small indivisible, indestructible particles called atoms.
2. All atoms of one element are exactly the same, but different from all other elements.
3. When elements combine to make compounds their atoms combine in simple numerical proportions such as one to one, two to one, four to three and so on.

1811: Another clever comte, Amedeo Avogadro, stated that equal volumes of gases under the same conditions of temperature and pressure contain equal numbers of molecules (Avogadro's law).

1817: The one that got away. Friedrich Stromeyer, a German scientist, sneakily discovered cadmium.

1818: Louis Jacques Thénard accidentally discovered hydrogen peroxide. I wonder if he became a blond?

ASTRONOMY

Pierre Simon Laplace, rather cheekily called 'le French Newton', demonstrated the stability of the solar system and solved many astronomical and mechanical problems. Astronomers and philosophers finally trashed the Aristotelian idea that everything in the universe is static and had been looking about the same since its creation. Kant and Laplace introduced the theory that the universe evolved gradually and called it the nebular hypothesis.

Telescopes were getting better and better. Uranus, and quite a few new satellites, came into view. William Herschel quit Germany to get out of the army and came to England where he became a musician. With his sister Caroline he got into astronomy and became the greatest observer in history. It was he who spotted Uranus which made him instantly famous. He and his kid sister were the first to realize how very, very big the universe actually was, although no one could prove it for over a century.

Some Great Breakthroughs in Astronomy 1735–1819

1744: Jean Phillippe Loys de Cheseaux was still puzzling over why the sky was dark at night. After lots of research he proclaimed that slight loss of light in space accounted for it. Absolutely amazing, Jean.

1752: Great Britain and the American Colonies adopt the Gregorian calendar by making September 14th come directly after September 2nd. I don't somehow think Britain became great making decisions like that. I bet a lot of those mingy factory owners gave their workers holidays during that period.

1754: John Dollond of London invented the heliometer, a brill new telescope that produced two images that could be played around with to work out angular distances. This eventually led to working out how big the sun was (the answer is – VERY). It might, or might not, surprise you to know that there are still opticians' shops that bear his name – though he is probably retired by now.

1761: Joseph Nicholas Delisle sent a few of his astronomer mates to good observation points around the world to keep an eye on the movements of Venus. The trouble was that wars and clouds tended to get in the way, but the few observations that came back were used to calculate solar parallax and the distance from the Earth to the sun.

1770: Anders Jean Sewell observed for the first time a short-period comet, but naughty old Jupiter's gravity chucked it out into space before it could get back.

1782: A strange little 17-year-old deaf mute astronomer called John Goodricke was the first to explain the variation in the light from the star Algol, which caused an invisible companion star. All I can say is that he must have come from the planet Krypton (along with Superman), if he could spot invisible stars.

EARTH SCIENCE

All this industrial revolution stuff required lots more coal and metal ores. Suddenly everyone was scrabbling around, digging up fossils and rocks, which gave birth to the new science of geology. Up to the middle of the eighteenth century people still believed that all the fossils and rocks had been left after Noah's flood, which had apparently covered the whole blooming planet.

The French naturalist, Buffon, reckoned the Earth was at least 80,000 years old instead of the 6,000 that was thought before (from the Old Testament). Whenever the age of the Earth was talked about, you must understand, one was instantly on dodgy ground regarding the Church. Gottfried Wilhelm Leibniz cleverly got round that one by publishing his book when dead. He'd explained that the Earth probably went through a gas stage, then a molten stage, before turning into what we've got now.

Abraham Gottlob Werner was the first to introduce some sort of system into geology, showing that rocks were in layers – old ones at the bottom, and newer ones at the top. He reckoned that in the past the Earth had been covered by a muddy sea and that the Earth's crust was formed when all the wet bits dried up.

His ideas were called the Neptunist theory, while all those who thought the Earth was formed by volcanoes were called Plutonists. A chap called James Hutton (a Plutonist) although wrong, wasn't as wrong as Werner and the Neptunists, as at least he believed in an Earth that had always existed and would continue very much the same as it was in 1785.

Some Great Breakthroughs in Earth Science 1735–1819

1743: The first geological map ever was made of East Kent – England.

1744: That Comte de Buffon keeps cropping up. He proposed that the Earth was formed when a comet rather carelessly collided with the sun.

1752: Nicholas Desmarest shocked everyone when he declared that France had once been connected to England by a land bridge, since washed away by currents. I doubt whether the French like the idea much better than the British.

1755: We think we have catastrophes now. It's all relative. In 1755 an earthquake in the sea near Lisbon killed 60,000. Later in 1815, Mount Tambora in Indonesia exploded, killing tons of people and lowering world temperatures for a year or so. In fact, our Lord Byron penned a poem called 'Darkness' which described a year without a summer. Funny really; there must be a lot of eruptions even now, as the weather in England is still awful.

1766: Workers in a stone quarry, near the Meuse River in the Netherlands, found a load of huge old bones but didn't have a clue what they were until 1780 when a ginormous skull was dug up. They turned out to be the bones of the huge Meuse Lizard (mosasaur) – a 40ft sea reptile, the first prehistoric monster to be identified, when examined by Cuvier in 1795.

1768: Captain James Cook waved goodbye to everyone at home and set off on his first voyage of discovery. He was one of the chaps who was asked to take a look at the passage of Venus across the sun in 1768 – which he did from Tahiti. On the way he bumped into the biggest beach in the world – Australia.

1772: Captain Cook's second voyage to the South Pacific failed to find another southern continent.

Dear Mum,

Having a wonderful time – Weather good – Food terrible – Can't find any more continents, so coming home.

Love to all,

Jim.

1781: René Hauy, a French geologist, carelessly dropped a big lump of calcite. When it shattered he examined the bits, which led to the geometric law of crystallization.

1785: James Hutton, rather encouragingly, stated that although there was no sign of the Earth's beginning, there was no sign of it ending either. He reckoned that the geological features that he could see then, had obviously taken ages to get like that, and that any changes happened ever so slowly.

1786: German-Swiss Johann von Charpentier finally convinced everyone that there really had been an Ice Age in Europe.

1804: Jean Baptiste Biot and Joseph Gay-Lussac went up in a balloon to study terrestrial magnetism and the Earth's atmosphere. That's their story anyway.

1811: A twelve-year-old girl, Mary Anning, went down in history by stumbling across a 33ft-long fossil of the first ichthyosaur ever known.

PHYSICS

The good old French were the last to accept that our man Newton just might have been right about physics. Mind you, Newton's theories and calculations were only any good for working out planetary orbits and not much cop for anything else.

The nature of heat was giving problems too. Most eighteenth-century scientists, rather unbelievably (unless you were an eighteenth-century scientist), saw heat as a kind of invisible fluid. Clever Count Rumford wouldn't have this and spent his time boring cannons (no jokes please), measuring the heat produced and puzzling how something like a cannon could contain so much 'fluid'. He therefore struggled on and worked out that if heat is produced by motion then it must be a sort of motion itself. Most people thought he was a bit of a silly count.

The eighteenth century was also a time of extensive experimentation with electricity. Trouble was they still didn't know what it actually was.

Some Great Breakthroughs in Physics 1735–1819

1735: Don't blame me for this one. Francesco Algarotti wrote *Newtonianism for the Ladies* which was a much simplified explanation of Newton's physics. What do you think of that, girls? It was a huge best-seller by the way.

1738: Pierre de Maupertuis took his tape measure to Lapland and confirmed once and for all that the world is flattened at the poles.

1739: George Martine demonstrated that the amount of heat in an object bears little relationship to its volume.

1742: The Celsius scale was invented by Anders Celsius. His first centigrade thermometer was all about face, having the boiling point of water at 0 and the freezing point at 100. Don't test your bath water with one of these! Jean Christian switched them in 1743 providing the system we use today, which must have pushed poor Anders's temperature up no end.

1744: Mikhail Vasilievich Lomonosov (from guess where?) published a paper on what causes heat and cold. He correctly concluded that heat must be a form of motion.

Pierre de Maupertuis again. He originated the principle of least action. This stated that action is a quantity that is force × distance × time. The principle stated that nature will work in such a way that action is at a minimum. Modern physicists are apparently quite happy with this. What do *you* think?

1746: The Leyden Jar — the first proper way to store static electricity (caused by friction) — was invented by Pieter van Musschenbroek and Ewald von Kleist. Poor old van Musschenbroek knew he was on to something when he got a shock off the jar. He wondered if there might be a connection between electricity and lightning.

1747: Benjamin Franklin discovered that a pointed conductor can draw off electric charge from a charged body. This was the basis for the invention of the lightning conductor — which was a little odd as Franklin (or anyone else) hadn't yet proved that lightning was a form of electricity.

Abbé Jean Antoine Nollet, a French physicist, constructed the first electrometer, a device for measuring electric potential (like electric pressure measured in volts). It was said to consist of a suspended pith ball. Pleath don't athk what a pith ball ith.

1749: Jean-Jacques d'Ortous de Mairan in his *Dissertation on Ice* (urgh! I hate ice shows) described the Chinese refrigerator (velly, velly chirry), which recognized the cooling effect of evaporation.

Benjamin Franklin installed a lightning rod to protect his own house in Philadelphia. Nice one, Ben — sort yourself out first. Two years later he distinguished between positive and negative current and showed that electricity can magnetize or demagnetize iron needles.

1752: The year of Franklin's famous kite experiment. He fixed a metal key to his best kite by a thread of silk and flew it into a lightning storm. Electrical sparks flew between the key and the silk which he'd attached to the ground at the other end. What, in fact, he was doing was diverting some of the electricity from the lightning that was belting down into the earth. Dangerous you might think. You're not kidding! Several European scientists were well frazzled trying to do the same thing.

1761: Joseph Black discovered latent heat (the heat required to turn a solid into a liquid or liquid into a vapour). He found that ice, when melting, absorbs heat without changing its temperature.

1769: John Robinson measured the repulsion between two charged bodies (sounds like Friday night in the Cat and Fiddle) and showed that this force is inversely proportional to the square of the distance between them. This means, I suppose, that if you get too close to someone, the chances are you'll find them repulsive.

1771: Italian anatomist Luigi Galvani made his frog's leg (sans frog) twitch by accident. He touched Kermit's leg with two different metals and was amazed at the result. He mistakenly thought the leg contained a fluid (which he called 'animal electricity').

1775: Alessandro Volta let everyone know about his new device for storing static electricity (replacing the Leyden Jar). It was eventually to lead on to modern electrical condensers (which increase or accumulate electrical charges).

1776: Pierre Simon Laplace reckoned that if the forces on all objects at any one time are known, then the future can be fully predicted. I don't think there was too much future in that idea, Pierre.

1783: Horace de Saussure wrote about constructing a hygrometer from human hair to measure relative humidity. Sounds like the basis for a good business.

1787: Jacques Alexandre Charles proved that different gases expand by the same amount for a given rise in temperature. It became known as Charles's Law.

1791: Luigi Galvani was still chopping the legs off frogs at a fair rate. He finally got the message that the legs twitched from outside stimuli probably caused by the two different metals – even if there didn't seem to be any electricity around. This discovery was the first step on the path which eventually led to Volta's electric battery (and a load of relieved frogs).

1794: Alessandro Volta took this further and said that an electric force can always be obtained whenever two different metals are put in a conducting fluid (frog's blood?). By 1799 he had invented the electric battery, known as the Voltaic Pile. It consisted of a stack of alternating silver and zinc discs separated by felt and soaked in brine. The very first source of steady electricity.

1807: Hans Christian Oersted, a right brainiac, told everyone that he was looking for a connection between electricity and magnetism. Watch out for his name.

1810: Johann Wolfgang von Goethe didn't go a lot on Newton's theory of white light being a mixture of colours, preferring to think (wrongly) that colour is in our heads: which is a bit like what old Aristotle was going on about.

1816: If you think the kaleidoscope is one of the most put-downable devices known to man, blame Sir David Brewster, a Scottish scientist.

1819: Oersted was really getting stuck into his experiments and accidentally discovered that a magnetized needle was deflected by an electric current. The plot thickens.

TECHNOLOGY

At last we can use the word properly – the direct application of science to machines. It was really the steam engine that had this incredible effect on science, manufacture and transportation. The early machines were a bit on the crude side, but gradually engineers started measuring their efficiency, using scientific principles. In fact, the assessment and improvement of machines became a science in itself.

But not everyone who invented anything was a scientist. Most advancements in, for instance, the textile industry were made by joyful amateurs who had no time to call in proper scientists. It's reasonable to say that when the American inventor Eli Whitney standardized spare parts in technology, product manufacture changed drastically.

The other factor that helped technology on its way was the development of engineering schools throughout Europe.

Some Great Breakthroughs in Technology 1735–1819

1736: Charles de Lacondamine first brought rubber to Europe from Peru, where they'd been using it for centuries. People knew it came from somewhere over the 'Indies' way so called it 'india-rubber'. Practically speaking, its only use, at first, was 'rubbering' out pencil marks. Which came first, rubber, or 'the rubber'?

1738: Jacques de Vaucanson was obviously a scientist who liked a giggle. At the Paris show he exhibited a mechanical duck (maybe the first robot), which knocked everyone sideways. It flapped its wings, swam, smoothed its feathers, drank and pecked up food. Best of all – a masterstroke – it shoved the chewed up food out of its other end in a most realistic fashion.

1751: Bored with school? Perhaps you'd have preferred L'Ecole Supérieur de Guerre (High School of War) opened in Paris. Heaven knows what they did to you if you failed the final exams.

1759: A bridge over troubled waters. James Brindley built the first canal to pass over a river by means of a fixed aqueduct.

It seems that John Smeaton from Leeds built a lighthouse with mortar that set under water. Why should anyone want an under-water lighthouse? Submarines?

1760: Joseph Merlin seemed a sandwich short of a picnic. He was an eccentric Belgian who donned the very first rollerskates and careered into the ballroom of a party given in Soho Square, London, playing a violin. He was, unfortunately, rather badly injured when he hit a large mirror. Mind you, I've seen stranger things happen in Soho (but not on wheels!).

The first four-wheel rollerskates were invented by Joseph Plimpton of New York in 1863.

1762: A Frenchman called Dumas had this weird idea of cutting up maps into little pieces and then putting them together again. This early jigsaw was an educational aid, though anything that makes maps even more incomprehensible seems crazy.

1763: If you went shopping for crockery at this time in England, the chances were that it would have to be the cream-coloured earthenware patented by the late, great, Josiah Wedgwood. It became all the rage.

1764: Blackburn man James Hargreaves introduced his Spinning Jenny. Good news — it could spin eight threads at once; better news — later models managed a hundred and twenty.

1766: The first fire escape on record is one built by a London watchmaker. It was dead simple, consisting of a wicker basket on a pulley and chain.

Richard Arkwright 1732–1792

Richard Arkwright started his working life as a travelling barber and wigmaker, buying hair from servant girls at every opportunity (that's his story). His first achievement was to perfect a method of dyeing this hair to order. When wigs started to go out of fashion he turned his mind to the weaving industry. He became obsessive about bringing an independent power source to the looms, and with the help of a local clockmaker, patented the first spinning-frame in 1769. At first he tried horse power, but he soon changed to water power, as it was much more constant (and didn't need feeding every five minutes). The poor underpaid workers rioted all over the North of England, but our Arkwright, undeterred, went on to become a great industrialist having loads of factories of his own. He helped make weaving England's most important industry. In 1785 he was the first to use James Watt's fab new steam engine. He was knighted and made so much loot that he bought his own castle and a church to be buried in. Not bad for an ex-barber.

1769: Nicholas Joseph Cugnot, a French military engineer, built a steam carriage that carried four speed-crazed passengers at the unheard of rate of 2.25 miles per hour. Mon Dieu! That's faster than a Reliant Robin (turbo)!

1772: The scourge of all children, papier-mâché, was patented by Henry Clay.

1774: The first hotel ever, Low's Grand Hotel, was built in Covent Garden and became famous for its grub. Poor David Low sold it in 1780 because he couldn't make a profit.

1775: American David Bushnell invented a hand-cranked, propeller-driven, one man submarine called the 'American turtle' because it looked like one. He used it unsuccessfully to attach a bomb to the British ship *The Eagle* during the American War of Independence.

The tram, a carriage pulled by horses, running on rails (the carriage, stupid!) was invented by Englishman John Outram and named after half of him.

James Watt 1736–1819

Mention the Industrial Revolution and most people think of James Watt. Perhaps it wouldn't have happened without him. He was born a rich kid, having a dad who owned and built ships. It was while hanging around his dad's workshops that James became fascinated by machines and mechanical instruments.

One day, while in his own instrument-making and repair shop, a guy walked in with a model of Newcomen's early steam engine which was broken. Watt, while fiddling around with it realized how jolly crude it was and built a model of his own, which, believe it or not, was 75 per cent more efficient and cheaper to run. He was soon flogging the real thing all over the country to every sort of industry. By 1800 he'd off-loaded 500 machines and was seriously rich. He was elected 'Fellow of the Royal Society' but, being quite shy, turned down a baronetcy. He spent his last days up in his garret workshop doing what he knew best – inventing things. What Watt didn't know, was that the 'watt' (what is a unit of electric power) was to be named after him.

1777: The invention of the torpedo is often credited to David Bushnell (the sub-man). 'Fraid not, 'torpedo' was the name given to mines and Bushnell invented the first one. It consisted of an underwater keg of gunpowder, supported by floats, which was fired by a trigger mechanism whenever it struck anything. Just about all great American inventions at that time seemed to be used against the British. Bushnell's 'torpedo' was used to blow up the *Cerberus*, in the Connecticut River. It missed, unfortunately (if you're a Yank), but blew up a parked schooner next door – a sort of consolation prize.

Joseph Bramah 1748–1814

One of the all-time bad jobs in history must have been that of the 'night soil men'. It was their job to go round at night emptying the cess-pits under the houses of the well-off. When Alexander Cummings invented a practical water-closet (lav.) he used Joseph Bramah to install them. Joe soon worked out a much better system (and cistern) and patented the 'Bramah' in 1778. It was to lead the field (if you can call it that) for a hundred years until the loo we know today, 'The Jennings', was invented.

JOSEPH BRAMAH
(FLUSHED WITH SUCCESS)

But Bramah is also famous for the invention of the Bramah lock which he exhibited in a store window offering 200 guineas to anyone who could unlock it. This was unbeaten for 67 years when an American locksmith managed it, after 51 hours' hard toil, at the Great Exhibition in 1851.

1778: A very dubious invention was that of the building society. The first was advertised in Birmingham by Richard Ketley. In those days, the members saved between themselves enough for each in turn to buy a house – and who got the first one was decided by ballot. Once everyone had a house the society was closed. The modern 'permanent' building society, which now seems to control all our lives, was started by an Arthur Strachey and his Western Life Assurance and Annuity Society.

A much more important revelation that year was a report from Captain Cook describing surfing in Hawaii. It didn't reach its true home, California, until 1900 and didn't become the cult sport until the 50s.

Samuel Crompton mated Hargreaves's 'Jenny' with Arkwright's water-frame machine (verrry interesting). The offspring was called a mule and was the first machine capable of spinning either warps (lengthwise threads) or wefts (crosswise 'filling' thread).

1779: The first iron bridge was built by Abraham Darby and still crosses the River Severn at Telford. It cleverly has not one screw, rivet, nut or bolt – being constructed using only perfect dovetailed joints.

1780: The inexplicable fascination some weird people have with war games was started by Helvig, the Duke of Brunswick's master of pages. In 1837 the general in charge of the Prussian Army made the playing of war games compulsory military training. That I almost understand, but when it gets to insurance salesmen in Croydon, well . . .

1781: James Watt patented a way to make his engine go round and round instead of up and down.

1783: Brothers Joseph and Étienne Montgolfier, who made paper in France, noticed the way scraps of paper floated up the chimney when lit, due to the current of hot air. They then experimented with paper bags and soon moved on to a vast 110ft diameter paper-lined fabric balloon, which floated for a mile or so. The French king and queen watched the brothers' next attempt which for some reason carried a sheep, a duck and a cock (sounds like the beginning of a rude joke); the first farm animals (or anyone else for that matter) to fly. In 1783 two people flew successfully for 5 miles.

Although Leonardo da Vinci first thought of the parachute (apart from the Chinese, who'd thought of everything) he never had the bottle to try it out. In 1783 a Frenchman L. S. Lenormand jumped from a high tower and survived (just). Next was Andre-Jacques Garnerin, who tied a large bucket on to a huge sort of sunshade and threw himself (and it) out of a balloon above Paris in 1797. All was successful except that his bucket swung around so much that when he reached the ground, much to everyone's disgust, he promptly threw up. It seems he also invented airsickness!

1784: Henry Shrapnel of the Royal Artillery had this charming idea of inventing an iron shell filled with bullets that would kill and maim lots of people all in one go. The Shrapnel shell was instantly loved by everyone (it wasn't fired at), and was adopted by the British Army in 1803.

1785: Sadly Pilâtre de Rozier, a French balloonist, invented air crashes, becoming the first terminal casualty when his balloon caught fire (which is pretty serious), popped and crashed (or splashed) in the English Channel.

1786: Where do little nails come from? From the nail-making machine invented by Ezekiel Reed.

1787: George Washington and Benjamin Franklin were invited to a strange demonstration on the Delaware River. John Fitch was showing off his crazy steamboat which was propelled by oars attached to a long wooden rod, powered by a steam engine.

1790: George Washington had probably needed a good laugh. His dentist had just invented the very first dental drill. It was around this time that proper false teeth were being made from plaster casts in Paris. Up until this time false  teeth had been carved from the bones of familiar or even rather exotic animals, hippopotamus being the most popular. OK, they were pretty strong, but after a short time they had a habit of turning brown and smelling dreadfully (a bit like a hippo).

The celeripede was the ancestor of the push-bike, only this had no pedals and had to be kicked along by the rider's feet. It was invented by the Count de Sivrac and renamed the velocipede or dandy-horse. They tried to cheer up its appearance by making it look like a lion, a horse or even a dragon.

It was either Marie Harel, her mum, or a priest she once sheltered with at the start of the French Revolution, who first came up with the recipe for Camembert. The cheese, which smells a little bit like a tramp's socks, was an instant hit throughout France.

1792: All commercial or domestic use of gas, can be traced back to William Murdock in the 1790s. From a little iron retort in his backyard which provided the gas for the lamps in his own house, Murdock was to see his invention develop into the street lighting that was everywhere by the early nineteenth century.

Napoleon's personal doctor, Baron Larrey, was most concerned about the way injured men were hauled back from the battlefield in awful wooden carts. He took a new cart, put springs underneath (to stop the jolting) and then put a canvas cover over the top. It was known as the 'one-horse flying ambulance' and was a great success. Funny thing was, however, that no one thought that civilians might possibly need ambulances, and the first one took 80 years to appear, in Margate of all places, pulled by hand and having only one wheel. Hardly worth inventing I'd have thought – I'd rather walk.

1795: That Napoleon had a great approach to science. When he needed something, he offered a cash prize to anyone who could solve the problem. This year he wanted a practical method for preserving food (no fridges yet). Nicholas Appert won with a sterilization process for food by bottling, canning, heating or sealing. TV dinners start here.

1796: A strange metal-domed cylinder was the first-ever diving suit. It was invented by a German called Klingert. The brave incumbent's arms and legs stuck out of it and there was a tube going to the surface to provide air. Two little glass-covered holes were thoughtfully put in so that the diver could see where he was going.

1800: English General William Congreve re-invented the rocket engine still powered by gunpowder. This stayed the same until the twentieth century. The rockets used today still only use an internal combustion engine. Atomic or electrical engines are still only in the development stages.

Joseph-Marie Jacquard 1752–1834

French weaver/inventor Jacquard tried to develop a mechanism that would automatically lift the threads of the weft which had, up to that time, been lifted manually. He constructed this brilliant machine in 1801, which he fully completed in 1806, using punched cards which told the needles what to do, and when. It did the work of five people. What Monsieur Jacquard didn't know, was that he had predicted the first computers which were to work on the same principle.

1801: Richard Trevithick went to all the trouble of inventing a full-scale steam carriage and then forgot to top up the water, causing it to catch fire.

1804: Fresh from his success winning Boney's competition, Nicholas Appert spent his winnings on opening the first canning factory (canned frogs' legs?). He also invented the bouillon cube (like Oxo, etc.).

1806: Joseph Bramah invented a printing machine that individually numbered banknotes.

Humphry Davy 1778–1829

Humphry Davy was one of those inventors who all the old films are made about. He insisted on sniffing and tasting every new gas or substance himself. Some of them had riotous effects (laughing gas) but others really knocked him for six and he was to die very young having become an invalid at 33.

Humphry also discovered the technique called electrolysis to

decompose water into its elements hydrogen and oxygen. Electrolysis involves putting electrodes into a fluid and passing an electric current through it. His discovery (in its modern form) is still widely used in industry to extract metals from their ores.

He will be remembered mostly, however, for the invention of the miner's lamp which saved thousands of lives. His lamp burned cooler than the ignition point of the explosive gas, methane, also burning with a bluish flame if the gas was around. In 1808 he developed the first electric-powered lamp, the arc light.

1813: Mention photography, and most people think of the Frenchman Daguerre. Not fair, I think; Frederick Scott Archer of Bishop's Stortford thought of the idea of using a negative and made prints as early as 1813. His day was to come, however, in 1851 when he developed the 'wet-collodian process' which was much faster and better than the Frenchman's method.

1814: Black date for pigeons. The first records of organized shoots date from this time. Big celebrations in the pigeon world came in 1880 when clay-pigeons replaced them.

George Stephenson 1781–1848

This clever, self-taught British inventor became known as 'the founder of railways'. When Stephenson first put his mind to railways, he was chief mechanic at a colliery up north. His boss asked him to develop a new locomotive for carrying the coal out of the mines. Stephenson invented the steam blast technique, which allowed trains to go much faster. It is generally regarded as the most important innovation in the history of the steam locomotive.

The 'Blucher' developed in 1813 pulled up to 30 tons at speeds that would have made horses collapse. The 'Locomotion' in 1822 drew the world's first passenger trains at speeds of, can you believe, twelve miles an hour. But it was his 'Rocket' which really made him famous. It won the Rainhill trials reaching speeds of 35mph and completely blew away any rivals being used on the brand new Liverpool–Manchester line.

1815: Scottish engineer John McAdam thought that crushed rock might make a rather good road surface. The name macadam for modern road surfaces is used in his honour, though in those days he didn't use tar or asphalt to stick the bits together.

American Seth Hunt was, almost unbelievably, the first person to patent a machine for making one-piece pins (what's a two-piece pin? I hear you ask). Up to this time England had been pin centre of the world since John Tilsby had founded his pin works in 1625.

Hunt's machine was improved by Englishman Henry Shuttleworth who apparently invented a less dangerous pin. Surely a pin is only as dangerous as where you stick it!

1819: The omnibus was invented in England by George Shillibeer, a coach builder. It carried 22 seated passengers and was pulled by three horses. The conductors wore sailors' uniforms for some obscure reason.

CHAPTER 7

From Guano to Generators –
19th Century Science – 1820–1894

Scientists at the back end of the eighteenth century had become more and more obsessed with electricity – and why not? This culminated in the year 1800 with something called the Voltaic Pile (which isn't a nasty medical condition). Another term for this 'pile' was the now more familiar 'battery'. Before its discovery electricity could only be used 'fresh', so to speak, as no one could think of a way of storing it. Once having stored it, however, the next brainteaser was what to do with it, and what 'it' actually was.

It wasn't until 1828, when Danish physicist Hans Christian Oersted accidentally discovered the link between electricity and magnetism, that boffins like Faraday realized they could put it to some practical use. OK they might have realized, but it took the rest of the century to make anything happen.

Electromagnetism was the key, however, and it wasn't that long before you could turn night into day at the flick of a switch, chat to your chums miles away without shouting, use motors that you didn't have to shovel coal into every five minutes and, eventually, buy little boxes that talked and played music at you in your own  front room. By the end of the century these electro-pioneers were fiddling around with cathode ray tubes. These were oblong glass tubes with all the air sucked out and two metal plates called electrodes stuck at either end. When connected to a battery, there was an invisible discharge of electricity and a faint glow from the negative plate called the cathode. Very nice, I hear you say, but what was the infernal thing for? It became an essential piece of apparatus on the road to X-rays, the electron and, arguably, natural radioactivity.

So What Else?
New fields of activity brought new words with them. Anthropology (the study of man as an animal); archaeology (the study of very old things); cell biology (how living things are made and work); psychology (the study of our minds and souls) and organic chemistry (the study of carbon compounds).

The Men Who Did It
It was well known, if a bit annoying, that before the nineteenth century you could only 'do' science if you were either I. Rich, or 2. Had a mate (called a patron) who was. During this century the study of science became a proper job, particularly in Germany where the clever Germans built brill universities which led the way in research. Mind you, it's fair to say that they had a lot to catch up on, as they'd been a bit slow dropping the mystical paraphernalia of the Middle Ages and Renaissance.

Through get-togethers, called congresses, scientific knowledge became much more international and ideas started flying, particularly in Europe.

Boney Beats the Brits
France, our old rival, led the scientific field at the beginning of the century (which probably started their belief that they invented absolutely everything). This was largely due to the enthusiasm of their clever (if rather small) Emperor Napoleon who was très keen on science. He was probably mostly into medicine as he had just about everything possible wrong with him.

Wissenschaft
Many of the better German scientists dashed down to Gay Paree

where all the action was, much in the way that British scientists export themselves now to make more loot (called the brain drain). They called science 'Wissenschaft' which might just have confused the poor old Frogs as this term included history, philosophy and philology (the study of language – NOT stamps!). They tended to be purists, science-wise, unlike our British lads who were a bit more practical.

God Gets His Way

You still couldn't get a half-decent scientific education in Britain, however, as the technical colleges were pretty mediocre, and the universities worse. Oxford and Cambridge were still suffering from a severe attack of the Church. Their connection to the dear old Church of England not only meant that the tutors had to be clergymen, but also it seemed that God didn't really like the students cutting up things like dead humans or animals, rather essential in anatomical and medical research. Even their attempts to import very advanced Continental mathematics went down the pan as, when it arrived, no one could understand any of the symbols.

Scots Sense

Up in Edinburgh the situation was a bit better. The university wasn't connected to the Church so the canny Scots were able to develop a tradition for being good at learning that still holds true today. Just as well really, as in epidemic-ridden Britain the Scottish-trained doctors were the only ones who knew their stuff.

Science, Who Needs It?

Stateside, the Yanks, true to form, had no time for silly old research. They were much more interested in inventing things that would save them time and sweat. The magic combination of a small working population who earned loads of dollars propelled brilliant technical developments from industries led by inventors like Alexander Graham Bell (a Scottish-American), George Westinghouse, Thomas Edison and George Eastman (whose family later invented

Linda McCartney). The Americans didn't get worked up about theoretical science until well into the twentieth century when your average Yank had all the cars, Hoovers and pop-up toasters, etc. that he (or she) could use.

Science and the Great British Public
You might think that the general public were grateful for all this wonderful new knowledge. No such luck! People who held religious beliefs (and in those days they were the majority) thought it was all the devil's work (clever chap), and were highly suspicious. And it wasn't just bishops like George Berkeley, who busied himself chastising scientists like Newton and Halley. The newspapers were full of cartoons taking the Mickey out of the rest of them.

Earth's Birthday
The trouble had all started when new-fangled geologists came up with a very good case for the Earth being much older than the Christians and Jews had hitherto believed. They'd reckoned that you could cram all the events in the Bible into 6,000 years, so it couldn't be older than that. The Buddhists and Hindus seemed to have the right idea, but nobody seemed to care much what they thought (history take heed). Strangely enough, the opposition

wasn't organized by the main ruling body of the Church, but much more from little local parish priests and their fiery flocks.

Darwin Go Home

If the fuss over the 'older Earth' theory was bad, you should have seen the palaver that Charles Darwin caused when he casually suggested that we'd all once been monkeys, in his book *On the Origin of Species*. 'Speak for yourself!' one can almost hear the masses cry. His theory of evolution caused a storm that went on for generations.

PLEASED TO MEET YOU MR. DARWIN. I HEAR YOU THINK WE'RE RELATED.

What Is a Scientist?

In 1883 William Whewell came up with the idea of calling scientists scientists. Before then they'd been labelled 'natural philosophers' which I think sounds rather flash. Well, they might have called themselves scientists, but we wouldn't have let them get away with it now, as they were mostly amateurs or hangers-on. A scientist (as we all know) is supposed to form a hypothesis (idea), conduct an experiment to try it out, then announce his theory to the waiting world. As it happens, most science wasn't practised by this method (and still isn't). Some scientists don't even do experiments, while others get their facts by experiment and then never even bother to produce a theory. Having said that, this was one of the most productive periods in scientific development – especially in Europe.

Some Great Breakthroughs in Astronomy 1820–1894

1820: John Herschel and Charles Babbage decided it would be rather a hoot to meet all their mates regularly and founded the Royal Astronomical Society in London.

1826: Heinrich Olbers came up with a real puzzler. If the stars are evenly distributed through space, how come the sky's as black as a bag at night. Nice one, Heinrich – it became known as Olber's paradox.

1830: Mary Fairfax Somerville wrote *The Mechanisms of the Heavens,* an easier to swallow translation of Laplace's *Mécanique Céleste.* Laplace declared patronizingly that she was the only woman to understand his book. Could be that she was the only woman that got to read it.

1835: Here comes Halley's Comet again. This time the little devil was spotted sneaking over Rome.

1837: Johann Franz Encke discovered a small gap in Saturn's outer ring and it was named after him. Imagine becoming famous for a gap.

1838: Friedrich Bessel was the first to find a way of measuring how far away stars are. While doing this he discovered that the star Sirius must have a little unseen companion. It was later called Sirius B (I hate serious bees) and was the first of what came to be known as White Dwarfs (caved-in stars).

1842: A very important total eclipse of the sun was observed by astronomers. A chap called Majocci tried to take the first snap of the event but surprise, surprise, it didn't come out. Could it just have been too dark?

1845: Edgar Allan Poe, the hit writer, was the second to try to explain why the sky is dark at night. He reckoned it proved that there was a limit to the size and age of the universe. Olber's paradox seemed to be solved. But was it?

1846: Another German, Johann Galle, discovered Neptune, the most distant of the known planets. He must have had a jolly good telescope as Neptune's 2,794,000,000 miles away.

1848: Julius Mayer reckoned the sun would cool down in 5,000 years. Sounds like 6848 might be the time to get out of the travel business.

1850: The American astronomers William Cranch Bond and his boy George, discovered another ring inside the B ring surrounding Saturn and after much hard deliberation called it, rather brilliantly, the C ring. That year, also, Cranch took the first decent daguerreotype (snap) of the moon.

1862: Alvan Clark and his son Alvan (confusing or what) while testing out their new telescope, spotted Sirius's little mate, called Sirius B (a White Dwarf) which, wait for it, was dark.

Foucault measured the distance from the Earth to the sun as 91 million miles. We now think it's 92.96 million miles. It's still ever such a long way whichever way you measure it.

1863: Annie Jump Cannon should go down in history for her name alone. Her work formed the basis for Henry Draper's *Catalogue of the Stars* which listed 225,300 different models (and none of them for sale).

1864: Sir William Huggins demonstrated that bright nebulas such as Orion are just full of gas, and later, that Sirius and the White Dwarf (sounds like a Spielberg movie) are moving away from us.

1873: Richard Proctor suggested that the moon had a rather bad complexion because of impact by meteorites instead of volcanoes as was originally thought.

1877:   Giovanni Schiaparelli was convinced he'd observed 'canals' on Mars. He probably had some spaghetti stuck to his telescope lens.

1879:   George Darwin reckoned that the moon was made one day as bits of the Earth were thrown off because it was revolving so fast. Don't laugh, this theory held strong until the late 1960s.

1881:   An American philanthropist offered $200 to anyone who discovered a comet. Edward Emerson Barnard of Nashville, Tennessee, went out and found 20 and was paid $3,200. Either my maths is useless, or poor Eddie's still owed $800.
    N. I. Kibaltchich invented a rocket. Unfortunately he also invented the bomb that killed the Czar of Russia. He was therefore promptly executed. Maybe he should have stuck to rockets.

1891:   Maximilian Wolf discovered the first asteroid (a tiny body revolving round the sun) while examining a photograph. He looked closer and found 500 more.

1892:   Barnard the Great White Comet Hunter tracked down the fifth moon of Jupiter, the first satellite of Jupiter found since Galileo, and the last satellite to be found without using photography or space probes.

BIOLOGY

Biology, as such, still didn't really exist in the eighteenth century, as the classification of plants and animals was all lumped together as natural history, and their physiology came under physics.
    Carolus Linnaeus had begun a proper system of classification that resulted in the sort of names they have today, but Comte de Buffon thought it was a bit silly to group things just by what they

looked like as Carolus has done. He much preferred a system based on their reproductive history. After all, he said, a fox is only different from a dog because, when mated, they either produce a sterile offspring or no nipper at all. Could that be why a giraffe is a different species to a gerbil?

George Cuvier got stuck into the study of extinct species, and his work led fairly directly to the theory of evolution, which would have annoyed him no end, as he didn't believe in it.

The Cell Theory

Robert Hooke started the ball rolling in 1665 when he observed and named cells (they looked like cells in a monastery) in cork. He didn't know that he'd grabbed a tiger by the tail and made one of the great discoveries about life. Even in 1831, when microscopes were much better, Robert Brown, noting that all cells have a 'little nut' in the centre, still didn't realise what he was dealing with. In 1838 it was proposed by a chap called Schleiden that all plant tissues are made from cells, and a year later Schwann proposed that eggs are made of cells and that all animal tissues are too.

Schleiden and Schwann (try saying that with a mouthful of cornflakes) had the basic gist of the cell theory. But it wasn't until years later, when cell division was understood, that the full picture emerged, and the cell theory became the backbone (or should I say vertebrae) of modern biology.

Some Great Breakthroughs in Biology 1820–1894

1822: Jean Lemarck was the first to distinguish between vertebrates and invertebrates. At last animals knew whether they were spineless or not.

1825: Henry Walter Bates spent eleven years making insect noises in South American jungles and contributed evidence to support Darwin's theory of evolution. I'm surprised after all that time chatting to insects, they could understand a single word he said.

1827: Estonian naturalist Karl Ernst von Baer discovered that mammals (including baers) develop from eggs, but don't often lay them.

1831: Charles Darwin got the job of ship's naturalist on HMS *Beagle*. His two year trip turned out to be five. Just long enough to run out of sandwiches and clean socks.

1836: The first living lungfish, though extremely unattractive, was caught. It's now regarded to be an important link between fish and amphibians. They didn't meet my old biology teacher!

1838: Theodor Schwann tried to convince people that yeast is made of living organisms, albeit little ones. Nobody would hear a word of it until Louis Pasteur convinced them a few years later.

1842: Samuel Dana spent much of his time up to his elbows in muck. He discovered that it was the phosphates in manure that made it so good for your dahlias – but bad for your friends.

1842: Anders Adolf Retzius, a Swede, introduced the theory on head forms, which basically recognized that different races have different-shaped heads.

1844: Gabriel Gustav Valentin cracked the secret of digestion when he discovered that pancreatic juice broke down the food in your tummy.

1847: Jeffries Wyman and Thomas Savage give the first detailed description of a gorilla (very big, very hairy and very cross?).

1851: French bacteriologist Charles Chamberland was a very clean chap indeed. He became famous for sterilizing medical equipment and filtering out bacteria. His filters were to lead to the discovery of viruses (organisms that cause diseases).

1852: Hermann Ludwig von Helmholtz became the first to discover the speed a message travels along a nerve. He had a nerve! – taken from a frog.

1857: Austrian monk Gregor Johann Mendel, while experimenting with his peas in the monastery garden, made discoveries that led (apparently) to his working out the laws of heredity. Who wants to know about a pea's background?

1858: Rudolf Carl Virchow reckons that all cells come from cells and that diseases are caused by cells falling out with each other. True in cancer and lupus but not in infectious diseases.

1863: Louis Pasteur revealed the micro-organism responsible for souring wine. That's what I call a bad micro-organism.

1865: German botanist Julius von Sachs discovered that chlorophyll is only found in small bodies (later called chloroplasts), and is the key compound which turns water and carbon dioxide into starch while releasing oxygen.

1868: Zoologist Sir Charles Wyville Thomson while mucking about on the sea-bed discovered that there are lots of weird, hitherto unseen, lifeforms down there. He should see cities like New York now.

1871: Charles Darwin discussed evidence of evolution of humans from lower lifeforms, comparing people to animals (not difficult). He introduced the concepts of sexual selection to explain hairlessness and group selection to explain our rather wimpish lack of natural weapons.

1876: Louis Pasteur, who obviously liked a drink, wrote a book on beer, the diseases related to it (not to mention drunkenness) and what caused them.

1883: The last quagga, a close relative of the zebra, died in the Amsterdam zoo. (I wonder if it died wearing striped pyjamas?)

1884: Friedrich Loffler discovered the bacillus (microscopic organism) that causes diphtheria and also the fact that some lucky animals never catch it.

1886: William Rutherford proposed 'the telephone theory' of hearing, which assumes that the whole ear cavity (cochlea) is made to move by sound. William had it a bit wrong, as we now know that there are weeny hairs growing in this cavity, that vibrate and pass sound to our waiting heads.

1887: Eduard Joseph Louis Marie van Beneden discovered that he had the longest name of any living biologist. A great feat! By the way he also let it be known that each species has a set number of chromosomes. Chromosomes, to put it simply, are the gene-carrying bodies of the cell tissue which transmit hereditary features from mummies and daddies to their nippers.

1892: Russian-British bacteriologist Waldemar Haffkine tested himself with a strain of cholera bacteria. A risky business. He then, however, went on to use a vaccine on 45,000 Indians which reduced the death rate by 70 per cent.

MEDICINE

Steady progress was made during this century in understanding our bodies and how they worked, but it would be the discovery of anaesthetics and nasty germs that really rang the bell. Alcohol had been known to deaden the senses (you bet), but was not that good for use in surgery, because 1. It took too long to get the patient drunk and 2. The amount needed to make him pass out was just as likely to kill him. Dentists came to the rescue in the 1840s when they found that ether, chloroform and nitrous oxide knocked you senseless (but still gave you a hangover).

All the old 'bad air' theories of disease were also chucked out when our little enemy, the germ, was finally recognized. Once routed out, the germ could be attacked in all its favourite hidey-holes. Louis Pasteur and Robert Koch got so on top of the 'germ theory of disease' that they even managed to immunize people against some of them. This was all the more incredible when one considers that the immune system as such hadn't been discovered.

Hormones were also being recognized at this time. William Beaumont, being a bit of a grisly opportunist, found a patient with a stomach wound that refused to heal up. Bill thought this a wonderful opportunity to fiddle around in the guy's stomach, and for years was in and out of it, discovering how the digestive system enabled all those powerful chemicals to break down food in our tummies. These chemicals are hormones from the exocrine system. Knowledge of the endocrine system and its relationship to diabetes came much later due to work on a dog's pancreas.

Some Great Breakthroughs in Medicine 1820–1894
1820: Pierre Francis Perry (see unlikely names for French surgeons) invented wire sutures for stitching open wounds. Not that impressive when you realize that in the tenth century the

Hispano-Moorish surgeon Abalcis was doing the job with catgut. He found its suppleness and strength purrfect. I bet his poor moggie wasn't that thrilled with this wonderful discovery.

1821: Two other Frenchmen, pharmacists called Pierre Joseph Pelletier and Joseph Bienaime, managed to isolate quinine from the bark of the Chinchona tree. The secret and sacred bark was used exclusively by the Peruvian Indians until the Jesuit missionaries, two-a-penny in those days, managed to wheedle the secret out of them. Quinine, by the way, is a drug used to treat the effects of malaria.

An English company, Fry's, started selling 'chocolate lozenges' for medicinal purposes. I hardly think putting on weight could ever have been described as medicinal.

1831: Everyone was knocked out by American Samuel Guthrie's discovery of chloroform (a new anaesthetic). The textbook describes the effects of chloroform as follows: 'At first a slight choking feeling is felt; followed by a hot flush; then the senses become less acute; voices become distant; a ringing in the ears; followed by a feeling of being unable to move, precede unconsciousness. Sickness occurs within 24 hours of consciousness.' I think, all in all, I'd prefer the pain.

1832: The Warburton Anatomy Act allowed second-hand-body salesmen to flog corpses for dissection. This put a stop to murdering and grave-robbing as a way of providing stiffs.

1836: Anatomist Wilhelm Gottfried von Waldeyer-Hartz (phew!) was first to note that the nervous system is built from separate cells; and that the cells do not actually touch each other. He also invented the word chromosome, to describe the rod-like structures which crop up in pairs (cosy) in the nucleus.

1844: The Commission for Enquiring into the State of Large Towns established the connection between dirt and disease in England. I think we must be ready for another one.

Sir Patrick Manson (known as Mosquito Manson) suggested for the first time that mosquitoes were the carriers of malaria – dirty little devils.

1847: German Karl Friedrich Wilhelm Ludwig invented a device for recording blood pressure which he used to prove that the circulation of blood is purely mechanical. It might be purely mechanical to you, mate, but it's life or death to most of us.

1849: Aloys-Antoine Pollender discovered the anthrax bacillus. The disease anthrax preys on all animals apart from cats (for some reason) and can be passed on to us humans. The result used to be called wool-sorters disease, but no one seems to know why (unless you're a dead wool-sorter).

1852: Karl Vierodt spent much of his time counting blood cells (red). Although there didn't seem to be a great deal of point at the time, it later became an important tool in detecting anaemia. Count on, Karl.

1853: Aspirin or acetylsalicylic acid (you can see why they called it Aspirin) was synthesized by Frenchman Charles Gerhardt who didn't seem that interested in finding out what it could be used for (silly homme). In 1893 a chemist working at the German company Beyer took some home to treat his dad who had a touch of rheumatism. The company quickly caught wind of it and began manufacturing the stuff. At the Treaty of Versailles in 1919 the poor old Germans had to give up the name Aspirin to the Allies as part of their punishment. We now swallow a thousand million a year. I bet poor old Monsieur Gerhardt would have had a terrible headache if he'd known.

1854: John Snow of York solved the cholera problem near his sewage-contaminated well by removing the handle. Brilliant!

1856: Ludwig again. He managed to be the first person to keep animal organs alive outside their bodies by pumping blood through them. No consolation to the late beast.

1858: Franciscus Cornelis Donders from the Netherlands found out that farsightedness (which means you can't see things close up) could be caused by too shallow eyeballs. Did that mean that shortsightedness (when you can't see things far away) was caused by sticky-out eyeballs?

1861: Pierre-Paul Broca knew this man that couldn't talk properly. When the guy died, Pierre-Paul did an autopsy and found that he had a lesion on the bit of the brain that Broca had always thought might control speech. He had discovered conclusively that different bits of the brain do different things.

Women and Gorillas

A difficult subject this. The now famous French anthropologist Broca declared that the brains of women were, on average, seven ounces lighter than men's. His student, Gustave Le Bon (not Simon), then said that the female brain was closer in size to a gorilla's. (How are we going so far?) He then dared to say that all psychologists recognized that women represented an inferior form of evolution and were closer to the child and savage.

Twentieth-century scientists, I'm relieved to report, found that the size of the brain had nothing to do with intelligence and that all that stuff from the nineteenth century was pure nonsense. Women are smaller than men therefore have smaller brains (phew!!!).

1864: Franciscus Cornelis Donders (again) discovered that astigmatism was caused by an uneven curvature of the lens or cornea of the eye. One must presume that the word 'cornea' was named after him.

1865: Joseph Lister introduced carbolic acid as a disinfectant in surgery, reducing deaths by 30 per cent and making much more complicated operations possible. Carbolic soap was popular until relatively recently.

Poor Hungarian physician Ignaz Semmelweiss having worked for years trying to prevent childbed fever, often caught by women after childbirth, suddenly caught it himself and died. There ain't no justice in this world.

1872: Physician Jean Martin used hypnosis as a form of therapy. Sigmund Freud, his student, listened very very carefully.

1877: Charles Darwin's *Biographical Sketch of an Infant* written after watching his lad's development carefully, became the first source of child psychology. Bet the lad was a right little monkey.

Louis Pasteur noted that some bacteria hate being with others and die. It wasn't until 1939 that a bright French spark called René Jules Du Bos discovered the first antibiotics produced from a bacterium.

1879: Monsieur Pasteur, not discouraged, found that weakened cholera bacteria failed to kill his chickens and that these chickens became immune to the normal virus. This discovery led to the development of vaccine against loads of diseases for which the whole human race (and a load of chickens) is extremely grateful.

1881: Pasteur again. This time the clever chap produced an artificial vaccine to fight anthrax. He demonstrated on a few extremely grateful sheep and cows that an injection with his new vaccine prevented them getting sick when further injected with the horrid bacteria. To prove it, he then injected a few, extremely grumpy, unvaccinated animals with this live bacteria, who promptly fell over and died. You win some and you lose some.

1883: Francis Galton introduced the term eugenics which suggested that human beings could be improved by selective breeding. I might be wrong, but wasn't that the same idea that nasty Mr Hitler came up with 50 years later.

Victor Horsley showed that some lack of growth was due to lack of thyroid secretion.

Danish physician Niels Finsen told everyone that red light reduces the symptoms of smallpox. He was proved to be wrong, however, but Niels went on to establish that ultraviolet light kills bacteria and cures the horrid skin disease lupus.

Sydney Ringer discovered that a frog's heart in saline solution would beat longer if calcium and potassium were added. I expect the frog could have told him that it would have beat even longer if it hadn't been whipped out in the first place.

1884: Czech-American Carl Koller used cocaine as a local anaesthetic. Oh yes, a likely story.

1885: Louis Pasteur mixed up a great new vaccine against rabies and tried it out on a kid bitten by a very unpleasant rabid dog. It saved his life.

1887: Leonardo da Vinci was the first chap to think of contact lenses, but it wasn't until this year that Louis Girard of Houston, Texas, found a way of making them.

1889: Charles Edouard Brown-Séquard was a funny bloke. He injected himself with hormones in the hope of finding renewed energy. I think I'll stick to Lucozade.

Surgeon William Halstead introduced the practice of wearing rubber gloves during surgery (and washing up?).

Oskar Minkowski and Baron Joseph von Mering snatched a dog's pancreas to see if it was essential to life – a nice way to treat your pets. It was! Apparently the pancreas supplies a hormone essential to the production of insulin (and keeping dear Fido alive).

1892: New York surgeon Theobald Smith discovered that Texas cattle-fever was spread by ticks. It gave extra clout to the earlier theories of how diseases like malaria and typhus are spread. Nobody seemed that interested in tick ranching.

1894: Baron Shibasaburo Kitasato and Alexandre Yersin separately discovered the bubonic plague bacterium. I bet they were cross.

CHEMISTRY

With phlogiston out of the way the path was clear for chemistry to really flourish in the nineteenth century, and the discovery of atoms and elements made chemistry top science. If there was a hitch, however, it was because all of the brilliant new finds and discoveries covered up a lack of knowledge about how things actually worked. Chemistry was not alone in this. Everyone loved 'gravity' but nobody really understood what was going on (until the mega-brainiac Einstein came along to let us in on it). Unlike your average darts player, however, chemists had more bullseyes than misses. The atomic theory was a good example so, although there were quite a few who thought it mumbo-jumbo, by the end of the century it was generally accepted.

When in 1828 Wohler synthesized the first organic compound almost magically from inorganic components, organic chemistry was allowed to join the bigger club, especially when entrepreneurs realized there were pocketfuls of hard cash to be made in industry.

Some Great Breakthroughs in Chemistry 1820–1894

1820: Anselme Payen discovered that charcoal can be used to remove impurities in sugar (black sugar?).

1823: Scotsman Charles Macintosh soaked some cloth in a mixture of molten rubber and paraffin and invented the Macintosh or Mac. It became 'the' waterproof topcoat worn by men in the nineteenth century. Women, one supposes, carried on getting soaked.

Michel Eugene Chevreul and Joseph Louis Gay-Lussac patented a new method of making candles from fatty acids, as opposed to tallow which is obtained from the kidney area of ruminating animals (yuk).

1825: Michael Faraday isolated benzine by fractionally distilling whale oil. Recipe: Take I large whale ... etc. etc.

Hans Christian Oersted of electromagnetism fame, discovered aluminium by using electric currents and chlorine to produce anhydrous aluminium chloride from alumina. He then dissolved the resulting compound in mercury and distilled the aluminium from the solution, as if you didn't know. Even though, a year later, Freidrich Wohler found a better way of doing it, aluminium remains the most pricey metal on Earth – eat your heart out gold and platinum. Aluminium jewellery was much sought after in the nineteenth century.

1826: One day John Walker, a Stockton-on-Tees chemist, was happily stirring a mixture of potash and antimony sulphide (as one does). He then scraped the stick he'd been stirring it with on his stone floor (as one also does). It burst into flames (the stick, silly) and John realized he'd found another way of making matches. His invention enabled their manufacture on a huge scale, and within a year they were being widely sold in boxes of 100.

1828: Herr Wohler again, proved that organic compounds can be got from inorganic compounds. The world is amazed.

Conrad Johannes van Houton dissolved a soluble cocoa powder and invented cocoa, the ultimate evening-time beverage. He slept well that night, probably dreaming about how much money he was going to make.

1834: Spoilsport Robert Wilhelm Bunsen discovered an antidote to arsenic poisoning. He's probably more famous, however, for inventing the bunsen burner in 1855. Except that he didn't. The credit should have gone to his assistant C. Desaga – who did.

1839: Charles Goodyear, fed up with his rubber-soled shoes getting stiff in winter and soft and shapeless in summer, set his mind to solving the problem. Having spent all his (and his poor family's) money and ruined his health (rubber sniffing?) he accidentally found the answer to stabilizing the dratted stuff. He let a mixture of rubber and sulphur touch the stove and instead of it melting, it just charred slightly. He called the perfected process vulcanization after Vulcan the god of rubber (or is it fire?).

1840: German chemist Christian Schonbein discovered ozone. I wonder if he'd have been cross if he knew we now seem to be going flat out trying to destroy it.

1841: Johan Jakob Berzelius managed to convert charcoal to graphite. No lead in HIS pencil!

Jacob Schweppe, German founder of the British soft drinks company, developed Indian tonic water. Schhhh...don't tell anyone. Tonic water is a soda containing sugar and quinine which was first used by the Indian army as part of the fight against malaria.

1845: Christian Schonbein, flushed with success at having discovered ozone, gets it in the neck from Frau Schonbein when, using her apron to clear up a spilled acid solution, the apron vanished in a puff of smoke. That was the bad news; the worse news was that he'd accidentally discovered guncotton (nitrocellulose).

1847: Italian chemist Ascanio Sobrero one day poured some

SHALL I SHAKE IT A BIT MORE ALF?

glycerine into a mixture of nitric and sulphuric acid. So far so good; but he discovered that he'd invented nitroglycerine when it blew up when lightly shaken. Despite terrible accidents the Swedish Nobel brothers carried on the study. They did quite well except one of them was blown to pieces by it. The other one (Alf) went on to fame and fortune giving away smashing prizes to other scientists who tried to avoid the same fate as his poor brother. The Nobel prizes for science, literature and peace are still paid for out of the fortune he made from explosives.

1855: Benjamin Silliman lived up to his name. He helped develop petrol but didn't see much use for it apart from as a stain remover. There are some amongst us, however, who sometimes wish it had stayed as that.

Cleaning must have been all the rage at that time for in France J. B. Jolly dropped some turpentine on a dress and noticed that it cleaned it, rather than the reverse. Perhaps Jolly and Silliman should have started a company together. Now what could it be called?

1856: Sir William Perkin produced the first artificial aniline-based dye. He'd been working in his dad's shed when only 18 (long before he was Sir'd), trying to produce quinine, when he accidentally stumbled upon this brilliant purple liquid. Unfortunately, he only managed the one colour but it was enough to start a fashion craze in England known as the Mauve Age. As for young Bill, he retired at 35 with loads of money and 'dyed' a happy man in 1907 – the founder of the modern synthetic dye industry.

Plastic

Alexander Parkes, a professor at Leicester University, experimenting with nitrocellulose and camphor came up with a hard flexible material which he cockily called Parkesine. It was, in fact, the first

THAT COLOUR REALLY DOESN'T SUIT YOU.

plastic, but poor old Parkie couldn't think of anything to do with it. It wasn't until 1869 that John Hyatt, an American, thought it might make rather good billiard balls. He managed to make it cheaply, renaming it celluloid.

1861: Ernest Solvay settled the problem of cheap production of sodium bicarbonate (and a lot of stomachs) by making it from salt water, ammonia and carbon dioxide.

1863: Johann Friedrich Wilhelm von Baeyer developed the first barbiturate which he named after his girlfriend Barbara. What if her name had been Gladys?

1866: Alfred Nobel found a way of absorbing the highly unstable nitroglycerine into a dry form of silica called kieselguhr. It could then be exploded at will, and was called dynamite.

1871: Max Bodenstein of Germany developed the concept of chain reactions, where one change in a molecule causes the next and so on, and so on.

1874: Othman Zeidler made some DDT but didn't realize that insects hated it. Later a Swiss went on to develop it and got the Nobel Prize for his trouble. Although it did the trick directly after the war, if Alfred Nobel had known what a terrible environmental polluter it was to become, he'd never have given him first prize.

1877: Shampoo, from the Hindi word champo (to knead or massage), was developed in England and made by hairdressers by boiling soft soap in soda-water.

1878: Luis Paul Hillaire Bernigaud, Comte de Chardonnet (Lu for short) developed and later patented rayon (artificial silk) because he was sick of his sick silkworms dying. I bet Joseph Swan was a bit miffed as he and his chum Edison invented it a couple of years earlier as a filament for their light bulbs. They failed to see its full potential. Mind you, inventing the first light bulb wasn't bad.

1879:   Constantin Fahlberg, an American, licked his hands after working with coal tar derivatives and discovered a sweet taste. This led on to the discovery of saccharin, a much healthier sweetener than sugar – or was it? Years later it was found that saccharin was poisonous when consumed in large quantities. I don't know how many spoonfuls that actually means.

1884:   Otto Wallach, a German organic chemist, isolated terpenes from various essential oils, such as menthol and camphor. His work always had the right smell about it, and it became the basis for much of the perfume industry.

1886:   Alfred Nobel discovered Ballistite, a type of nitroglycerine that doesn't produce smoke. I'm sure if you'd just been blown up you wouldn't care a tinker's cuss whether there was any smoke or not.

After loads of unsuccessful and dangerous attempts by chemists to isolate the element fluorine, Ferdinand Frederic Henri Moissan finally managed it. Fluorine didn't like being alone and poisoned Moissan causing him to die early, aged 54.

PHYSICS

When it was discovered that magnetism and electricity were related, the boffins quickly realized the influence it would have on science and technology. The same was true with thermodynamics (the science of heat) which first appeared as a concept in 1824 and was fully fledged by 1865.

Everyone knows these days that the ordinary batteries that you have in your Walkman turn chemical energy into electrical energy and most know that friction turns the energy of motion into heat energy (that's why we rub our hands, or anything else, when cold), but before the 1840s no one had a clue about these things.

James Prescott Joule and Herman von Helmholtz independently worked out that no energy is lost as it's turned from one type to another. Apparently these concepts were essential for old Einstein to prove that energy and mass (or matter) are basically the same thing.

The study of wavelengths was also top of the pops in those days, beginning with the Doppler effect in which it was discovered that wavelengths produced by a moving source are raised in pitch when the object is coming towards you and lowered when moving away. This accounts for the strange change in pitch when a police car is racing towards you, from the sound when it's passed (not to mention a strong feeling of relief!). Not only did these techniques help measure the speed of light and sound, but they also helped find out how fast the Earth was whizzing through space.

As the century was drawing to a close, lots of physicists were playing around with the first vacuum tubes producing rays and stuff. Crookes made the best tube and his discoveries were to lead to yet another scientific revolution in 1895.

Some Great Breakthroughs in Physics 1820–1894

1820: Dominic Arago demonstrated that magnetism isn't only affected when electricity is passed through iron, when he did the same with copper wire. Conclusive, I'd have thought.

André-Marie Ampere (Amp to his friends) came up with the basic law of electromagnetism which dealt with the influence of electric current on a magnet and called 'The Right Hand Grip Rule', a method of sorting out the direction of a current with your right hand. He proved that two wires, each carrying an electric current, would repel each other depending on whether the currents were going the same way (or not).

His poor old dad, by the way, was executed (not by electric chair) following his involvement in a rebellion against the French government. His mum died shortly after, and the shock nearly sent poor Amp off his trolley. His name is still used to describe a unit of electricity (no, not the 'André').

The science of electrodynamics (the study of electrical currents and their effects) kicked off to a good start when Hans Christian Oersted discovered electromagnetism. He later invented a meter for measuring electrical currents which he generously called an Amperometer. Come to that an Oerstedometer would have been a bit difficult to get your tongue around.

1821: The clever Englishman, Faraday, was fiddling around with electromagnetism as well. He suspended a piece of copper wire from a hook so that its lower end touched a dish of mercury. When he passed a current from a battery through the hook, the wire moved in a circle, stopping when he switched off. He had, in fact, stumbled upon the first primitive electric motor. Fine if you were really looking for a motor to make a bit of wire go round and round.

1827: Botanist Robert Brown, using his nice new microscope, discovered that pollen grains suspended in a liquid were rushing around all over the shop. This became known as the Brownian motion. It took a 100 years to realize that Botany Bob had provided the first concrete evidence that molecules really exist.

1829: New Yorker Joseph Henry found that wire when coiled produces a greater magnetic field than when straight, and that insulated wire wrapped round an iron bar can produce a great electromagnet. Poor Joe beat our Faraday to the idea of the dynamo but forgot to publish it right away. Faraday, therefore, got all the glory.

1831: Neck and neck still, Henry and Faraday independently discovered that electricity can be induced by changes in a magnetic field, a discovery that led to electric generators.

Faraday did a dead clever experiment in which he set up a copper disc on a spindle between two magnets. When he fitted a handle to the spindle and turned it — Hey Presto — a continuous supply of electricity. It was the prototype for the dynamo.

John Frederic Daniell invented the Daniell cell, the first reliable source of electric current, based on the interactions of copper and zinc.

1846: James Prescott Joule discovered that an iron bar miraculously changes length when magnetized.

1849: James Thomson predicted that if you apply pressure to water it lowers its freezing-point.

1851: Leon Foucault hung a pendulum in a church and demonstrated the Earth's rotation.

Oliver Lodge reckoned the sun might emit radio waves but no one detected them until the 1940s (that's what I call hot radio).

1852: Jimmy Joule and William Thomson got together and established that as gas expands, it gets cooler.

1862: Swedish physician Allvar Gullstrand got stuck into the physics of vision and developed a pair of specs to correct astigmatism. They were also rather useful after lenses had been removed during cataract ops.

1863: Geophysicist Augustus Love from Weston-super-Mare

discovered the Love wave (sounds a bit racy). Calm down, it was an earthquake wave that now helps scientists to measure the thickness of the Earth's crust.

1871: James Clerk-Maxwell could only explain his new work by inventing a mythical creature called Maxwell's Demon (weird or what?). This little chap apparently could see and handle individual molecules.

Ernst Mach, an Austrian, gave the world his philosophy that knowledge is simply sensation. Well, I suppose you could see it that way, Ernst . . . (?)

Funny old James Clerk-Maxwell. This time he remarked that atoms remain in the precise condition in which they first begin to exist. Sounds like a Volvo. Great for the second-hand atom market.

1872: Belgian Zenobe Gramme invented the dynamo – a generator of continuous and reversible electric current. This great breakthrough really began electrical technology.

1880: Pierre Curie discovered the piezoelectric effect. This means that certain substances produce an electric current as a result of pressure on them. This can easily be demonstrated in the back row of any cinema. Curie went on to say that this effect has many applications. I'm sure it has, Pierre.

1882: John William Strutt (Lord Rayleigh) found that the ratio of the atomic mass of oxygen to that of hydrogen is not 16 exactly, as had been assumed, but 15.882. Sounds like someone fouled-up somewhere.

1885: James Dewar invented the Thermos flask which keeps hot liquids hot or cold liquids cold, due to a vacuum between two glass walls. Beats me how the flask knows whether to be hot or cold.

1887: Ernst Mach. This time our Ernst noted that airflow becomes disturbed at the speed of sound. I'm not surprised – I get disturbed going downhill on a bike.

1888: Heinrich Hertz produced and detected radio waves for the first time and calls them Hertzian waves. Marconi rather meanly, I think, renamed them radiotelegraphy waves.

1889: George Francis Fitzgerald formulated the principle that things shrink a bit in the direction they are going. I wonder if that means they get bigger on the way back?

1894: J. J. Thomson announced that he'd found that cathode rays go much slower than light (which still isn't that slow).

EARTH SCIENCE

Geology was in its infancy at the beginning of this century but grew into a major science by the end. Charles Lyell's work with fossils embedded in rock strata led to a proper geological time scale, and caught the attention of Charles Darwin who was busy at home working on his controversial theory of evolution.

Around this time geologists were digging up brill fossils (like dinosaurs) and bone-hunters were scouring the world, particularly in America, trying to find bigger and better trophies to impress their mates with. Georges Cuvier reckoned that all these fairly dim monsters had been wiped out by catastrophes, but Darwin wouldn't have it, preferring to believe that only little changes had gradually sent them packing.

Strangely enough, the catastrophe theory gained more strength when Jean Louis Agassiz promoted the idea of an Ice Age, and current thinking is beginning to look at the idea again.

Some Great Breakthroughs in Earth Science 1820–1894

1820: William Buckland of Oxford University proposed that all geological research be directed to confirming the old Noah's Ark yarn and other whacky biblical tales. Try again, Bill, I think you might just be heading up the wrong path.

1821: Ignatz Venetz, a Swiss, was the first to propose that the Earth was once covered in glaciers. Come to that, Switzerland still is.

1822: Mary Anne Mantell claimed the credit for finding the first fossil of a dinosaur. It was named Iguanodon by her hubby, Gideon Algernon Mantell. It's now reckoned that it was he who really discovered it. Sounds like there might have been a few arguments in the Mantell household. Either way, I'm glad he didn't name the poor old thing after himself (a gideonalgernonodon).

1827: Jean Baptiste Fourier suggested that human activities have an effect on the Earth's climate. I wonder if he'd have been taken more seriously now?

1830: Charles Lyell embarked on a massive study that showed that the Earth must be several hundred million years old, which upset religious people no end.

1840: Jean Louis Agassiz proved the existence of the Ice Age by describing the motions and deposits of glaciers.

1841: Geologist Clarence Edward Dutton studied volcanoes and earthquakes. This led him to the conclusion that the continents are made of lighter rock than the oceans and that mountains 'float' in lighter rock. Sounds as if he had water and rock a bit mixed up.

1842: Richard Owen was the first chap to use the word dinosaur ('terrible lizard') to describe those rather large, rather loopy-looking beasts, that were around for 175 million years (not each individual one!).

1843: Geologist Thomas Chrowder Chamberlin not content with one Ice Age suggested there were several.

1846: Lord Kelvin (British) took the Earth's temperature and worked out that it was 100 million years old. Silly chap didn't take into account heat from radioactivity (mind you, it hadn't been discovered yet). Either way he was very, very short of the mark.

1855: Luigi Palmieri invented the first crude seismometer to measure the first crude earthquake.

1859: Geophysicist Harry Reid worked out that earthquakes are caused by rocks on a fault plane moving one against another and called it the elastic rebound theory. Up till then his geophysicist mates had reckoned that it was the earthquakes that caused the faults, which just shows how wrong experts can be.

Edwin Laurentine Drake drilled the first oil well in Titusville, America. He hit the 'black gold' on August 28th, memorable because it kicked off large-scale geological research. Not in the desire to further mankind's knowledge. They just wanted more oil.

1860: Hermon von Meyer found a fossil feather which he

145

reckoned came from the earliest bird (well he would, wouldn't he). Strangely enough, later that year, an almost complete fossil (probably missing a feather) was found and thought to be the same species.

1863: Francis Gallen introduced the term anticyclone and founded the first modern way of mapping the weather. I hope he wasn't as boring as the weathermen (sorry! weatherpersons) we get on the telly these days. Six years later, meteorologist Cleveland Abbe sent out the first weather reports from his observatory in Cincinatti.

1880: John Milne invented a modern seismograph to measure earthquake waves properly.

1882: Balfour Stewart had been getting his kilt in a twist over the changes in the Earth's magnetic field. He suggested, correctly, that there must be an ionosphere (a layer of ionised molecules in the upper atmosphere).

1883: Krakatoa, a volcanic island between Java and Sumatra, blew up and killed 40,000 people. At least it gave John Milne something to measure with his new toy.

1890: Arthur Holmes used radioactivity to date rock formations and worked out that the Earth is 4.6 billion years old. I bet poor old Lord Kelvin felt silly.

TECHNOLOGY

The nineteenth century must have been just about the most exciting period to have lived (technology-wise). At the beginning of the century, it would take weeks for a message to sail across the oceans. By the end, thanks to electromagnetism and the telegraph, one could communicate instantly over any distance. Imagine the concept of the first telephone, if you'd never seen or heard one before. Lights that switched on instantly, made possible by an electricity supply

in your own house. Railways that criss-crossed the country, which meant no more sitting behind smelly horses, in rickety glorified carts, for hours, or even days, on end. And ships that didn't have to rely on the wind to get anywhere.

In 1885 Karl Benz was driving what we now call a car – little knowing that in a hundred years it would be one of the world's great polluters and that in most cities there'd be nowhere to leave the stupid thing.

These cities, of course, were getting bigger and taller thanks to materials like Portland cement and cheap steel. The gobsmacked man in the street gazed in awe as skyscrapers, suspension bridges and long tunnels were laid out in front of him.

In the country new machinery took a lot of the sweat (and a lot of the jobs) out of the work in the fields. All this was very necessary, as the human race were breeding fast (like rabbits) and needed feeding and clothing (unlike rabbits). In a hundred years, the world as we knew it would be almost unrecognizable thanks to science and technology.

Some Great Breakthroughs in Technology 1820–1894

1820: An enterprising Peruvian beachcomber, noticing the amazing amount of guano (bird droppings) on the beach, decided (maybe) to take some home to see if it would be any good as fertilizer. Being very rich in nitrogen and phosphates it turned out to be the best available. So started the guano industry which was to reach its peak between 1853–7. During this period 8,000,000

tons of this Peruvian seagull guano was
exported all over the world. Sometimes
it was even found to be 100 feet
thick. They carried on
excavating in Peru until
the supply was
practically exhausted.

I expect the birds were too. In America, just to be different,
they used fish droppings (or floatings). Please don't ask your
next question.

1821:   C. Buschman, a German inventor, did the world a dubious
favour by inventing the harmonica (sorry Mr Wonder) as a tool
to tune his piano. What I'd like to know is how the dickens he
tuned the harmonica? (Don't say with his piano!)

1825:   George Stephenson's Locomotion No. 1 made its first
trip. It was the first locomotive to regularly carry passengers and
freight. His 'Rocket' won the Rainhill Speed Trials in 1891, reaching the unheard of speed of 35mph.

William Burt of Detroit produced the first typewriter to 'go'
almost as fast as one could write.

1829:   Queen Nyu Wa is said to have invented a sort of accordion
in 2500BC. Sadly it didn't stop there and on 2 May 1829, Austrian
Cyril Demian patented the one we know (and love) now.

Baked beans were first made to be eaten with pork. They were
soaked overnight, seasoned with mustard, salted pork and molasses
and baked in an oven all day. They weren't tinned until 1875 (not
the same ones) when they were used by fishermen in Maine, USA.
The baked beans we love today (in tomato sauce) didn't arrive
until 1891.

Louis Braille invented a system of raised dots on paper to help
blind people read. He'd been blinded himself when three (not
intentionally) by one of his dad's tools – which makes him even
cleverer.

1834:   James Chalmers of Dundee, Scotland, printed the first stamps but they weren't licked and used until the Penny Black in 1840. Queen Victoria was on the frontside and the glue on her backside.

James Sharp invented the gas stove to use in his own kitchen. He flogged the first one to the Bath Hotel, Leamington Spa, and manufactured them in 1836. He used the Bunsen principle from 1855 onwards.

1835:   While Babbage was desperately trying to get his computer to work, his friend Ada (Countess Lovelace), who was Lord Byron's kid, busied herself writing the first simple programmes.

1836:   Although fibreglass, as we know it, didn't appear until 1960 it was actually invented by a Frenchman in 1836. He made fine threads from glass fibres and coloured them with metal particles. When mixed with silk, they made a brilliant cloth. He provided the draperies for the hearse used to re-bury Napoleon's ashes in 1840.

1837:   Samuel Finley Breese Morse patented his own version of the telegraph. He became most famous for giving the world a series of dots and dashes that, when untangled, became Morse Code. Unbelievably, his invention is still used if more modern methods go on the blink.

Augustus Siebe invented a suit that, although not much good for everyday use, was brilliant underwater. Air was pumped down from the ship above, so you had to be on good terms with the chap doing the pumping.

1839:   Daguerreotypomania spread all over the world when Louis Jacques Daguerre produced photos the like of which had never been seen.

Crookes and Cunningham invented a machine that produced 18,000 bricks in 10 hours.

1840:   John Draper took the oldest surviving picture of a person.

I wouldn't imagine the subject's in quite such good condition.

1843: The French state-owned factory, Manufacture Français des Tabacs, manufactured cigarettes for the first time. The cigarette was actually invented by Spanish beggars who collected cigar ends in the street, wrapped them in paper and smoked them (doesn't everyone?). Shame they couldn't have made a few pesetas out of their idea.

1844: André Fichet, a French locksmith, invented the first safe. He probably shoved one of his patented burglarproof locks on the front (just to be on the safe side).

1846: While monkeying around with his bass-clarinet a Belgian, Adolphe Sax, invented a new instrument, the Adolphophone. Is that right?

1849: The first bombs were dropped from a pilotless Montgolfier balloon. They made quite a splash, as they were dropped on Venice.

1850: Stanislav Henri Laurent Dupuy de Lome developed the first high-speed fighting ship. It was called, predictably, *The Napoleon*. Good job too; they'd never have got all Lome's name on the side.

Unbelievably, the first dishwasher was developed in America. It was (of course) steam-powered.

If you're bored by all those daft macho jeans ads on the box,

blame Oscar Levi Strauss who cut the original pair out of a tent.

In the constant search to conquer sea-sickness, Henry Bessemer invented a ship in which the first-class lounge stayed horizontal at all times despite the roughness of the waves. The poor common-folk threw up over the side as usual.

The guitar as we now know it was developed by Spanish instrument maker Antonio Torres. It wasn't 'plugged in' until a switched-on guy called Richenbacher designed the Electro-Vibrola Spanish guitar in 1935.

Isaac Merrit Singer produced the first successful sewing machine (invented by Elias Howe) in Boston, USA. It must be said that this was the culmination of developments dating from a hundred years earlier when an Englishman, Charles Weisenthal, invented the double-pointed, central-eyed needle that made it all possible.

An unknown, and probably drowned, inventor, built an aquacycle where the rider (or sailor?) was supported on floats and had paddles attached to his feet. The device was used for wild-fowling but I expect the poor quackers probably died from laughing.

1852: The first balloon not to go wherever it damn well wanted was invented by Frenchman Henri Giffard who managed to strap a little steam engine to its rear end.

The first lift for the general public (if they dared) was built by American Elisha Graves Otis for a New York store. Much more interesting was the very first lift built for Louis XIV in 1743 who had it stuck on the side of his palace so that he could, with very little effort, nip upstairs to see his jeune fille – Mme de Chateauroux. Mind you, I'd have thought with him being king, she should have come to see him.

1853: Sir George Cayley was a clever chap inventing a toy helicopter that went 90ft in the air. He did, however, copy the idea from the even cleverer ancient Chinese. He went on to develop the first manned glider.

Henry Cole has a lot to answer for. Too busy to communicate with all his chums at Christmas, he invented the Christmas card.

1854:   English inventor Henry Bessemer developed a process for producing inexpensive steel. Some say that he might have nicked the idea off a chap called William Kelly who also invented it with four Chinamen several years earlier.

1855:   A British inventor named Cowan looked thoughtfully at a turtle and proceeded to invent a turtle-shaped armoured car, based on a steam tractor.

Toilet paper was invented by American Joseph Gayety and sold in 100 sheet packs of shiny (how horrid) paper. In Roman times

a sponge on a stick was used in public toilets (only one?) and kept in a pot of salt water. In medieval times, the more wealthy folk used pieces of blanket; and monks would cut up their older habits into squares (what a filthy habit!). Hindus and Moslems simply used their left hand and washed it afterwards with water from a jug, thus giving rise to the Hindu and Moslem habit of only eating with their right hands. Now, are you really surprised?

1856:   Who'd have thought when riding on Jesse Reno's 'moving staircase' at the Coney Island fairground, that they were witnessing the first escalator. They've even got a spiral one in a Japanese department store. Trust them to go one better.

1858:   At last America and the UK could communicate. The first transatlantic telegraph cable was laid.

1860:   Jean Joseph Etienne Lenoir built the first 'horseless carriage' to use an internal combustion engine. Steam was now a thing of the past.

Frederick Walton oxidized linseed oil mixed with resin and cork dust on to a cotton backing, and so invented linoleum.

1862: American Richard Gatling invented the machine-gun to enable people to shoot each other lots – and quickly.

1863: The first underground railway was inaugurated in London. It was three miles long and used steam traction. Anyone travelling on the Northern Line recently would agree that it hasn't changed much.

It is little known that mailbags were transported round London via an air-tube railway. (Funny little unmanned carriages whizzed along pneumatic tubes at a speed that would make us envious today.) It is even less known that they still are.

1865: An anonymous American engineer invented a flying machine that never really got off the ground. It consisted of a circular frame to which were attached, by individual harnesses, ten eagles. The passenger sat in the centre of the frame holding the eagles' reins. This invention appeared in a serious American science magazine.

The first manufactured pet food was made by Spratts in America (of course). It was a sort of cake for dogs. The Earth-shattering invention of bone-shaped dog biscuits took another 50 years.

1866: Robert Whitehead was the British manager of an Italian engineering company. He first thought of a boat filled with explosives, guided by wires, as the ultimate sea weapon. Unfortunately, because it was on the surface, the victim was able to get out of the way quite easily. He therefore decided to make it go underwater. The torpedo, as it was called, did the trick nicely.

1868: The first traffic lights were seen in London outside the Houses of Parliament. They were gas-lit lanterns, just red and green, set on poles and operated by policemen. They were put there to stop the traffic in order to let members cross the road. How tempting.

Another early robot was invented by Americans Zadoc Dederick and Isaac Grass. It took the form of a steam-powered man pulling a little cart. One of the latest and most sophisticated 'androids' was presented by Frenchman Pascal Pinteau in 1988 and called Leonardo da Vinci.

American photographer Thomas Adams was experimenting unsuccessfully with a natural substance called chicle as a substitute for rubber in the production of rubber goods(?). One day, for totally obscure reasons, he shoved some in his mouth and so invented chewing gum. He then added flavouring and opened the Tutti-Frutti Company. The sensible Brits didn't much like the idea of chewing rubber and it didn't catch on until 1911 when the now famous firm of Wrigley re-introduced it.

Emperor Napoleon Bonaparte strangely organized a competition to find a butter substitute for the 'less prosperous classes' (cheek!). Hippolyte Mege-Mouriez reckoned that anything a cow could do he could do better. He came up with a compound of, wait for it, suet, skimmed milk, cow's udder, pig's stomach (yum yum)  and bicarbonate of soda. I bet you'd need the bicarbonate after that disgusting lot. Having said that, Hippo won the competition and claimed the invention of margarine. In 1910, you'll be relieved to know, its production switched to vegetable oils.

The rickshaw was invented in Yokohama by an American minister, Reverend Jonathan Scobie, whose Mrs had a bad leg. The first chaps to pull rickshaws were the poor Japanese who Scobie had managed to convert. Imagine being converted to life as a substitute horse.

1869: Astide Berges, a French papermaker, reckoned he could harness the power of the alpine waterfalls for his factory. He eventually made it, creating the first proper hydro-electrical power.

1870: American inventor S. R. Mathewson solved the problem of horsedrawn vehicles charging all over the San Francisco streets every time a steam tram appeared. He designed a gas-fired, horse-shaped steam tram that didn't belch smoke. All it proves is how stupid horses are.

1874: Major Walter C. Wingfield nicked an Indian game and patented it as his own. He called it Spairistike, and it became probably the most popular of all outdoor games. You might know it better as tennis.

American Farwell Gideon realizing that the huge ranches of the wild and woolley west had to be contained, developed barbed wire and fenced in a fortune for himself.

1876: Karl Paul Gottfried built the first fridge that was any good, even though Aussie-Scot James Harrison had been flogging his version for 15 years.

Although Henry Heinz invented the tomato ketchup we know today, the Chinese had been using a sauce called 'ke-tsaip' for donkey's (or panda's) years. By the way, did you know the official standard for best quality ketchup insists that it doesn't leave the bottle faster than .00522mph.

Alexander Graham Bell patented the telephone three days before spilling battery acid down his trousers. He casually made the first phone call to his assistant to come and give him a hand (or some new trousers).

Thomas Alva Edison invented the phonograph, but although it made him even more famous, he wasn't that impressed with the sound quality and moved on to other things. Bell took it up, but it was Charles Tainter who got the patent and called the machine the graphophone. The first modern 'discs' were made of rubber and demonstrated in 1888 in Philadelphia.

Remarkably, solar energy was first seen at the Paris Exposition, when clever Frenchman Augustin Mouchot produced enough energy to power a little steam engine. No one did any further work on the idea till 1948.

1878: Amazingly Sir Thomas Swan, an Englishman, and Thomas Edison, an American, both independently invented the electric light bulb. After they'd finished suing each other to no avail, they joined forces and made a pile – of cash and light bulbs.

James Ritty, bar owner of Dayton, Ohio, was fed up with his staff constantly nicking the takings and customers fighting over their bills. He set about inventing a cash register which he then sold to other saloon owners having the same problems. He never needed to worry about money again.

1880: Clever Dan Ruggles, an American inventor, used his hot-air balloon to lift explosive charges into the clouds to create rain. It took his admirers quite a while to realize that old Ruggles only sent it up when it looked like rain anyway.

1882: Another attempt at building a Channel tunnel was commenced following Napoleon's daft plan to invade Britain underwater in 1802. It was given up for political reasons.

1883: After many attempts Gottlieb Daimler developed the first truly efficient, high-speed internal combustion engine.

1884: Irish engineer Sir Charles Parsons invented the steam turbine engine based on Hero of Alexandria's principle (AD200). This engine revolutionized marine propulsion, power stations, and public lighting generators.

Lewis Waterman, an insurance salesman, wrecked a policy when his pen deposited its ink all over it. He set himself the project of inventing a pen with its own ink supply. He became the creator of the first practical fountain pen.

1885: George Eastman's invention of flexible roll film and, four years later, the Kodak camera, meant that photography became possible for the man in the street.

Mrs Benz became the first car thief when she 'borrowed' hubbie's new motor to show the world it really worked.

1886: A German ship, *The Gluckauf* was the first purpose-built oil tanker. There's so much oil in the oceans from these wretched ships these days that before long we'll be hearing reports of water slicks.

1887: Esperanto, the international language, was invented by Lazarus Zamenhof – a Pole. Although still spoken throughout the world, it has a slightly amateurish, 'enthusiast' feeling about it. Having said that, it looks very much as if it might become the pivotal language of international translation machines. Esperanto might go to the ball after all.

1888: John Boyd Dunlop did the world's bums a great service by inventing the air-filled rubber tyre.

Louise Glas installed a primitive juke-box at the Royal Palace(?) in San Francisco. It worked with cylinders and was apparently not that good. Despite many attempts, the juke-box we know and love didn't really take off until the 1950s with the arrival of the '45'.

Poor American William Kemmer pushed forward the bounds of

science by being the first chap to get executed by electric chair. Thomas Edison, always one to see an opportunity, arranged for prisons to have alternating current as a foot in the door to getting it installed in American households.

Whitcomb L. Judson devised the father of the first zip-fastener as a way of doing up boots. Unfortunately, it was clumsy and came open easily (which would certainly have limited its use). Gideon Sundback, a Swedish engineer, invented the zip as we know it today, in 1913. For years they were regarded as improper if used on women's clothes and weren't seen until 1930.

1891: The Bristol Electric Co. was responsible for the first torch. It was a bit on the big side, weighing four pounds (including battery).

1892: In 1841 artist John Rand developed a collapsible tube for oil paint. It took another 50 years for anyone to think of putting toothpaste in it. Up to that time it was packed in little pots.

The first four-function calculator that really worked appeared on the market. It was called the 'Millionaire' and probably made its inventor one.

H. D. Perky (an American lawyer) invented the first breakfast cereal, Shredded Wheat. At the same time, the Kellogg Brothers were running a sanitarium in Michigan, USA. Being total spoil-sports, they wouldn't let their prisoners – sorry, guests – have their usual ham and baked beans for breakfast. Will Kellogg had been boiling wheat in an effort to find a digestible substitute for bread, for his brother Dr John (the boss). One day a batch was left out accidentally. The brothers tried again and found that the standing had tempered it. Will then devised a way of slicing the compressed wheat and Hey Presto — Cornflakes.

It is little known that head boy scout, Baden-Powell, used the box kite of Lawrence Hargrave to lift people into the air. Apparently lines of them were sent up at a time but I can't seem to find out why.

CHAPTER 8

....

Science and Wartime – 1895–1945

Hold on to your seats. If you think it's been complex up to now, catch a load of this lot. In this section we will be introduced to new terms like X-rays, radioactivity, subatomic particles, relativity and the quantum theory. These discoveries were to lead scientists to look at matter and energy in a completely new way, and eventually – with the invention of the atom bomb in 1945 – to learn how to blow ourselves to kingdom-come at the press of a button. It's not surprising that science was to develop in leaps and bounds during this period, when you realize that there were more actual scientists hard at it at the beginning of the twentieth century, than in all the previous eras put together.

Although all this study was to become a much more communal effort, a few all time one-offs like Einstein, Bohr and Rutherford, were thrown up (if you'll pardon the expression). Science became like a ginormous jigsaw puzzle with hordes of researchers beavering away at each individual piece. It took brains like Albert's (Einstein) to fit all the bits together so they could see the bigger picture.

All this new-fangled science had a staggering effect on the everyday life of us lesser mortals, unlike the Renaissance or the Age of Enlightenment which only really influenced the way we thought. As soon as some bright spark discovered something, another bright spark was seeing what use it could be put to. For example, the discovery of the electron (the lightest known particle) led to electron tubes in only twenty years, followed by a flood of uses like radio, telly and the ability to talk to your mates practically anywhere in the world (providing they had a phone).

Industry itself was to put its money where its mouth was and set up research outfits of its own, like the Bell Labs in the States, founded by the American Telephone and Telegraph Company.

Germany Pulls Ahead

By the beginning of the twentieth century the clever Germans were streaking ahead in the science and technology race. They'd become world leaders in the production of dyes and chemical products, which was to give birth to the vast German pharmaceutical industry. They were knocked off the number one spot around the time when a certain Mr Hitler came to power. This was probably because so many European brainiacs (a lot of them Jewish), sniffing imminent trouble, set up home in the very welcoming America, which laughed all the way to the bank and consequently took over the lead. In fact, many of America's subsequent Nobel (remember him?) Prize winners had spent more of their lives in Germany than in the States. The poor old Russians, always good at missing the boat, wouldn't have any of these brainy ex-Germans in the house, which probably accounts for their only having two Nobel Prizes to put on their mantelpiece in the last sixty-odd years.

Wars are always good for science, and science is always good for wars. The First World War was no exception, with Germany having over 100 laboratories churning out more and more stuff to hurt us with. After this extremely nasty scrap, governments started pouring loads more cash into the science game, except in Germany, of course, as the naughty Nazis had frightened most of their scientists away. All this, as we now know, was to come to a head with the Second World War and that blooming bomb.

Brand New Philosophies

In the first half of the twentieth century whole bunches of preconceptions about mechanisms of chemical reactions, the way the actual universe was constructed, or for that matter – matter itself, were to fall apart. This new way of looking at things had a heavy influence on the way we humans looked at ourselves (animals didn't seem to care too much), a bit like it was during the Age of Enlightenment.

In America the philosophical school of pragmatism held views similar to the late Ernst Mach: reality can only be explained by experience alone. At the same time it became clear that science must also be based on logical reasoning (especially maths). The scientific view soon became the only way acceptable to all (except the deeply religious) of looking at reality, and in many cases became the model for philosophical thought as well.

By now very few scientists were giving Darwin's theory of evolution a hard time and it was becoming the backbone of the social sciences and psychology.

Quantum Reality

Around the end of the nineteenth century, Newton's theories were beginning to become a bit ragged at the edges and, in some areas, actually fell apart. It became a bit obvious that one cannot trace all physical phenomena back to pure mechanics. To get things straight, scientists developed the quantum theory and quantum mechanics, chucking out loads of old obsolete classical physics. Wolfgang Pauli and Werner Heisenberg added theories which wouldn't even attempt to visualize phenomena (as in classical physics).

In 1927 Heisenberg came up with what was to be one of the fundamental principles of quantum mechanics. He reckoned that it just wasn't possible to work out the actual position and speed of a particle (such as an electron) with absolute accuracy; it was only possible to work out the *probable* position.

This became known as the principle of uncertainty and a chap

named Bohr tied it up with his theory of complementarity (whew! hang on). If you observe a system, you actually get involved with it, and disturb it. Bohr then made out this theory was a fundamental principle of the natural sciences (well he would, wouldn't he?).

It included the complementarity between 'the wave' and 'the particle' theory of light. Light can be seen as a wave, for example, especially when it is diffracted passing through a narrow slit, or as a particle, when ejecting an electron from a metal surface.

The Quantum Theory

Most science books spend chapters describing the development of this theory. I haven't got the time or the inclination, but the bare bones seem to go like this. All processes consist of a series of leaps. Matter absorbs energy and loses its quanta. The energy of a particular quantum is obtained by multiplying the frequency of radiation by h, 'the quantum of action'. Consequently the quanta of high-frequency radiation (like X-rays) will have more energy than the quanta of low-frequency radio waves. Look, I know this probably doesn't make much sense. Try and get hold of Stephen Hawking's brilliant *A Brief History of Time* in which the staggering, physically helpless, non-speaking, non-writing genius describes the whole business in a way that even you or I can understand (well, almost).

ANTHROPOLOGY AND ARCHAEOLOGY

In 1805 Eugene Dubois brought home to Europe a Javanese fossil now known as Homo erectus. He was reckoned to be the first man-type species different to us. Unfortunately, Dubois caused so much aggro that he had to hide his new mate under the floorboards. It wasn't until another Homo erectus was found in China that the discovery could be taken seriously.

Sadly, one of the largest groups of these fossils disappeared during the bombing in the Second World War. Homo lostus!

Another great discovery was made by Raymond Dart who was given the head of a child (fossilized, of course!) to have a look at. The kid was thought to be yet another form of man which he named australopithecus africanus. Interpretations and arguments about this young head are still going on today.

Most cries of fraud and forgery regarding late nineteenth-century findings of bones and cave paintings, were silenced when four young boys stumbled upon the Lascaux cave paintings in 1940. Their realism, and the information they contained about early man, were so impressive that the cynics had to shut their mouths. Just about all the major discoveries in anthropology were made around this period and the oceans were chock-full of expeditions setting out nearly every day all over the globe from Siberia to the Americas.

In archaeology, Arthur Evans astounded everyone in 1900 with his discovery of the Minoan civilization on Crete, closely followed by Hiram Bingham's discovery in 1911 of Machu Picchu, the vast mountain-top city, way up in the Peruvian Andes. This city was to reveal the story of the Incas from the first to arrive to the last to leave.

The ultimate and most astonishing find was in 1922 when Howard Carter and Lord Carnarvon discovered the tomb of the now legendary Tutankhamen. 'King Tut' was the sort of find that all those knobbly-kneed, pith-helmeted explorers had dreamed about. Having said all this, archaeology was gradually to shift from chasing more and more spectacular finds towards a much more scientific approach to the past.

Some Great Breakthroughs in Anthropology and Archaeology 1895–1945

1902: Pierre Boule reconstructed the skeleton of a Neanderthal man.

A French expedition to Susa, the ancient capital of Elam (Persia), discovered a lot of old tablets engraved with the first set of laws ever recorded. Whatever did they start?

1908: A black cowboy, George McJunkin, discovered the first known Folsom points (primitive spearheads), associated with fossilized bison bones in New Mexico. I personally think that the discovery of a black cowboy named McJunkin was slightly more spectacular.

1911: The first fragments of the infamous Piltdown man were found in England. For years and years (until 1953) this part-skull was thought to be the oldest evidence of the human race, until it was discovered to be a huge hoax. It appears some joker put together an ancient human skull with a nice new chimp's jaw.

1919: F. Wood Jones argued that we humans said goodbye to the great apes at a stage similar to that of the modern tarsier (lemur to you). This suggested that no common ancestor of humans could possibly be like a monkey. Funny, I know of quite a lot of very common people who seem to disprove that.

1926: Roy Andrews, who doesn't sound much like an explorer, found no traces of the human remains he was looking for in the Gobi Desert. He did, however, find the first dinosaur eggs known to science. I bet you can now get them by the half-dozen in Sainsburys.

1927: Davidson Black, a Canadian, found a tooth which turned out to have once resided in the mouth of 'Peking man' (half a million years old). It's now reckoned to be the discovery of the race Homo erectus.

1928: Franz Boaz was one of the first anthropologists to attack theories of racial superiority; although he also believed in equality of the sexes he apparently wasn't wild about the idea of having only one wife.

1932: A chap named Edward Lewis, while in India, found a bit of the jaw of a primate which, for the next 50 years, anthropologists believed was from man's earliest known ancestor. Unfortunately, it has only recently been established that ramapithecus, as it was called, grew up to be what we now know as the orangutan.

1935: While shopping in a Hong Kong apothecary shop, German paleoanthropologist, Ralph von Koenigawald, found some teeth belonging to the gigantopithecus (the largest primate known). You deserve to become extinct if you do things like leaving your teeth in junk shops.

ASTRONOMY

Most astronomers at the beginning of the century thought that the sun was just one of the stars in the Milky Way. It was also thought that all those fuzzy objects, like the Andromeda Nebula, observed for two hundred years through rather crappy telescopes, were all part of the same thing. Edwin Hubble found out the truth; that they were an enormous distance from our galaxy and that Andromeda was a galactic system every bit as big as ours.

Hubble made another surprising discovery. During the 1920s he found out that the further a galaxy was from the Earth, the faster it was trying to get away from us (can you blame it). This was the basis for theories that the universe was getting bigger and formed the model for what came to be called 'the Big Bang' theory.

In solar system astronomy, one of the most notable achievements was the expansion of the solar system into nine planets when Clyde Tombaugh discovered Pluto in 1930. These days, however, nobody much cares about poor old Pluto and don't feel he really has much significance (I bet Mickey and Goofy still love him).

One of the astronomical breakthroughs of this period was the understanding of the life-cycle of a typical star. As stars were classified into gas giants and white dwarfs, etc. it became apparent that stars of different ages must be categorized differently.

How Big is the Universe?

The answer seems to be — very! As early as 1745 Kant had said that our solar system belonged to a flat rotating system which was one of many 'island universes' that existed in the whole 'big' universe. As telescopes got better, what had been fuzzy patches — which astronomers had probably tried to wipe off their lenses — were seen to be myriads of stars. By the twentieth century it became clear that old Kant was right.

In 1912 Henrietta Leavitt, an American astronomer, studied cepheids, which are a type of variable star in which the brightness is periodic over time. By measuring the variations she could calculate their brightness and therefore how far away they were. Ms Leavitt also studied what were known as the Magellanic Clouds (two distant universes), using the above method, and found that they were a distance twice the diameter of our galaxy away.

That's nothing, said Edwin Hubble when he established that Andromeda, and similar nebulae, were even further away than that. When he discovered that the further the galaxies are from Earth the faster they are moving away, and that the speed is proportional to the distance, it supported the theory that the universe was created by one huge explosion, and the stars are all the bits flying all over the place.

A Belgian priest, Georges Lemaitre, also went along with the idea that the universe had started with the explosion of a 'primaeval atom' (which was the whole universe crammed into very little space). This explosion came to be called 'the Big Bang'.

A slightly spooky confirmation of this theory happened by chance in 1965 when two physicists from the Bell Telephone Company in the States were fiddling around with a really sensitive microwave antenna. They heard this strange hiss at a wavelength of 2.35cm with an intensity much stronger than it should have been. So what? you and I might have thought. Not them; they realized that this hiss was caused by radiation emitted by a body at a temperature of −454°F. So what? we still might have thought. Apparently this temperature is precisely that which the universe is believed to have cooled to, as a result of the Big Bang. Science fiction, eat your heart out.

BIOLOGY

Experimental biology really began in the nineteenth century. In 1857 Gregor Mendel had discovered the laws of heredity, but no one wanted to know. His work was later rediscovered by accident in 1900. The idea of a 'gene' being a unit of inherited characteristic, like the colour of eyes or the length of a nose, made it possible to understand how things could be passed down from generation to generation. Basically this means if you're an ugly creep, blame your mum and dad, and tell them to do the same. The role of these genes in the production of enzymes (chemical catalysts) in the cells of organisms also became understood, and led to the 'one enzyme – one gene' theory. The penny only fully dropped in the 1940s when the biologists finally got their heads round DNA, the substance that transmits all this genetic information.

When examining the fruit-fly (as one often feels like doing), whose chromosomes (antibodies containing genes) are clearly visible, it was noticed that such things as mutants appear – having slight changes in wing shape, etc. This gave huge clues in the study of evolution.

Biology began to look over its shoulder increasingly at chemistry to such a point that they mated and spawned the new science of biochemistry. Suddenly the role of these things called enzymes and hormones began to be understood, especially the relation of the hormone to illness. (A hormone is a substance secreted by certain glands into our blood which stimulates the action of certain organs.)

Some Great Breakthroughs in Biology and Biochemistry 1895–1945

1895: A chap named Rabl confirmed that chromosomes keep their own personality during cell division. This was ever so important as it led to the assumption that chromosomes carry our 'heredity'.

1897: Eduard Buchner, a German biologist, stumbled on the fact that a cell-free extract of yeast can convert sugar to alcohol. (Jesus did it with water . . .) This was the very beginning of biochemistry, as before this chemists believed that processes of this kind could only happen in living cells.

1900: Biochemist Frederick Hopkins of Eastbourne, discovered tryptophan, an amino acid (a basic part of protein). He proved that it's essential to rats (are rats essential? I ask). This became the first-known essential amino acid.

1901: The last big mammal to become known to science, the okapi, was discovered, minding its own business, up Africa way. He turned out to be a relative of the giraffe. They still exchange cards at Christmas.

Jokichi Takamine of Japan not only discovered adrenalin (a hormone secreted by the adrenal gland), but synthesized it too.

1902: Ivan Petrovich Pavlov was a well-known dog annoyer. He formulated his law of reinforcement by giving his dog its dinner at the sound of a bell. After a while he only had to ring the bell and the dog would drool and jump up and down. Pavlov became famous but the dog probably died of malnutrition (with a strange ringing in its ears).

1905: Clarence McClung (surely the silliest name in science) found that female mammals have two X chromosomes and males have an X and a Y. Why? Search me.

1906: Fred Hopkins again. This time he told us that food contains other ingredients essential to life that aren't proteins or carbohydrates. We could now have told him they're called vitamins.

1907: Hans Hugo Selye proved that stress can affect our physical functions. R u b Bi#sh !

1909: Archibald Garrod, pathologist, discovered that some genes function by blocking steps in life processes that would otherwise take place.

1910: Karl von Frisch showed that frisch − sorry, fish − can see different colours. Well, Karl, we're all really relieved to know that.

1913: High-school teacher Johann Regan used his new telephone to find out whether it was true that a male cricket's call is a mating signal to a female cricket. When the male cricket chirped over the phone, the female cricket immediately headed for the earpiece. So that's what you must do if you want to date a cricket.

1914: John Broadus Watson proposed the use of animal experiments in psychology. I know this frustrated cricket . . .

1919: Whacky old von Frisch again, discovered that bees communicate through body movements. Ouch!! Right again, Karl.

1922: Elmer McCollum discovered vitamin D in cod liver oil and used it for treating rickets. He must be right, I've never seen a rickety cod.

1925: At the Scopes 'monkey trial' held in Dayton, Ohio, John Scopes was prosecuted for teaching evolution to a group of chimps – sorry, children.

George Hoyte Whipple found that iron is an important constituent of red blood cells.

1926: Hermann Muller obviously had something against fruit-flies. He increased their mutation rate by a factor of 150 by zapping them with X-rays.

1928: Albert Szent-Gyorgyi von Nagyrapolt discovered vitamin C at the same time as Charles King. If you're ever asked, I wonder which name you'll remember?

1931: I'm not making this up, honest. Eloise B. Cram proved that if a threadworm infects a grass-hopper, it becomes an easier prey for chickens. I didn't even know that chickens liked grasshoppers. I'd have thought they'd rather have eaten the stupid worm. Thanks, Eloise.

1932: Julian Huxley wrote a book which stated that the specific growth rates of the organs of the body stand in constant ratio to each other. How come some people grow huge ears and noses then, Julian?

1933: The last Tasmanian wolf died in a zoo, though there are some reports that there are still a few hiding in the Tasmanian bushes (and who can blame them?).

1934: Adolf Butenandt prepared the first pure progesterone, a female sex hormone.

1935: Not to be outdone, along comes testosterone, the chief male sex hormone, discovered by Swiss chemist, Leopold Ruzicka.

1936: Ruskie Andei Nikolaevich isolated pure DNA for the first time.

Another Soviet biochemist, Alexander Ivanovich, in his book *The Origin of Life on Earth* put forward a theory that we still like today. He thought that life evolved in random chemical processes in the ocean, which became like a vast biochemical soup out of which early lifeforms crawled. Yum, yum, sounds kinda tasty.

Robert R. Williams synthesized vitamin B which proved very, very vital for beriberi (a horrible Eastern disease).

1938: Trofim Denisovich Lysenko, a Soviet botanist, one of the infamous Joe Stalin's blue-eyed boys, became head of all Soviet biological research. He imposed his view that acquired characteristics can be inherited. This is now known to be incorrect, but with Stalin's methods, practically anything became possible. Ve have Vays of changingk your karakter!

A weird-looking thing called a coelacanth was caught live off the African Coast. Lucky really, it was believed to have been extinct for 60,000,000 years. Perhaps as fish go, it was just rather old.

1940: Remember the Russian botanist Lysenko (Stalin's mate) who insisted that acquired characteristics can be inherited; well, another Russian, Vavilov, said he didn't think it was true. In typical Russian democratic manner, he was arrested and sentenced to death. I do like a reasonable discussion. Vavilov wasn't executed but died of ill-treatment in prison three years later. Obviously, Russian prison-guards didn't need to inherit any horrid old characteristics.

1944: R. B. Cowles and C. M. Bogert proved that desert reptiles regulate their body temperature by specific behaviour patterns (they probably take their jackets off).

CHEMISTRY

Now that scientists had got the hang of atoms they were much better equipped to explain many of the chemical properties of elements and compounds. Linus Pauling in the 30s told of the role of electrons in the formation of the molecule (the smallest portion of a substance able to retain that substance's characteristics).

Atoms, he said, can be tied together by either electrostatic forces or by sharing electrons, which all sounds very cosy. The newly developed quantum mechanics just served to underline, theoretically, all that chemists were finding. The study of things called polymerization reactions helped them develop new compounds made up of macromolecules, so along came many new artificial fibres and early plastics.

Silicones had a chemistry all to themselves and their synthesis led to really important industrial compounds after World War Two.

Marie Curie (Sklodowska)

Marie Sklodowska was of a Polish disposition and travelled to Paris, though penniless (or francless), to study her passion, science, at the Sorbonne. She nearly died of starvation while there, but still managed to come top of her class in 1894. She met her husband Pierre Curie (what a coincidence) in the same year and together they became by far the most famous husband and wife team ever known to science. (Mind you it's difficult to name another one.) Together they discovered polonium and later radium (used in the treatment of cancer). Marie is probably best known for confirming the existence of (and coining the word) radioactivity, ushering in the atomic era.

The Curies were excited by a mineral ore called pitchblende and set about refining it, as it appeared to be far more radioactive than anything they'd seen so far. The Czechoslovakian government sold them tons of the stuff, and delivered it to their leaky old shed near their laboratory. Unfortunately, they had to shift the ore by hand to their lab.

The element it contained was polonium which turned out to be a hundred times more radioactive than uranium. But they also realized it contained an even more radioactive element, nicknamed radium, but in tiny quantities. Despite the tons of ore they processed, they only managed to extract a tenth of a gram of this new element. Sounds like it might have been

better to take their gear down to the shed and do the refining there. Anyway their health was so broken from exhaustion and malnutrition that they were unable to collect the Nobel Prize awarded to them in 1903.

Pierre, unfortunately, got run over by a lorry in 1906, but Mrs Curie carried on until awarded a Nobel prize in her own right – the first person ever to get two.

The last years of her life were spent pioneering X-rays and radium treatment which became essential in her work with cancer patients. Unfortunately, poor Marie had been handling the stuff too long, and died of leukaemia in 1934, the greatest woman scientist who ever lived.

PHYSICS

Practically everything that was known on the subject was turned on its face during the first half of this century. Thanks to a jolly clever man called Einstein and his theory of relativity, all the Newtonian ideas about space, time, continuity and what caused what to happen were changed drastically. Before all this happened, however, they had to understand how the atom was made up, which they did by a series of discoveries.

Up till 1900 physicists thought that everything they encountered could be explained by Newton's laws of motion. Unfortunately, it could not explain things like the distribution of energy in molecules of gas, and that of radiation emitted by hot bodies. Max Planck, in 1900, threw everyone by saying that energy can only be given off by matter in small packets called quanta. Trouble was nobody seemed to know what this quanta was until Einstein introduced the concept of the photon. Photons were the small packets of travelling light – a bit like Newton's idea that light consists of vibrating particles. Einstein reckoned that as well as being given out in small packets, light could only be absorbed in small packets. Physicists, trying to keep up, observed that certain metals give off electrons when placed in a strong light and the speed that they whizz off doesn't depend on the light's intensity, but on its colour or wavelength. This got called the photoelectric effect. Clever Einstein explained this effect by saying that an electron only leaps away if hit by one of his photons (are you still with me?) and it's not dependent upon how intense the light is, but on its wavelength (or colour).

The other problem that the physicists solved was that of the cathode ray. They found out that the rays consist of tiny particles with a negative electric charge, called electrons. The discovery of X-rays and radioactivity seemed to open up this hunt to understand the structure of the atom. Ernest Rutherford managed to identify the little particles that were given off by radioactive substances and what happened to the atoms that they leave. He mercilessly bombarded these atoms with alpha particles and found that some of them rebounded back along the same path. Rutherford concluded that an atom must consist of a very dense nucleus of positive charge surrounded by negatively charged electrons orbiting around it, a bit like the planets in a miniature planetary system. Unfortunately he wasn't quite there, and it took Niels Bohr to put him right. He said that electrons occupy fixed energy levels in the atom and can only absorb or give off energy by jumping from one energy level to another.

So far so good, but Bohr's theory had its own problems. It was all right as far as it went, but it couldn't explain atoms more complex than hydrogen on which it was modelled. In 1905, however, Albert

Einstein had published his theory of relativity, a theory of mechanics which seemed to be happy with electrodynamics. This was eventually to tidy the whole thing up nicely.

Einstein's Relativity

This was Albert's theory to describe how objects behave when moving jolly fast (near the speed of light). You won't get a shorter version than this. He maintained that the universe was made up of continuous space and time in the form of a mind-blowing four-dimensional curve. This implied that the force of gravity, which Newton had been going on about, was actually created by bending the actual fabric of space, caused by the presence of mass, such as stars and planets. So now you know.

Most scientists were blown away by all this and didn't understand a word of it (not like us, eh?). When Einstein proved it all, in 1919, it caused a sensation and the poor overawed scientists had to take his genius seriously. In later life, Einstein's work was to lead directly to the development of the atom bomb, a bit of a dilemma for someone who was a confirmed pacifist.

Even so, he died the world's most-admired scientist.

> Albert Einstein's the man we must credit
> For being the man who first said it.
> The name of the game
> That brought him to fame
> Was $E = mc^2$ – Geddit?   *Stanley J. Sharpless*

(Energy contained in any particle of matter is equal to the mass of matter multiplied by the speed of light – the basis behind the idea for the atom bomb.)

EARTH SCIENCE

The idea of a continental drift (continents gradually drifting to their present positions), dreamed up by Alfred Wegener, was not really accepted until the 1960s. In fact, poor Wegener got the cold shoulder from most of his contemporaries.

Geologists had been too busy sticking their noses down volcanoes and measuring earthquake waves to try to find out what the Earth was made of. It was only now that they realized that it has an outer crust (like a pie), an upper mantle and lower mantle (between the crust and the core), then an outer core, and, in the middle, an inner core.

Some geologists, at this time, put on masks and flippers and became oceanographers. Using sonar they discovered the huge ridge in the mid-Atlantic, and then discovered that there were even deeper parts of the oceans.

Studying weather came on a storm (sorry), with the role of air masses being fully understood. Meteorologists (weathermen) started using numerical methods for sorting out whether one needed to take an umbrella.

Some Great Breakthroughs in Earth Science 1895–1945

1895:   The Rev. Jeannette Piccard let go of the string and sent the first balloon into the stratosphere.

1897:   Jacob Aall Bonnevie Bjerknes, a Norwegian/American, worked with his dad to sort out the first mathematical theory of weather forecasting. They still probably got it wrong, but at least their sums were OK. The British were still hanging seaweed on the kitchen door.

1899: William Thomson (Lord Kelvin) sounded a right cocky so and so. In a book he reckoned that life probably evolved quickly, so there was no need for geological time to exceed 100 million years. This just happened to be the age he'd given the Earth way back in 1862. OK, Bill, if you say so.

A year later Thomas Chrowder said this was all a load of baloney. Thomson had used the Ice Age as evidence of his steady cooling theory, but Chrowder maintained there had been several – with nice warm bits in between.

1902: Oliver Heaviside and his partner, A. E. Kennelly, worked out that there must be an electrified layer in the Earth's atmosphere that reflected radio waves. We now call it the ionosphere.

1905: There's a large hole in the middle of Arizona that was thought to have been caused by a volcano. Daniel Barringer reckoned, rightly, that it was caused by a runaway meteor, and it was named after him (the hole or the meteor?).

1907: Bertram B. Boltwood discovered how to find out the age of rocks by determining the ratio of uranium to its final decay product, lead. Next time you want to know how old a rock is . . . there's your answer.

1910: Frank B. Taylor proposed again that the continents just won't sit still and are constantly shifting around on the Earth's surface. He also claimed that Africa and South America were once joined.

179

1914: Beno Gutenburg, a German-American geologist, spotted something odd in the behaviour of earthquake waves at a depth of about 1,860 miles (what a dig!). This was found to mark the boundary between the Earth's outer core and the lower mantle.

1922: Sonar was used during a German expedition called 'The Meteor'. It was organized to find gold under the sea, needed to pay Germany's huge war debt. They didn't find any and I think it serves 'em right. They did, as you know, find the mid-Atlantic ridge, but they couldn't exactly flog that.

1929: M. Matuyama discovered that the Earth's magnetic field, for reasons of its own, reverses direction from time to time.

1930: Charles William Beebe and Otis Barton dived to an amazing 1,368ft in their brand new bathysphere. Four years later, they let out the rope a bit more and got down to an ear-splitting 3,038ft.

1935: Charles Richter developed a scale for measuring the strength of earthquakes based on seismograms. It's still known as the Richter scale.

1938: The first green warning. G. S. Callendar told the world that human beings, and what they get up to, are increasing the amount of carbon dioxide in the Earth's atmosphere. What would old G. S. say now, I wonder.

1943: Some poor old Mexican farmers had a bit of a shock

when they noticed a lump growing in one of their cornfields. It turned into Mount Paricutan – a very nasty volcano. And we worry about the odd spot.

MEDICINE

In the nineteenth century Koch and Pasteur started identifying the organisms that cause disease, and this work was continued by other scientists throughout the twentieth century. Also several of the toxins secreted by those nasty little micro-organisms which often cause disease were identified and made to stand in the corner. And then there was penicillin, a funny fungus with wonderful properties, that was discovered accidentally by Alexander Fleming. The introduction of this penicillin and other antibiotics made terrible diseases, like tuberculosis, curable.

By the 1930s several infectious diseases were known, but the nasty little secret agent, called the virus, turned out to be so small that it remained invisible under normal microscopes. When the electron microscope was invented, its cover was blown and scientists even managed to take its picture.

Hormones and vitamins also came onto the centre stage, the latter being linked closely to health care. It was discovered that that nasty disease beriberi was caused by an absence of a vitamin called thiamin, and that the failure to produce insulin causes a certain type of diabetes. By nicking the insulin from animals, diabetes could finally be treated.

Psychology went through great changes, largely due to the kind help of animals who underwent all sorts of weird and wonderful experiments. Sigmund Freud became both famous and infamous owing to his obsession with childhood experiences and sex, which he seemed sure had a lot to do with mental disorders. His work caused a right uproar, not only with society at large, but with the staid old scientists as well. At that time there were several schools of thinking, each with different ideas for treating psychic disorders.

Some Great Breakthroughs in Medicine 1895–1945

1900: Talk about dedication – James Carroll deliberately let his pet mosquitoes, that had lunched on a yellow-fever victim, have supper on him. This was all in an effort to prove that the little perishers carry the disease. He survived the fever, but it caused a heart disease that did for him a couple of years later.

Jesse William Lazear, not to be outdone, died of yellow fever in a brilliantly successful attempt to link our little mosquito friends with the disease.

Sigmund Freud interpreted dreams in terms of hidden symbols that revealed the unconscious mind. I'm glad Siggy never got to listen to some of my dreams. He'd probably think I'd *lost* my unconscious mind.

1901: Freud introduces the 'Freudian slip' concept. A Freudian slip is when you say something that has a double meaning. The meaning that you didn't mean, means more than the meaning you did mean. If you see what I mean.

Never polish your rice even if tempted. Gerrit Grijns showed that it removes a certain nutrient and causes the dreaded beriberi.

1903: German surgeon, George Perthes, discovered that tumours (which grow in cells) hate X-rays and suggested X-ray treatment for cancer.

1905: Alexis Carrel managed to join severed blood vessels. Hold on – here come the transplants.

George Washington Crile performed the first blood transfusion without killing someone.

If you think artificial joints are relatively new, think on. J. B. Murphy was fitting them in 1905.

1907: Englishman John Scott Haldane developed a method for divers to get to the surface safely without getting 'the bends' (drink all the water?).

1909: Charles Jules Henri Nicolle discovered that typhus is transmitted from a dirty rotten body louse.

1911: A London doctor developed the gastroscope, a tube that can be swallowed by the patient so that the doctor can see what he's had for lunch *and* if it agrees with him.

1914: Alexis Carrel did the first successful heart surgery – on a dog. Weak-hearted dogs heaved a sigh of relief.

1917: If you are worried about catching Rocky Mountain Spotted Fever – fret not. Ralph Parker developed a vaccine against it this year.

1918: Neurosurgery (brain repair) was first introduced in the States in 1918 by Harvey Cushing. It would have been more appropriate if his first name had been Peter, after the great horror film star. In 1936 two surgeons worked out a way of operating on the brain while the patient was simply sitting down. Mind you, I reckon I'd need to lie down.

1921: Alexander Fleming had a very runny nose. He was mucking around with some bacteria on a culture plate, when he dripped on it. When the bacteria dissolved he realized that mucus (also saliva and tears) contains something called lysozyme which must be anti-bacterial.

1923: George and Gladys Dicks, who sound more like a comedy team, found that scarlet fever is caused by streptococci (a bacteria) and developed an antitoxin (a toxin that neutralizes another toxin) for it. What clever Dicks!

1924: Unbelievably acetylene was first used as an anaesthetic. Yes, I should imagine being set upon by a blowtorch could have some rather deadening effects.

1927: The first version of the iron lung had been seen in 1876 but was not that brilliant. I think if you're going to use an iron lung it's probably better if it works. American Philip Drinker came up with the answer in 1927. The machine was developed to help people who had lost (or were losing) the use of the muscles which control the opening and closing of the lungs. Drinker worked out that if you put your patient in an airtight box (with his head sticking out one end I hope), you could use the combination of a rhythmical pump and atmospheric pressure. It did the trick nicely.

1928: Dr Alexander Fleming of St Mary's hospital, London, stumbled upon penicillin by accident. He apparently went on holiday leaving in the lab some jelly on which he was growing bacteria. When he got back he found the jelly covered in a strange mould which had devoured all his bacteria. Although he proved its benefit in treating a couple of badly infected people, his drug was ignored by colleagues. As Fleming had insufficient chemical knowledge, he had to wait eleven years before two brill biochemists, Florey and Chain (with whom he shared the 1945 Nobel prize for Medicine) perfected a method of producing penicillin.

1929: Schizophrenia (a mental disease) was treated with insulin shock treatment by Manfred Sakel (who goes first – me or me?).

1932: Armand Quick introduced the Quick test for measuring how long it takes blood to clot. I expect this allowed him to get home a bit earlier.

184

1933: Grantly Dick-Read wrote *Natural Childbirth*, a still-popular book that advocates the use of exercises instead of drugs in childbirth.

1935: Gerhard Domagk's daughter was dying from a streptococcal infection so with nothing to lose, he tried the first sulphur drug 'Prontosil' on her – the first human ever. Her miracle recovery heralded the emergence of Prontosil as the first worldwide 'wonder drug'. Nice one, Gerhard.

1936: Alexis Carrel made a rather good artificial heart to keep his patients going while tinkering with their real ones. Wish they could do that with cars.

1937: Big year for hay-fever sufferers. Pharmacologist Daniele Bovet came up with the very first antihistamine. A discovery not to be sniffed at.

Ugo Celutti and Lucio Bini develop the first ECT (electroconvulsive therapy). This treatment is used widely these days to sort out all sorts of mental disorders. Its other names are the dreaded 'electric shock treatment' or 'brain zapper'.

1943: Dutch doctor Wilhelm Kolff developed the wonderful kidney dialysis machine, which acts as an artificial kidney, purifying the blood.

1944: Blue babies turn pink. Alfred Blalock corrected the blood supply to the lungs of a little girl. Blue for a boy – pink for a girl.

1945: Fluoride was first added to the water supply in the States in an effort to reduce tooth decay. Maybe they should have tried nicking the kids' 'candy' first.

TECHNOLOGY

From an age when technology was the master and science the chief assistant, the twentieth century turned things round the other way. Electronics was born out of the discovery of the electron and was as important as the discoveries that led to the vast German chemical industry. The electronic vacuum tube was top invention – most important because it made audio signals louder (telephones), and could generate, amplify and detect high-frequency signals (radio waves). It was the heart of the phenomenal development of radio (in the 20s and 30s) and of the telly in the 1940s.

Cars came into their own. From a slightly wheezy, unreliably fragile start they became a top mode of transport – unless you happened to be Polish.

Planes love wars and the First and Second World Wars were no exception. It seems impossible to think that, in less than 50 years, we saw planes go from daft-looking crosses between kites and prams to highly grown-up machines that can not only fly quickly, but also take off vertically.

Computers, though a bit thick by today's standards, were also born in wartime. Alan Turing invented one to break the Germans' 'unbreakable' wartime code called 'Enigma' which it did brilliantly much to their annoyance.

The first recognizable computer was invented in 1945, although in those days they looked a bit like something out of *Dr Who*.

Some Great Breakthroughs in Technology 1895–1945

1895: Otto and Gustav, the Lilienthal brothers, designed and flew the first-ever glider to get above chin height. In fact it flew so high that Otto was able to be killed the following year (a different flight, I hasten to add).

Off we go to the pictures. The Lumière brothers invented the Cinématographe. The first showing in Paris drew crowds and was to lead to the vast cinema industry. The audience, not knowing what to expect, were all terrified when faced with a simple moving picture of a man walking into a station, shot at rather a strange angle. They should see *Psycho*.

Bicycles have to answer for the daft invention of Frenchman François Barathon – the pedal-driven lifebuoy. The survivor of the shipwreck sat on a rubber, air-filled bag which kept him and the machine afloat – and worked two sets of cranks (I think poor François was one of them), one with his hands and the other with his feet. These cranks turned propel-  lers – one to keep him upright and the other to get him home safely. It even had a nice little sail fitted.

The first 'One-armed Bandit' (or fruit machine) was invented by a Chicago wheeler-dealer, H. S. Mills. He installed these 'Kalamazoos' at all his famous lemonade stands. By 1932 the Mills Novelty Company was knocking out 70,000 of the updated machines a year.

It's interesting to note that in 1967 a survey made in Las Vegas found 10,000 licensed slot machines, each one paying $250 a year to their inland revenue, plus an income-based tax to the state. The average machine was set up to return $61 on an outlay of $250. Do you ever feel you might be in the wrong business?

1896: John Pemberton, an Atlanta (USA) chemist, developed this drink that was to become quite popular. It was made from a nut extract, sugar, caffeine, coca leaves (with the cocaine removed) and vegetable extracts. Sounds pretty disgusting, eh? A few months later his assistant added some soda water which the punters seemed to find more palatable. This drink did quite well until 1985 when they decided to change the secret recipe. There was nearly another civil war in America, so the company went back to the original mixture. All imitations were thwarted by the development of a rather whacky bottle shape based on the shape of the cola nut. The drink was called – all together now – Coca-Cola.

1897: Charles Algernon Parsons invented the first turbine-powered steamship. At a naval formal review in front of Queen Victoria it whizzed past the rest of the ships. The fastest steam launch was sent out to catch the *Turbinia* but gave up.

There's a place near Calcutta called Dum-Dum. It was here that hollow-tipped bullets were tested by the British. The wounds these Dum-Dums produced were so horrid that the Hague Convention banned them in 1908. The crafty British hung on to them and used them to make mincemeat of the Dutch settlers during the Boer War. Don't go thinking the British were always the good guys.

1900: Count Ferdinand von Zeppelin constructed his own steerable air balloon which flew on 2 July. By 1939, 52,000 Germans had flown in (or under) a Zeppelin, but after the Hindenburg went up in flames in New Jersey in 1937, killing all the passengers, there seemed to be a marked cooling off (enthusiasm-wise) for this method of travel. By the way, the first air hostesses were seen (and disappeared) on this early means of travel.

One never really considers where the paperclip comes from. It was invented in 1900 by Johan Waaler and patented in Germany. The pinnacle of German technology.

When I was young all the clever kids used to make things with their Meccano sets. Meccano was invented by Frank Hornby (of little train fame). It was originally called 'Mechanics Made Easy' which doesn't exactly roll off the tongue, you must admit.

1901: Hubert Booth, an English mechanical engineer, invented the first vacuum cleaner when he suggested that dirt should be sucked not blown. His first model was horse-drawn and dragged round from door to door. The trouble was, it was so blooming noisy that all the other horses in the street would bolt when the thing was started up.

The vacuum cleaner as we know it was invented in 1907 by W. H. Hoover (surprise, surprise), who'd seen a caretaker in an Ohio department store using a contraption incorporating a motor which sucked, a paper bag and a broom handle. Sounds like something you could be arrested for!

King Camp Gillette, who sounds a bit like a gay blues singer, responded to an idea thrown to him by his boss, a bottle-top maker, to invent something that could be thrown away after use. As shaving had always been slightly dangerous and a hassle, Gillette came up with the idea of a sliver of steel clamped into a holder. The first model went down like a lead balloon, selling only 51 razors, but the following year, for no apparent reason, the idea took off and the American Safety Razor Company sold 90,000 razors and 12,500,000 blades.

Shaving with a safety razor sure beat rubbing your chin with pumice stone which had been common in Charles II's day.

Guglielmo Marconi received the letter 'S' in St John's (Newfoundland). Astounding! I hear you cry. Well it was, when you consider it was the first transatlantic telegraphic radio transmission.

Millar Hutchinson invented the first electric hearing aid. Although much better than the Victorian 'speaking trumpet' it wasn't that convenient as it was the size of a large portable radio. Hutchinson also invented the Klaxon horn for cars – so loud, it was guaranteed to send you deaf. Wait a minute, I think I see the makings of a great business. Make 'em deaf, then flog 'em a hearing aid.

1903: Wilbur Wright, part of the Wilbur and Orville team, flew in the first powered plane from Kitty Hawk, North Carolina. OK, it only lasted 59 seconds, but you've got to start somewhere. The

'Flyer's' take-off was from a trolley that ran along rails. So they invented the first flying train as well.

It seems incredible that at a time when you couldn't fly anywhere, and cars looked like Meccano, it was possible to make photocopies. American G. C. Beidler, recognizing the constant need for copies of essential documents, produced a machine which he patented in 1906. Photocopiers didn't, however, become popular until the 1960s.

A German company was granted a patent for a gramophone that played records made of chocolate covered in tinfoil. After you'd listened to the record you ate it (the record). I think it says all that needs to be said about early German popular music. A year later, Emile Berliner, a German living in the States, invented the flat disc phonograph (non-chocolate) which was quickly taken over by the record industry.

I HOPE IT TASTES BETTER THAN IT SOUNDS

French scientist Leon Guillet invented this brilliant material called stainless steel but didn't realize that it didn't corrode. Silly homme.

The symbol of middle-class respectability 'Ovaltine' was invented by Swiss doctor George Wander. It had been called Ovalmaltine, but the daft clerk at the English patents office typed the name wrong, and it stuck. I wonder what George felt about that.

1905: Almon Strowger, an American undertaker, was a bit narked because his competitor's Mrs, who worked at the local manual (or femanual) telephone exchange was hearing about all the best potential burials first. Resourceful to the last, Almon invented the automatic telephone exchange which solved the problem. He should just have buried the rival's wife.

The first helicopter to carry anyone daft enough to try was invented by E. R. Mumford and had six propellers and a petrol engine. Its best flight was up to six feet in the air. The trouble was, it had to be fixed to the ground to prevent it flying away. The first one to take off and fly any distance (be it only a foot off the ground) was built by Paul Cornu, a French bike-seller. Good as far as it went, except it had the annoying habit of falling completely to bits on landing.

1906: A German called Nestle living in London invented a way of making hair curly using hot air. Obviously the Brits liked their hair straight, as he took the idea of 'the permanent wave' to the States and made a fortune.

1908: The method of shooting people nice and quietly was invented by Hiram Stevens Maxim who developed it so that it could also silence cars.

1909: A breakthrough in bread technology The toaster was marketed by the General Electric Company. Even more fabulous, the self-timed, pop-up-automatic-done-on-both-sides toaster was developed to our eternal gratitude by Charles Strite from Stillwater, Minnesota.

There was a time when everything seemed to be made of Bakelite. It was a hard plastic that went even harder on heating, instead of melting like most others. It was invented by Leo Baekeland and replaced all sorts of traditional materials like wood, ivory and hard rubber.

Hydrofoils aren't that new. This device for lifting the hull of a boat out of the water to reduce drag, was developed by Italian Enrico Forlanini.

Eugene Schueller founded what was to become L'Oréal in 1927. The hairdressing industry was revolutionized by the invention of Imedia, the first organic hair dye.

1910: Rayon stockings appeared for the first time in Germany. Sheer nylons weren't seen until 1938 when introduced by the Du Pont company led by Dr Wallace Carothers. Nylons didn't reach Britain until the Second World War when the American GIs traded them with British girls for various things.

We've heard of planes taking off from trains, now one takes off from a ship, predicting aircraft carriers.

It would have been rotten luck to have lived next door to the first person to invent the drum kit in New Orleans. The modern 'shiny' ones weren't seen until the 1950s.

1911: Escalators were designed by Jesse Reno, as a fairground attraction at Coney Island in 1856. The first commercial ones came to Earls Court Station, in London, where a man with a wooden leg was hired to ride up and down to prove its safety. He couldn't have been that safety-conscious otherwise he wouldn't have lost his leg in the first place.

Bombs were first chucked out of an aeroplane by Guilio Gavotti during the Italo Turkish war. It was all a bit hairy, as the pin was pulled out of the bomb while still in the plane and then dropped on the enemy.

No wonder we still associate Nivea cream with old ladies, it was invented by Paul Beiersdorf, a German chemist, in 1911. He also invented the sticking plaster.

1912: It must have been cold that winter, as Sidney Russell designed an electric heating pad for beds. It was shortly to become the electric blanket.

1913: Henry Ford was in a hurry to make cars (and cash) as quickly as possible. He developed the very first assembly line for car manufacture. The conveyor-belt method cut the assembly time from 12.5 to 1.5 hours.

What has nine letters and is a totally infuriating (I think) game for bored people. The crossword was invented by Arthur Wynne and first appeared in *The New York World*. If he only knew what he was starting.

If you'll believe there was once an American Indian called George Crum, then you might believe that he worked as cook in a heap big wigwam, the Lake House Hotel, Saratoga Springs, New York State. One day he was asked for some French fries (chips to you) cut thinner, from a rather pernickety punter. Anyway, the result was the Saratoga Chip which turned into the crisp as we know and love it. The first person to manufacture them in Britain was Frank Smith. The rest is crisp legend.

1914: Although Britain was embroiled in a new war, over in the States much more important things were afoot. In the eternal quest of womankind to keep everything in the right place, Caresse Crosby, a young New Yorker, always abreast of current fashion, asked her maid to create a bra out of a couple of handkerchiefs and two ribbons (she sounds more like a conjuror). Her friends were well impressed (we don't know what she looked like before!) and asked her to make the 'garment' for them. After this uplifting little event nobody was that interested until she flogged the idea to the Warner Brothers Corset Company for 15,000 dollars (paid in two instalments?). Suddenly the brassière took off (interesting). Poor Caresse could have made $20,000,000 had she known.

1915: French scientist Paul Langevin invented sonar, which was used mostly for detecting icebergs. Not surprising really, as it was only three years earlier that the *Titanic* went down after hitting one.

Our old chums, the Germans, decided to use poison gas against the British and the French this year, during our first test match against them.

The gas mask was invented which contained a chemically-treated pad that fitted over the nose and mouth. During the second test match, the entire British population (except pets) were issued with these masks — just in case.

1916: Nikala, the first synthetic detergent, was invented in Germany. It enabled water to penetrate the fibres, but didn't know how to remove dirt. The world had to stay (slightly grubby) and wait until the twenties and later, for modern detergents and cleaning fluids.

Lux Soap Flakes (the oldest) came in 1921 made by the British Unilever Company. Also Vim (1923), Persil (1932), Omo (1952), Lux washing-up liquid (1959) and the famous Ariel (1968).

1917: Clarence Birdseye was in Labrador doing a wildlife survey, when he noticed that the fish, when caught, instantly froze solid. He wondered if the same could be done with vegetables (if you can catch them) as a way of keeping them fresh. The rest is legend and Mr Birdseye became seriously rich. The company, I'm sure I don't have to tell you, was called . . . Findus (only joking).

1918: Car hire was first seen when a second-hand car dealer in Chigago hired out twelve old bangers (and some cars as well). His company was bought by the famous Yellow Taxi Cab Company and renamed Hertz Self-drive.

The Racine Universal Motor Company was responsible for the very first hairdryer. My sources tell me that they were manual. What does that mean, I wonder?

1921: Due to the over-fishing of oysters for natural pearls (at one time more valuable than diamonds) by unscrupulous dealers, the clever Japanese found a way of making them artificially. They fooled the unsuspecting oysters (not an easy task) by planting a bit of grit inside their shells. A pearl takes three years to form. Pity they couldn't trick the stupid things into hurrying up a bit.

Would you believe that I invented the lie detector? Don't believe the nasty rumour that it was invented by John Lawrence of Nova Scotia.

1922: The first portable radio weighed 22lb and was invented by J. McWilliams Stone. God knows what a non-portable one weighed. Apparently one was fitted in a Model T Ford in the same year by American George Frost, making it the first car radio.

Another landmark in the history of mankind – the choc-ice was invented by Iowa-born C. K. Nelson who called it (oddly) Eskimo Pie.

1923: Although John Logie Baird (I can never resist calling him Yogi Bear) was credited with the invention of the first proper telly, the idea had been worked on for years. If he hadn't got there first it might well have been Vladimir Zworykin, a Russian, who got the credit. The first regular programmes reached the eager British audience (of about 10) in 1936.

1924: Inventions and gadgets were coming thick and fast and 1924 was no exception. We saw the spiral-bound notebook, the self-winding watch, Kleenex tissues, insecticides, the deep-freeze and Sellotape, to name but a few.

The first real motorway was built as a race-track as well (so, what's changed?). Designed by Karl Fritsch in Berlin, it eventually became a fast two-lane highway. Anyone seeing the average motorway at holiday times would wonder if they're fast becoming parking lots.

1926: The first we saw of the aerosol was in 1926 when it was invented by Norwegian Erik Rotheim. It wasn't manufactured until 1941, however, when Lyle Goodhue developed an aerosol for zapping insects. The spray particles are quite small, one-fifty-millionth of a millimetre to be precise.

1928: Time for a shave. Colonel Jacob Schick invented the electric shaver. The company still bears his name.

1929: Frozen foods became available to the average American, along with the electric organ and the dreaded sliced bread.

1930: The principle of the tape recorder was discovered in 1888 but the first machine had to wait 10 years before going on show at the Paris Exhibition. Nobody showed much interest which was a touch short-sighted. The first proper tape recorder using magnetized plastic tape was developed in Germany in 1930.

The turbo-jet engine was developed by Englishman Frank Whittle. It wasn't ready to stick on a plane until 1941. Turbo-jets are still used, even on Concorde.

1931: When Prohibition was enforced in America, people were stuck for things to do in bars and clubs. The pinball machine helped while away the alcohol-free hours. The first electric pinball was invented by Sam Gensberg, a Pole, and it was called 'The Beamlight'.

1933: Whatever you think of Monopoly, you're by no means the first. It was invented by Charles Darrow, an American, who was unemployed owing to the Great Depression (which I get when I play it). The game has since earned the company that bought it from Darrow £700 million.

1934:   The first streamlined car to break from the old boxy shape was the Chrysler Airflow. If anyone's got one they don't want . . .

Percy Shaw, a road repairer, was driving home in a fog and couldn't see where he was going (that's his story). He saw a cat sitting by the road and noticed how its eyes reflected the lights from his car. It gave him the idea for illuminating dark roadways, so instead of nailing loads of cats to the roadside, he set about reproducing their eyes in glass.

They were particularly useful during the blackout, as enemy aircraft couldn't see them from above.

1935:   Now we're getting somewhere. The first beer cans were seen in New Jersey, USA.

The bane of my life, parking meters, were thought up by journalist Carlton Magee and were put up in Tulsa, Oklahoma, USA. These wonderful things first came to Britain in 1958 and their ever-loving bee-like attendants in 1960.

1936:   The first paperback books came from Penguin of London. They cost 6d (2.5p). Suddenly loads of people who hitherto couldn't afford books, started buying them regularly. They couldn't read, but at least they bought them.

1937:   They'd been trying to come up with a quick way of making coffee since 1867. Nestlé, the Swiss firm, cracked instant coffee in 1937 and called it Nescafé. Didn't it do well! There are now over 100 different brands throughout the world.

The British sure lead the world in the field of invention. Take Constance Honey, who invented the chocolate spoon for bribing kids to take medicine.

In 1937, American Earl Hass became the hero of most women when he patented the tampon. The company was called Tampax.

Humpty Dumpty sat on a supermarket trolley. The owner of a store of that name, in Oklahoma City, realized the trouble his customers were having carrying their goods, so he converted some folding chairs into carts, shoved wheels on the legs, and put a basket on the seat. The new trolley was pushed from behind.

1938: Ferdinand Porsche built this funny little car that he somehow thought would sell. He called it Volkswagen VW and produced 37 vehicles in the first year. The 'Beetle', as it was nicknamed, did sort of OK – selling 23,000,000 until being recently discontinued. Porsche went on to design another car that didn't do badly either. Three guesses what he called it? (The Ferdinand?)

The first machine to learn from its mistakes was invented by T. Ross, a US engineer. Apparently this thing could find its way out of mazes all by itself. Creepy, I call it.

This year also saw for the first time, the ball-point pen, light-sensitive sunglasses, nylons and the non-stick pan.

1939: Even murder became mechanized with the invention of the hand-held electric carving knife.

Don't ever drink a Molotov cocktail (unless you really want to get wrecked). This simple invention was just a glass bottle filled with petrol which explodes when

198

thrown at your foe. It was first used by the Finns against the Russians.

The Jeep was thought to have been named after one of the mates of the cartoon character, Popeye. The vehicle was born on the 10th of June having taken only 75 days to develop. Over 585,000 vehicles were built for the American war effort and the design, with certain modifications, is still used today.

The bazooka or rocket launcher has been claimed by several inventors. This charming weapon allows a rocket to be fired by a single soldier (with another one loading) and can go through armour like a hot knife through butter.

1942: Here's a good one! During the Second World War the British were becoming well fed up with the amount of ships the blasted U-boats were sinking. The best defence was by air patrols, but because our planes couldn't fly too far, there was a severe limit to the area they could cover. In 1942 a British inventor came up with the idea of building vast artificial icebergs which could be used as floating airstrips. Inside would be workshops, hangars and comfy crew quarters. The project was called Habakkuk after a small-time biblical prophet. It was found that if 10 per cent wood pulp was added to the ice, it would make it as strong as concrete, but the cost of building these things would be much more than building a conventional aircraft carrier. The plan was abandoned.

1943: Few people are aware that Jacques Cousteau who starred in those seemingly endless films about fish and stuff actually invented the aqualung with his underwater mate, Gagnan.

1944: The bad news; the Germans invented the first rocket-powered plane, the ME 163-BI Komet. The good news: it had this annoying (if you were German) habit of blowing up on take-off.

A particularly unpleasant invention (if you were British) was the German V2 rocket. This liquid-fuelled weapon was designed by the brilliant Wernher von Braun and terrorized London throughout

1944 and 1945. After the war, von Braun very sensibly went to the States and developed the rocket engine for his nice new masters.

That nice Mr Hitler rang his old motoring mate Mr Porsche and asked him to build the biggest, strongest tank in the world, as all his little ones were getting well and truly clobbered on the Russian front. The Mouse, as it was called (I think that's a German joke), was 20ft high and powered by a 1500hp diesel engine. The troubles were that 1. It could only go at 12mph. 2. It was so heavy that it smashed all the roads it travelled along, and sank rapidly in anything but hard ground. 3. It shattered windows and deafened anyone near it.

John Presper Eckert and John W. Mauchly developed the ENIAC, now regarded as the very first all-purpose, stored program electronic computer.

Percy Le Baron Spencer applied to bring radio waves into the kitchen with a patent for a microwave oven. Spencer, a physics boffin, discovered the power of radar to produce heat. He directed the energy towards a bowl of maize and Hey Presto! got popcorn. (No! that's not the invention!) The machine, however, was huge and expensive, so microwave ovens lay low until 1967.

Bang the Bomb – 1945
Just about the most important thing to come out of the war (apart from Vera Lynn) was the harnessing of nuclear energy and the development of the atomic bomb.

Albert Einstein (the cleverest man in the world) was pressured into writing to American President Roosevelt informing him that uranium could be used to create lovely big bangs. Scared that the

Jerries would get there first, the President went along with the idea, and put 43,000 people to work (the largest enterprise in the whole history of science).

Believe it or not, the whole operation was kept secret and many of the scientists didn't even know what they were working on. The actual bombs were knocked together at Los Alamos, New Mexico, under the directorship of a rather bright physicist called J. Robert Oppenheimer.

The whole caboodle went up in smoke (mushroom-shaped) when a uranium-235 bomb was dropped on Hiroshima killing 80,000 Japanese and wounding a further 50,000. Just to make sure, they lobbed another on Nagasaki a few days later. OK, it finished the war with Japan, but the world would never be the same again.

CHAPTER 9

Science Up Till Now – 1946– . . .

As I've said before, there's nothing like a huge war to promote new inventions and scientific discoveries. Although there'd been quite a bit of pre-war research, we can thank World War II for the arrival of radar, synthetic rubber, DDT, nuclear fission, jet-planes, helicopters, ballistic missiles (thanks a bunch) and the electronic digital computer. These things were to transform our day-to-day lives and cause society to change almost as much as the Industrial Revolution or the introduction of farming 10,000 years earlier.

Some scientific research, however, actually slowed down during the war. Telly, for instance, stayed practically dormant while we were all busy killing each other, though it seems to have done all right since. Funny really, these days it seems that a war isn't a proper war unless you can see it on the box.

Scientists back in the forties weren't too hot at predicting the future, their view being much like those of their contemporary film-makers. If you've ever seen any futuristic movies made in the forties or fifties, they'd have had us all dressed up like oven-ready turkeys, driving around in hovery things that looked more like flying juke-boxes.

The scientists reckoned that maybe a few large companies might own their own computers by the 1980s, not dreaming for one minute that kids could be getting them for Christmas to play games on. Come to that, whatever happened to nuclear power which was to solve all our energy problems? I expect a few people up Chernobyl way might have something to say about that. The wonder pesticide DDT was to revolutionize agriculture, yet it ended up being given the thumbs down in only 20 years, as it was beginning to kill us as well (I bet the bugs laughed!).

And who'd have thought, in the forties, that in the next 20 years we'd be strolling about on the moon (only to find out it was as boring as the average suburb on a wet Sunday), or be making babies by test tube (also rather boring).

Even the beginnings of the universe would become clearer, along with all the secrets of our heredity, and surprise, surprise, that that modern wonder the vacuum tube would soon be obsolete, replaced by transistors and other solid-state devices.

The trend towards groups of scientists working together became the norm, except perhaps in mathematics (mathematicians always were an anti-social bunch). The equipment used was becoming so darned expensive that it became impossible for the average scientist to have all the right gear in his own back room.

Although the population of the world had exploded, the number of people needed to produce food or manufacture articles for the growing monster was reducing. This was largely due to the widespread use of machines. By the 1980s, in fact, more than half of all the boffins in America were employed by business or industry. This, of course, meant that they suddenly became capable of making huge amounts of cash – a far cry from poor old Ms Curie who was broke most of her life.

Scientists these days hardly break wind without writing a learned paper on the subject in the thousands of journals which even seem to get on our news-stands. With all this information and knowledge being shovelled out, no one individual can keep up with even the smallest scientific area. Specialization, therefore, is very much the name of the game.

The Mating Game
Although every scientist has had to become a specialist, the actual sciences have merged as never before. Astrophysics with biophysics,

chemistry with physics, biology with chemistry, etc., etc. Practically every aspect of science seems to be making friends with its relatives. It all becomes a bit mind-blowing. Do you know, there are even some sciences which haven't yet got anything to study, such as exobiology, the study of extra-terrestrial living things. There could be a great future there — getting paid for waiting around for something to happen!

But don't go thinking that all these developments do us that much of a favour, or that the mass of the population think it all wonderful. Many of the things that the scientists have come up with in the last, say, fifty years have been of dubious benefit. Cars that can do 180 mph in the blink of an eye, huge luxurious airliners that can kill us in huge numbers at a time, and nuclear weapons that could stop the whole shooting match in one hit, are not necessarily essential for a nice quiet life.

In fact, half the things that our scientists have given us we might have been perfectly happy not having (before we knew they existed). I mean, the caveman who once dreamed of having something sharp, probably wouldn't have been any more thrilled with an electric carving knife. Mind you, I don't know if I could live without the little machine that removes wool-balls from my sweaters.

ANTHROPOLOGY AND ARCHAEOLOGY

By the mid 1980s complete skeletons of Homo habilis and australopithecus (remember the child's head?) had been found, and also remains of people like us, 10,000 years old. By this time, however, anthropologists weren't interested in a load of old bones, they were up to their necks in molecules, and using proteins and DNA to see how closely we are related to the great apes (ask Arnold Schwarzenegger). It turned out, in fact, that we're closer to chimps than the more easily recognizable gorillas and orangutans.

It now seems we fell out with the monkey world and decided to be hairless grown-ups only a few million years ago. It was thought, right up to the sixties, that the australopithecines gradually grew into the way we are now, but in the seventies it was discovered that they once shared the same territory with 'modern' man, which blew that theory apart. The search is still on for that 'missing link', or a common ancestor (and we've all got a few of those).

In archaeology one of the great breakthroughs had been Jacques Cousteau's development of sophisticated underwater gear. For the first time, the wonders of the deep could be examined closely and at length. In fact, some underwater sights were left to the future when, hopefully, equipment might be able to see them even better.

Some Great Breakthroughs in Anthropology and Archaeology 1946 to the present

1947: Two shepherd boys discovered arguably the most important Jewish religious documents in a cave at Khirbet Qumran. They'd been written around the time when Christ was alive and were named the Dead Sea Scrolls.

1956: Mr and Mrs William Clouser Boyd studied blood groups going back to the thirties and released a list of 13 races of Homo sapiens (like what we are). One surprise was that the Basques appeared to be the last survivors of an early European race (which might account for their stroppiness with everyone else).

1961: Louis S. B. Leakey and Mary Leakey found themselves a handyman. So what? you might think. 'Handyman' is the translation of Homo habilis. The lucky Leakeys found the very first fossil remains.

1963: Some ex-Ice Age skeletons were found hiding in a cave near Cosenza, Italy. One of the little group turned out to be a dwarf who was obviously accepted by those nice hunter-gatherers. Darling, you must meet the Hunter-Gatherers.

The Lascaux caves were closed to the public because people wouldn't stop breathing. Apparently their breath was increasing the humidity which caused a horrid fungus that was spoiling the paintings.

1967: A thirty-million-year-old ape's skull was found and called aegyptopithecus. He's the earliest known primate in the line that leads to our good selves.

1974: I love Lucy. A team led by Don Johanson (Miami Vice?) came across a little girl who they named Lucy. She was getting on a bit, 3,000,000 years old to be precise, but she was the first australopithecus afarensis anyone had met. She was apparently named after the Beatles' song 'Lucy in the Sky with Diamonds'.

1979: If you think builders are slow these days, what about the guys that built the temple of Apollo in Turkey. Lothar Haselberger discovered almost complete plans for the temple scratched in the stone. It was planned in 334BC to be the largest in the world but six hundred years later it was still incomplete. That's what I call a lunch break.

1982: After 17 years' hard labour, the *Mary Rose*, a sixteenth-century warship, was pulled out of the water in Portsmouth. It was found to be full of Tudor odds and sods.

1984: Andrew Hill, while strolling through Kenya, found a jaw-bone, believed to be 5,000,000 years old. Its owner was believed to be related to Lucy.

Richard Adams uncovered the first unlooted Mayan tomb found since the early sixties in the heart of the Guatemalan jungle. Nobody had been in since the fifth century AD. I wonder if Dick promptly looted it.

The appropriately named Andy Mould was cutting some peat one day when he dug up the now famous Lindow man, perfectly preserved after 2,200 years (Joan Collins eat your heart out). He was apparently a Druid who was killed in an incident involving a burned barley-cake. This priest who had got the cake was apparently sacrificed to the Celtic gods. Seems King Alfred got off lightly. I wonder if there's any money in peat-based face packs?

1986: Don Johanson again. This time, with his chum Tim White, he found a girl who'd gone completely to pieces, 303 to be precise. She was a Homo habilis (Handywoman) who they named, rather unromantically, OH62. Poor OH62 turned out to be only three feet tall and much more ape-like than they expected. Mind you, it was her 18,000,000th birthday.

A fisherman wading in the Acula River, Mexico, tripped over a stone with funny, unrecognizable writing on it. It was later dated back to the first century AD and probably said 'No fishing without a permit'.

1987: A team of scientists drilled into a chamber at the base of the Great Pyramid at Giza, to assess the air and the condition of a boat that someone had told them was buried there. All the old air escaped, but they captured the boat. What could they possibly want with horrible old Egyptian air?

1988: French and Israeli scientists found some fossils in an old Israeli cave that are not only 92,000 years old, but the remains of modern Homo sapiens. This effectively doubled the time that folk like us are supposed to have been around.

BIOLOGY

Biology was arguably top of the league progress-wise after the war especially in the area of molecule behaviour. Apes got the full works, especially in the wild, and there were almost as many scientists swinging around in the trees as the poor monkeys they were studying.

And then came genetic engineering. Watson and Crick finally found out how old Gregor Mendel's laws of heredity really worked. At about the same time, scientists, playing around with bacteria and the nasty viruses that jump on them, discovered a way to transfer genetic material from one organism to another. Voilà! We have genetic engineering. Just as important, all this nice new genetic information could now be used to learn about how proteins are built and, more to the point, what they do.

Some Great Breakthroughs in Biology 1946 to the Present

1946:   Max Delbruck and Alfred Hershey (not of Hershey Bar fame) independently discover that genetic material from different viruses can get it together and form a brand new one.

1947:   Karl von Frisch, the fish man (remember?) found out that bees used the polarization of light to see where they were going.

1950:   Embryos were transplanted into cattle for the first time. It's all the rage these days. The poor cows started having a rotten sex-life.

1952:   Joshua Lederberg discovered that viruses that go around attacking bacteria can (and will) shove genetic material from one to the other. This was, apparently, big news in genetic engineering circles.

Eugene Aserinsky couldn't take his eyes off his eight-year-old son when asleep. Using an encephalograph he discovered that rapid eye movement observed during normal sleep indicated vivid dreams. Some of my vivid dreams would make old Eugene blink!

Do you remember me telling you about the discovery of the coelacanth? – the allegedly extinct fish found in 1938? Well, James Smith offered a prize to anyone who could supply him with another. I suppose the old one was now extinct itself. It turned out that the fishermen around the Comoro islands had been casually catching the little devils for years and didn't think anything of it.

James Dewey Watson (American) and Francis Crick (British) made a fab model of the giant DNA molecule, which finally proved how it is capable of transmitting heredity in all living organisms (even you).

1957: G. E. Hutchinson defined the ecological niche as 'an abstract hypervolume with axes for each of the environmental and biological variables that affect the organism whose niche it is; that is, the niche is a region both in space and in possible behaviours that the organism occupies'. If you disagree with that (or understand even one word of it) please DON'T let me know.

1958: A Russian scientist discovered a funny little lizard species that only ever has females. Before you ask the next question let me tell you that it reproduces without the help of male lizards or, in other words, parthenogenetically (which sounds no fun at all). It was the first known all-female vertebrate species.

Harris, Michael, and Scott – who sound like a comedy singing group – demonstrated the direct effect of hormones on the central nervous system via the posterior hypothalamus – which sounds like a rude song, but is really a region of the brain.

1960: It's discovered that bottle-nosed dolphins use a kind of sonar to locate objects in water, a bit like bats do (only not in water).

1961: James V. McConnell reported that flatworms which have eaten other flatworms that have learned their way through a simple maze, learn it quicker than those who haven't. I wonder if this accounts for the old saying 'if you want to know the way, eat a policeman'.

1962: Ecology is the science of the relationship of an organism to its environment. Although it had been talked about since the 1850s it kicked off properly with a book called *Silent Spring* by Rachel Carson published in 1962 and grew up to, and through, the seventies. Many people believe that ecology is the science of avoiding pollution which is, of course, quite attractive – but wrong.

Computers have helped a lot, as ecology seems to need a great deal of maths. It stands to reason when you think how many individuals there are, and how many different physical situations they can get themselves into. With this wonderful new tool ecologists during the sixties and seventies spent their time finding out how the competition amongst species, or even individuals, for niches (ways of living) affected population.

1964: The International Rice Research Institute started the 'Green Revolution' with new types of rice that give double the yield if given sufficient fertilizer.

1965: Sex again. An artificial sex-attractant (pheromone) was developed for cockroaches. I should think the horrid little beasts would need something to make them attractive.

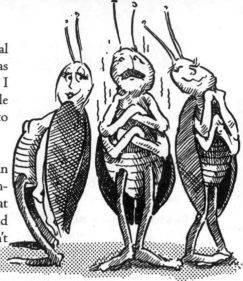

1966: Konrad Lorenz argued in a book that only humans intentionally kill one another. What about flatworms, Konrad? I should think eating your friend doesn't exactly do him much good.

1967: Casimir Funk (famous rap-biologist) died. He had invented the word 'vitamin'.

Arthur Kornberg announced that he and his mates had made the very first biologically active DNA.

Alf Porsild and Charles Arlington grew some mountain lupines from some seeds frozen since the Ice Age, setting a new record of 10,000 years for seeds to still remain viable. Seems rather a lot of fuss about nothing. If they'd asked me, I could have pointed them to my local garden centre who've got nice new ones.

George Schaller's *Deer and the Tiger* describes the interaction between a tiger and its prey. Can't think why it needs a book. Tiger eats deer – end of story.

1968: Shock-horror! Lake Erie was reported nearly dead. It was stated that even if the pollution stopped right away, it would still take 500 years to get it back to how it was 20 years ago. Erie's the word.

1970: A team of scientists announced the first complete synthesis of a gene. They would have used a natural gene as the template but this time they managed to cobble one together from its component chemicals. Later work by this team produced the first functional synthetic gene (no Levi jokes please).

1972: DDT was restricted to safeguard the environment, especially birds who were complaining because their eggshells were thinning.

1973: If you can believe this you'll believe anything. J. M. Diamond, in a book about birds in New Guinea, claimed that similar birds occur in a gradation in which each larger bird is 1.3 times bigger than its smaller relatives in all ways. He later goes on to prove, unbelievably, that this ratio applies to pots and pans, violins and many other inanimate objects.

1974: A halt was called to genetic engineering when a committee of 139 scientists from the US Academy of Sciences got their genes in a twist (sorry) over the insertion of the genes of one organism into another. They said that it could start again when the biologists involved knew what on earth they were up to.

1977: A baby mammoth frozen for 40,000 years was recovered in good shape in Russia. (Well, good shape for dead!)

1978: Stephen Harrison reported the first high-resolution structure of an intact virus. For some obscure reason it was called the tomato bushy stunt virus.

1980: The Supreme Court allowed a microbe for oil clean-up to be patented. Slick work by General Electric.

A team headed by Martin Cline succeed in switching a gene from one mouse to another. I've heard of sharing, but this is ridiculous.

1981: A black-footed ferret, thought to be extinct, was discovered living happily in prairie dog town in Wyoming. At least it wasn't down a cowboy's trousers (or genes).

1984: Wilson and Higuchi of the University of California cloned the first genes of an extinct species. They took the genes (striped) off a preserved skin of a quagga — a sort of old zebra. I don't, however, know what they did with them.

1986: A living organism produced by genetic engineering was licensed for the first time in the USA. It was a virus to be used as a vaccine to prevent herpes in pigs.

Hans Fricke hires a submersible and goes down to look at those old coelacanths at home. Instead of crawling around on the bottom, as was suspected, they were swimming about energetically, performing headstands and swimming upside down. No wonder the daft beggers were thought to be extinct.

1987: A sad story. 'Orange Band', the last lady dusky seaside sparrow, died in captivity — drawing a red line through the species. They did, however, mate the five remaining gentlemen sparrows with the look-alike Scott's seaside sparrow. It's such fun at the seaside.

1988: This all gets sillier. The US Patent and Trade Office issued patent no. 4736866 to Harvard Medical School for a mouse. This mouse had been developed by genetic engineering and was the first animal to be patented (how demeaning).

Medicine and biology (especially molecular biology) had become so close in recent years that one could hardly spot the join. Having said that, some innovations have been just pure medicine. These include: organ transplants; endoscopy; angioplasty (shoving tubes carrying a laser into arteries to blast away arterial plaque); amniocentesis (diagnosing and treating unborn kids); ways of dealing with fertilizing eggs (human, not chickens') to produce viable babies; ultrasound scanning and a whole bunch of new vaccines.

Genetic engineering has helped produce certain proteins needed by sick people, like human insulin or human-growth hormones; artificial vaccines have helped produce cheaper treatment for hepatitis B; and much better and more complicated transplants made possible by better tissue-matching.

Since 1946 there has been a whole new understanding of the immune system which helped doctors realize how diseases are caused and, more to the point, how they can be avoided. Our bodies, it seems, become activated when exposed to 'foreign bodies' (sounds nice). This became clearer with the discovery of blood types and artificial immunity with 'killed' or 'weakened' germs. Many diseases, like arthritis and diabetes, were found to be caused when our immune system turns round and rather daftly attacks itself. As bad luck would have it, just as scientists were getting to grips with how the immune system really works, a horrid new disease emerged that actually sets out to destroy the immune system. AIDS, the scariest of all the known diseases is still a mystery, and now threatens the whole world.

Some Great Breakthroughs in Medicine 1946 to the Present

1948: Philip Showalter became the saviour of rheumatoid arthritis sufferers when he realized that it could be treated by cortisone (a substance produced in the adrenal glands).

1951: Antabuse, a drug for preventing alcoholics from drinking, is introduced. I didn't know ants liked drinking.

Hearts and lungs got the full works with John Gilbert's fab heart-lung machine. He used it successfully to keep a woman alive in 1953 while patching up her heart.

1952: Polio struck America, seeing off 4,665 unlucky people.

Ever fancied changing sex? George Jorgenson did, and became Christine. What's wrong with Georgina? It was the world's first sex change operation.

Jonas Salk of New York cracks polio with a brand new killed-virus vaccine. He started inoculating in 1954.

Evarts Graham and Ernest Wynder discovered that tobacco smoke causes cancer in mice. Cigarette sales to the mouse community plummeted.

1954: Gregory Pincus and John Rock developed the contraceptive pill for women. The first tests took place in Puerto Rico in 1956 (the Year of the Rabbit?).

1956: Bruno Kirsh was a bit worried about his guinea pig when he discovered some peculiar dark bits in its heart cells. Nobody knew what they were for years until it was discovered they released hormones that regulate the circulatory system.

1957: The dreaded high-speed dentist drill was invented in the States. As far as I'm concerned it just makes the pain come quicker.

Interferons were discovered. They're the chaps, produced by our bodies, that fight those nasty viruses.

Heartfelt thanks must go to Wilhelm Kolff who invented the first proper artificial one. The first heart pacemaker was made by Swedeke Senning. It was capable of stimulating other organs as well as the heart (no rude comments please!). They can make them pretty small these days. In

1986 a three-day-old Manchester baby had one successfully fitted.

1961: Frank Horsfall Jnr. told the world that it is the changes in DNA structure in cells that cause cancer. What causes the change, Frank?

1962: Lasers were used for the first time in eye surgery. Ouch!

1964: A Professor Brooke's rat had cancer. His efforts to cure it caused another professor, G. Rosen, to use chemotherapy for the first time before trying anything else. Chemotherapy is the name given for the treatment of cancer by chemical substances.

1965: Harry Harlow demonstrated that monkeys reared in total isolation are affected emotionally for the rest of their lives. Nice one, Harry, but surely the average prisoner in solitary confinement could have told you that.

1966: Daniel Gajudusek of Yonkers, New York, transferred kuru – a disease that you seem to get by eating other people (cannibalism) – to chimpanzees. The first time a viral disease of the central nervous system had been transferred to another species. I just can't see what good that does (especially if you're the other species). It's now thought that the AIDS virus was originally transmitted to man from a monkey.

Careful with your next packet of peanuts. It was discovered by someone called Wogan (no! I don't think so) that mould grown on your nuts (please!) causes liver damage, or, worse, cancer. Big C. peanuts?

1967: Christiaan Barnard, a South African surgeon, became world famous for performing the first almost-successful heart transplant. Almost, because the patient lasted only 18 days – and who remembers his name?

The now everyday, run-of-the-mill, heart bypass operation was developed by Cleveland surgeon, Rene Favaloro.

1968: The wondrous contraceptive pill, first seen in the late fifties and loved by men and women alike, was suddenly found to cause blood clots in some women.

1969: Did you know that in 1969 it was discovered that some people can get an allergic reaction to exercise, causing spots, choking, low blood pressure and many other things. That's good, I was just going to take the dog for a walk.

1974: Chloroform used to be used in cosmetics and drugs, but was banned in the US because it was found to be carcinogenic. What's the use of looking pretty if it gives you cancer? they asked themselves.

1977: Two New York gay men were diagnosed as having a rare cancer called Kaposi's sarcoma. Unfortunately, it now looks like they were the first AIDS victims in the city. The disease was, almost unbelievably, not recognized until 1981.

1978: The first nipper to be conceived without sexual activity – a test-tube baby – was born, Louise Brown in the U.K.

1979: A Japanese doctor, Ryochi Naito, made some artificial blood (not like in horror films) and injected himself. It was made from a totally synthetic derivative of petrol and was milky white in colour. Science fiction creeps closer.

1980: A machine was developed to blast away kidney stones with sound waves – while still in the kidney! I bet a bit of Heavy Metal at full volume would also do the trick.

1983: There was an old postman from California ... A retired postal worker died after five years of amnesia caused by loss of blood to the brain. It was revealed that the cause of the amnesia was a small damaged region of the Hippocampus, which is the bit of the brain involved with memory. What did I just say?

1984: Fags got the thumbs down again. The American Heart Foundation connected smoking with heart attacks for the first time.

William H. Clewell performed the first successful operation on an unborn child.

1986: Two American scientists, Burke and Yannas, saved a hopelessly burned patient by creating the first artificial synthetic skin.

1988: Rudolf Jaenisch and his team announced that they had succeeded in implanting a hereditary human disease in mice — which would help the study of such diseases and improve treatment. I bet the mice would like to give those doctors a few mouse diseases. Mousecular Dystrophy?

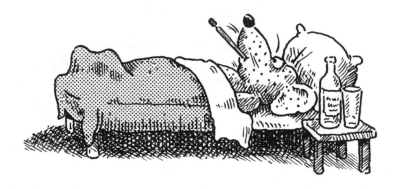

Whose Genes?

About 3,000 human diseases are caused by specific genes. Simple, find the gene and solve the problem. The trouble is, each of us contains about 2,000,000 genes and if that wasn't bad enough, each of us has different ones.

It is possible, however, to locate bits of the DNA molecule using a method, far too complicated to explain, called southern blotting. If some of your family are unfortunate enough to have a genetic disease you probably won't know which gene is causing it. You can compare the identifiable pieces of DNA from those who've got it and those who haven't. Often there's a bit of this identifiable DNA that is inherited with the gene for the disease. This makes the DNA a marker for the gene, and by separating and testing different chromosomes our scientists can use this marker to locate the chromosome on which the naughty gene is hiding.

This is where it all gets a bit tricky. Knowing the marker for a gene isn't as good as knowing the gene itself, but with persistence the gene can sometimes be found and copied. This is called cloning and the process, although still in its early stages, is already leading to loads of clinical applications. A huge effort started in the USA in 1988 to map all the genes relating to human beings. The trouble is that as individuals are being examined, all their genes, good and bad, are being revealed. On one side this is good, as deficiencies can be spotted and their children can be monitored accordingly. On the flip side, insurance companies are watching like vultures and vetting people before they're even born.

CHEMISTRY

To the general public in the twentieth century, chemistry has ceased to be our friend, having become a sort of monster that we cannot hold down. Every development that looked like making our lives easier and more comfortable is now showing signs of having terrify-

ing side effects. The use of herbicides and pesticides seems to be poisoning our rivers and wildlife. Aerosols, though hugely convenient, also seem to be busy destroying the ozone layer, which could eventually give us the ultimate suntan. Additives to make our food tastier, look brighter, and last longer, seem to be slowly killing us. Factories churning out all the consumer junk that we've convinced ourselves we can't live without are causing rain that would be an improvement on the acid in our car batteries. It is unfair, however, to blame the scientists. All they have ever done is to discover or invent. The use to which we put their work has to be down to us.

Some Major Breakthroughs in Chemistry 1946 to the Present

1949: English biochemist Dorothy Crowfoot was the first to use a computer to fathom out the structure of an organic chemical penicillin. She went on, a few years later, to use it to work out the structure of vitamin B12.

1950: The artificial sweetener cyclamate was introduced. This seemed like great news until artificial sweeteners came under scrutiny as a cause of cancer.

1952: Glenn Seaborg discovered einsteinium (the artificial element with the daftest name). It had an atomic number of 99 and was found in the debris of the first thermonuclear explosion.
Choh Hao Li isolated the human-growth hormone.

1962: Neil Bartlett of Newcastle demonstrated that compounds could be formed that include the so-called noble gases (thought not to enter any form of molecule) by preparing a concoction called xenon platinum hexafluoride. It had always been thought that these noble gases were far too grand to combine with any other atoms to form molecules.

1977: You've heard, no doubt, of racehorse doping. Alan Geeger and Alan MacDiarmid were into iodine doping which made poly-acetylene an electrical conductor.

1981: At last the sun is really beginning to work for us. Heller, Miller and Theil invented a liquid junction cell that could convert

11.5 per cent of solar energy to usable electricity.

1984: Garlic was found to contain a compound that almost certainly thinned the blood. You might not have any friends (including vampires), but at least your blood would be OK.

1988: If you think chemistry might become simpler the more we learn, just consider that there are 400,000 new compounds discovered every year. To date there are 10,000,000 specific compounds kicking around.

PHYSICS

While the chemists seem to be coming up with more things that can eventually kill the planet, the physicists had already got there with the two nuclear bombs that were exploded at the end of the Second World War. Huge amounts of cash were chucked into physical research after the war, especially in the areas of nuclear and particle physics. Later, governments realized how important physics could become in manufacturing, especially things like transistors and lasers.

As physics became more and more complex with the study of atoms, sub-atomic particles, quantum electrodynamics, etc., it was discovered that many things didn't act as predicted, a development of the quantum theorum of the previous chapter. This was worked into a theory called 'strangeness' and whole bunches of boffin-words started to appear, like 'quarks', 'flavours' and 'WIMPS' (weakly interacting massive particles).

'Strangeness' and all these new particles were lumped together and classified in a scheme called the 'eightfold way'. It could be explained by abstract maths (not by me, I hasten to add) rather than a physical understanding of how the thing worked.

In 1964 a chap called Murray Gell-Mann cracked it and came up with an explanation called the aforementioned 'quark model' although nothing was proved until 1977.

In 1976 a concept had begun to unravel called supergravity

which involved the brain-warping idea of a ten- or eleven-dimensional universe. I couldn't get my head round Einstein's four!

ASTRONOMY

In the 1940s Hale's telescope was built on Mount Palomar and was the best ever seen. It still is, though they reckon that could all change in the 90s. When radio astronomy took off in the 1950s, the universe was found to be twice as big as the astronomers had thought, and there was still some sneaking doubt as to whether it existed in a steady state of continual creation or had started with the Big Bang.

The sixties saw all the nearer planets being explored with satellites and space probes, as well as the surprises of the quasars and pulsars. Still, there was no evidence to discredit the Big Bang theory, even when, in the seventies, theoretical physics and astronomy came even closer.

Black holes were all the rage. Objects (probably collapsed stars) so big and dense that nothing, not even light, could help being sucked in by their terrific gravitational pull. Of course, with all these satellites and spacecraft whizzing about, it became possible to look even closer at things by having the telescopes on board. Mind you, even if it were possible, cruising near a black hole makes the Bermuda triangle seem like a picnic.

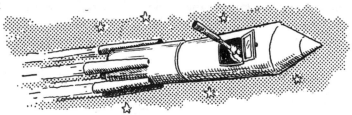

It must be said that space travel by proper spacemen, instead of a whole menagerie of hapless animals, was the great success of the sixties. Although spacecraft had been darting around since 1957, visiting Venus, Mars, Mercury, Eastbourne, Jupiter and Saturn (guess the odd one out), there's nothing like having a real live guy on board, and the punters loved it. Space travel was headline news for a few years and astronauts, and even some astronomers, were revered like rock stars.

After the Americans had succeeded in dropping someone on the moon, all their efforts went into producing a spacecraft that would function like a common-or-garden airliner (overcrowded, delayed?). This went well until Challenger, a US space shuttle, blew up on take-off and killed seven brave (or crazy) astronauts.

The Russians were more into fixing up home from home space stations in orbit which ended up with dizzy Soviets spending months going round and round the Earth. Now they're all swapped round. The Ruskies want a shuttle and the Yanks want a space station. It wouldn't take the brightest cosmic wheeler-dealer to work out some sort of arrangement.

All this space stuff isn't just pie in the sky, however, as the rewards to us little humanlings have been great. Communication satellites have reduced the world to the size of a pea, making the Earth a true global village (if we could only stop killing each other). Weather satellites have finally put paid to bits of seaweed. These days they almost always get the weather forecast right. Well, almost! Satellites can find lost planes and ships and even the odd, daft explorer stranded in some wilderness or other.

Like all things, there's the other side. Your average enemy can use satellites to spy on things that you'd prefer not to be seen, and rockets carrying horrendous fusion bombs are sitting ready and waiting to make us all into just another few specks in the universe.

Some Great Breakthroughs in Astronomy 1946 to the Present

1946: A V2 took a day off from terrorizing the British and carried a spectrograph up 34 miles to take a closer peek at the sun.

1949: American astronomer Fred Whipple suggested that comets are just dirty snowballs consisting of ice and rock dust (ouch!).

Tee-hee, the Americans captured a German V2 rocket and shoved a smaller one on top of it. This became the first multiple-stage rocket and soared to 240 miles, way above the atmosphere (and the cross Germans).

1951: Dutchman Dirk Brouwer was the first astronomer to take all the data from 1653, shove it on a computer and calculate planetary orbits. He even predicted ahead to 2060, though I doubt we'll be around to argue.

1957: Up goes a Sputnik, the first artificial satellite, launched by those clever Ruskies. Almost immediately a dog goes for the longest walk ever, trapped in Sputnik 2.

1958: The Russians thought they'd spotted a volcano on the moon. The oh-so-smart Americans were to derive a great deal of pleasure years later when they went up to have a look and proved them wrong.

Wernher von Braun, now safely working for the enemy in America, launched the first satellite to orbit the earth.

1959: The Russian satellite Luna 1 (renamed 'Dream') was widely hailed as the first artificial planet, when it completely missed the moon (where it was going) and ended up orbiting the sun. I hardly think that's something to write home about.

Thick and fast now, Luna 2 crash-lands on the moon and Luna 3 returns the first pictures of the far side. Guess what? It looked much the same as this side.

1960: Frank Drake ran a 400-hour project to attempt to find extra-terrestrial life in the universe. He, as you might imagine, didn't find any, unlike his ancestor of the same name.

1961: Yuri Gagarin went down in history as the first man in space. He orbited the earth for 108 minutes then came home for tea.

Al Shepard, not to be outdone, shot up in Mercury 3 and stayed up for 15 minutes. From then on, various Russians and Americans whiled away many a happy hour looking down on us mere Earthpersons.

1962: The Russians sent up their first Mars probe but promptly lost it.

The US space probe Mariner 2 took a trip to Venus to become the first man-made object to reach another planet.

1963: Alan Sadage discovered that galaxy M82 was undergoing a ginormous explosion. No need to panic, however, he reckoned it had been going on for 1.5 million years.

Valentina Tereshkova Nikolayeva was the first woman in space doing 48 orbits in 78 hours.

1964: US space probe Ranger 2 took the first good close-up snaps of the moon. 4,316 pictures to prove it's not made of green cheese.

1965: Trust Venus to be different. It was discovered to go round in the opposite direction to other planets. So the sun rises in the West and sets in the East.

A. Leonov took the first walk 'outside' his spacecraft wearing just his spacesuit. What, I ask, did they expect the poor Russian would be wearing? A fur hat?

1966: The Soviet spacecraft Luna 9 made the first soft landing on the moon. It touched down gingerly on the so-called Ocean of Storms. In the same year they sent up Luna 10 which orbited the moon.

Jocelyn Bell spotted the very first pulsar CP1919 but her boss Anthony Hewish got all the credit and a share of the Nobel Prize (men!). Poor Jocelyn didn't get a look in. In 1968, the first signals from the pulsar were taken to be from 'little green men' but it was soon shown that it came from a neutron star revolving really fast. What a shame!

Surveyor 11 from the States dug a little moon-trench and sent the pictures back to Earth. Everyone thought it looked a bit like Earth soil, but they were a bit off the mark. They did, however, report back that it was safe to walk on, which turned out to be correct.

1968: Borman, Lovell and Anders achieved the impossible – orbited the moon, and came back.

1969: Two Soviet space vehicles Soyuz 4 and 5 meet up, dock, exchange crews and come home, so breaking the world record for the most expensive pointless exercise.

The race is won. American Neil Armstrong became the first man to stand on the moon, Buzz Aldrin was right behind him. The other crew member stayed back on the spaceship, probably getting lunch ready.

1971: Alan Shepard and his crew got digging on the moon and brought back 98lbs of moon rocks. As if we hadn't got enough rocks at home.

Mars posed for the camera when Mariner 9 orbited. Unfortunately, Mars wasn't looking its best, being covered by a huge dust storm. Eventually some really good snaps came back and everyone was happy.

1972: Pioneer 10 became the first US space probe, or any other for that matter, to leave our solar system.

1973: The Americans sent up a Skylab. Three crews visited to do medical and other experiments. It re-entered the atmosphere in 1979 and some debris fell to Earth in Western Australia. Luckily no one was on board and, even luckier, no one was underneath.

1975: As the Vietnam war ends, the Russians and the Americans finally pool their resources and start working together. The Apollo-Soyuz test project carried out full docking operations.

1981: Joe Cassinelli discovered the most ginormous star ever seen. He called it, rather unimaginatively, R136a. It turned out to be 2,500 times bigger than our sun and 100 times brighter. I must go out and try a little R136a-bathing.

The first flight of the STS–I Columbia (later known as the Space Shuttle) was tested by Young and Crippen (sounds ominous). In the next year or so several shuttles were sent up and brought down, until 1986 when Challenger blew up killing its seven crew. The flights resumed in 1988.

1984: McCarthy and Low discover a 'cool' companion to the star called Van Biesbroeck 8 at a distance of eight million light years from us. This, I agree, sounds like pure rock and roll.

On the fourth Challenger mission, two loonies went out wearing jet-propelled back packs. It was the first time anyone had left a spacecraft unattached. On the same mission two satellites were lost.

1985: The construction of the hugest telescope ever seen, the Keck, began on the top of a Hawaiian mountain. Its mirror was 33ft across. I bet that's bigger than Madonna's.

1986: Science fiction looms again. A team of seven astronomers discovered that our galaxy, local galaxies and local superclusters of galaxies are being drawn towards 'The Great Attracter' in the direction of the Southern Cross. God knows who or what the Great Attracter is. Maybe Madonna again.

1987: Late-sleeper Ian Shelton was looking at the night sky on 24 February when he saw the nearest supernova to Earth since 1604. It became known as 1987A (original) and had once been the star Sk69.202. Neutrinos (uncharged particles with zero mass) from the explosion had reached the Earth the day before.

1989: Scientists travelling in an ordinary aeroplane looked out of the window and observed the atmosphere of Pluto, hitherto only suspected to exist. Don't ask me how they knew it was Pluto.

1991: Stop press! A planet about the size of Jupiter has been seen in orbit around another star by scientists at Jodrell Bank, England. The significance, if the find is confirmed, is enormous. It means that if one star in the Milky Way can have an orbiting planet, then maybe even thousands can. Still not impressed? Well, this really opens up the possibility that there is quite a chance that life-bearing planets might exist – and not that far away (well, if you call 180,000,000,000,000,000 miles not that far away).

EARTH SCIENCE

After the Second World War scientists suddenly got to grips with understanding the Earth's crust. Geologists worked out that it was broken into a number of plates all moving about relative to each other, which explained such things as earthquakes, volcanoes, mountains and rifts in the ocean floor (which all happened when the plates carelessly collided).

Meteorology is another bit of earth science. With all those satellites whizzing about, and radar as well, weather forecasts got much better. Computers were becoming quite sophisticated, which in 1961 helped Edward Lorenz establish that even weeny changes in initial conditions result in the weather going barmy. Scientists looking at long-term changes have noticed that all those nasty gases that we filthy humans give off are beginning to muck up the atmosphere. The 'greenhouse effect' is causing the poor old world's temperature to rise, probably because of carbon dioxide and other horrid gases trapping heat (just like the average greenhouse).

As mentioned before, our ozone layer that's kindly been protecting us from the bits of the sunshine that turn you brown, is thinning rapidly (like Elton John's hair!).

Some Great Breakthroughs in Earth Science 1946 to the Present

1952: James Alfred van Allen developed the rockoon, a rocket launched from a balloon (not a hip rodent) to poke around in the upper atmosphere.

1957: Frederick Lindemann (later Viscount Cherwell) somehow found out that the upper stratosphere is warmer than the lower layers of the atmosphere.

1958: Bachus and Herzenberg proved that the Earth's got a sort of dynamo in it, which creates a magnetic field.

1959: The US weather bureau started the temperature/humidity index as a way of judging how uncomfortable a hot summer day is. Goodness knows why anyone needed some bureau to tell them when to sweat or not!

1965: Jacques Cousteau's team of damp aquanauts surfaced after spending 23 days at a depth of 330 feet in the Mediterranean. I would imagine their air might have been running out.

1967: A team of scientists discovered that practically half the floor of the mid-Atlantic ocean consists of dust blown from Africa and Europe. I suppose that if Homo habilis (handyman) had had Hoovers, we wouldn't now have a mid-Atlantic ocean.

THIS COULD RE-WRITE HISTORY!

1968: Elso S. Barghoorn and his mates found amino acids in some three-billion-year-old rocks – perhaps the first sign of life.

1976: Next time you use a spray can, check that it's ozone friendly. In this year the US National Academy of Sciences reported that Freon, used in various aerosols, was chipping away at the ozone layer. A year later, chlorofluorocarbons were banned as spray propellants in the States. Was it too late we ask ourselves?

1980: Walter Alvarez and his clever chums found a funny layer of clay enriched with the heavy metal iridium in the Earth's crust. From this they reckoned that something big and nasty from space collided with us causing not only all this metally clay but the end of all our brill dinosaurs.

1982: If you were living up Mexico way and wondered why it wasn't quite as sunny as usual, it was probably because El Chichon (a mean hombre of a volcano) had just sent up loads of dust into the stratosphere. It hung around up there for over three years.

1984: Russians are very good at digging holes, their best place was called Kola and was 7.5 miles deep reaching the Earth's lower crust. I bet those poor Ruskies needed a Coke after a dig like that!

1985: The British Antarctic Survey found this horrible hole in the ozone layer over Antarctica. It had been growing for years. That's the trouble with holes.

1986: A Dominican miner in the La Toca amber mine found a dead frog. So what? you might think. The only thing different about it was that it was 35 to 40 million years old (and had croaked).

1987: Kevin Aulenback discovered a group of dinosaur eggs containing lots of little fossilized unhatched duck-billed dinosaurs. A quacking dinosaur?

The oldest-ever embryo of any kind, an allosaur (a kind of dinosaur), was discovered by Wade Miller. The poor little chap was less than an inch long.

TECHNOLOGY

New developments come in two different types. Velcro, for instance, solves a particular problem, whilst the laser is far more generalized and affects all kinds of things. Many new technologies have run riot in the last forty or so years changing our everyday lives far more than others. For example, since the war cars, although still having 4 wheels, an engine and a few seats, have improved no end, with the addition of steering, fuel injection, pollen and dust filters and, more importantly, leopard-skin seat covers and nodding dogs. Many items that weren't even a twinkle in the inventor's eye 50 years ago, are now becoming part of everyday life. I mean, how could we now live without personal stereos, fax machines, photocopiers and magnetic cat flaps?

I suppose it's fair to say, however, that the major contributions to our present well-being (technology-wise) have been solid-state electronics and digital computers. The transistor allowed the computer's plentiful offspring to become smaller and much cheaper. A computer that once cost millions of pounds and practically filled

231

an aircraft hangar can now fit into a shopping bag and give you change from 500 quid. Computer language (whatever that is) wasn't seen or heard until 1956 and the keyboard, which I'm working on now, arrived ten years later. If radios and televisions carry on shrinking we'll all need blinking magnifying glasses to see them. But who knows what the future may bring? There's probably some clever little Japanese chappie working on a machine right now that will be able to tell us just that.

Some Great Breakthroughs in Technology 1946 to the Present

1946: John Logie Baird died this year. We all know he gave us the telly but did you know he had also invented a gizmo that can find things in the dark? A mechanical nose?

Frenchman Louis Reard had this brilliant idea. He called it the bikini because he reckoned that it would cause as much of a fuss as the American atomic bomb, which had been exploded on the Bikini Atoll in the Pacific four days earlier. None of his models would wear it so he had to employ some rude dancers from the Casino de Paris.

The ejector seat was first tested by Bernard Lynch who flew through the roof of his Meteor at 82,000 feet. Anyone needing a similar test pilot, please don't ring me.

Frothy coffee, although first seen in the late nineteenth century, disappeared until 1946 when the Italian company Gaggia (who still supply most restaurants) invented a machine to make it.

1947:   Peter Goldmark of CBS Records in the States perfected the LP to replace the old 78s. The first recording was from the musical *South Pacific*. As far as I'm concerned it just prolonged the agony.

Ever since time began, people have been trying to create rain. At first, your average native would jump up and down and wave spears, but later in the eighteenth and nineteenth centuries they tried 'bursting' the clouds with cannon balls. Many opportunists, like American Dan Ruggles in 1880, would try to produce rain just when it looked likely to rain anyway. In 1947 the first practical technique was developed by Bernard Vonnegut, a leading cloud physicist (can you believe it). He sprayed the clouds with silver iodide crystals, which then served as nuclei for snowflakes.

1948:   After a walk in the woods with his dog, Swiss engineer George de Mestral noticed the poor critter was covered from nose to tail with burrs from the bushes. He looked closely at how they were attached and promptly invented the fastener Velcro. He became very attached to the dog after this.

If you had been at Yale University around this time, you'd have noticed some strange students throwing aluminium flan cases at each other. They'd bought them from a local baker who, by the way, was called Joseph Frisbie. Need I say more.

Edwin Land launched the instant camera, called Polaroid, in America. Kodak had shown no interest, but when they saw its huge success, launched their own version in 1976. Polaroid Corporation sued them for patent violation and after some of the longest proceedings in history won $1,000,000,000 in damages. Not exactly instant retribution.

If your idea of fun is strapping yourself to a large kite and flinging yourself off a cliff, then you'll be interested to note that the hang-glider was invented this year by Francis Rogallo.

1949:   Prepared cake-mixes hit the States for the first time.

1950:   One of the daftest-looking sports, artistic skiing, was

invented this year by silly Swede, Stein Eriksen. (Mind you, all Swedes are called Eriksen.) Artistic skiing looks about as graceful as a ballerina wearing wellies.

The dreaded credit card was first introduced by Diners Club of America. Things have got to such a pitch in the US these days, that actual folding, no-nonsense cash, is frowned upon.

1951: Why did the zebra cross the road? To stop cars from running us down. The first zebra-crossing was seen in the UK.

Univac 1 wasn't a cleaner, but the first commercially available electronic computer, and the first to store data on magnetic tape.

The first nuclear reactor was developed near Idaho Falls in the USA. Britain uses less than 17 per cent of nuclear-derived electricity, far less than other European countries.

1952: The first use of a transistor instead of a vacuum tube was in a hearing aid – A HEARING AID!

1954: Where else could TV dinners be introduced but the USA? Now the average American didn't have to leave his armchair at all, except for the obvious. I'm surprised no one has thought of bringing back the commode.

1955: The deep-freeze was introduced into the States this year. Another good reason for only going out once every few months.

Back in 1950 Christopher Cockerell reckoned he could make boats go faster by using the wife's vacuum cleaner. He cut a hole in the bottom of an old punt and made the cleaner blow instead of suck (otherwise he might have drowned). This cut the friction between the hull of the boat and the water. He refined the idea for years, then launched the first Hovercraft which blew the world sideways (and the boat forwards). There's now talk of huge hover-ships driven by atomic power.

Mickey Mouse was sixty in 1989. Lots of him can be seen at the Los Angeles Disneyland which opened to rapturous applause in 1955. It was the first theme park, invented by the late, great Walt Disney.

A Danish carpenter, Ole Christianson, designed some kids' building-bricks called Lego. Now just about every modern architect seems to be copying him. Chelsea Harbour, London – for instance.

1956: Now there's clever – and CLEVER! Stanislaw Ulam programmed a computer to play chess. The programme aptly called Maniac I enabled the computer to beat a human for the first time. That's nothing, a not-too-bright chimp could beat me.

1958: The unbelievably sexless Barbie-doll was marketed in the States by the Mattel Company. It became a plastic role model for millions of American pre-teenage girls. She was the first doll to have an adult body though, ask as I might, I can't find out just how 'adult' she was. The same goes for her boyfriend, Ken, who looks like a demented transvestite. I have a feeling they might have used the same mould for him as they did for his girlfriend. No wonder Americans have so many sexual hangups. Mind you, in England we have Sindy and Paul who even have their own fan club . . .

Peter Chivers, an English Rolls-Royce mechanic, invented the wind surfer, but had no interest in selling the idea on. It wasn't until 1968 that two American surfers started producing it commercially.

1960: Astroturf, a sort of artificial grass, was laid at the Astro-dome at Houston. Hayfever sufferers love it.

The first laser (using a ruby cylinder) was developed by Theodore Maimen of Los Angeles, California. It was first used medically in 1964 for treatment of lesions on the retina (foreign lesions?).

Materials that can remember their original shape began in the sixties. Thanks to this so-called memory, they can go back to the shape they were when they reach the temperature at which they were originally moulded. This development stayed dormant for years until the space industry took it up. Two patents are now granted every day. In 1988 the Japanese Walcoal Company started selling a flat bar that contained an alloy wire that remembered the shape it was when it was last worn. Mammaries are made of this!

This was the era of the back-combed hair. The L'Oréal laboratories developed the first hair lacquer which, when sprayed on, formed an invisible net which held the dreadful hairstyle in place, but disappeared when brushed out. It also, probably, helped make the hole bigger in the ozone layer.

1961: The tape cassettes which we know and love were designed by the Dutch company, Philips. They decided, kindly, to allow other manufacturers to have free use of the patent to encourage the spread of their system throughout the world.

If you ever want to get out of a sticky situation use a rocket belt. This was invented by Wendel More and can take you instantly 65 feet into the clouds!

1962: The first industrial robot packed its sandwiches and went off to work in the States. In 1983 Yamazaki of Japan gave robots the ability to reproduce themselves (but not the way you think).

The first live TV satellite transmission was between Andover, Maine, and Goonhilly Downs, Cornwall, and was called 'Telstar'. An appalling record of the same name savaged our ears around that time.

1963: The hovercraft went into lawn-mowing with the 'Flymo'.

You probably think that the felt-tip has been around since history began, it was in fact invented by Pentel in 1963.

Emmett Leith and Juris Upatnieks of Michigan University invented this fab method of producing 3-D snaps of an object by using lasers. It became known as the 'hologram'.

1964: Lyndon B. Johnson, top man in the States, announced the existence of an extraordinary plane that could fly at a speed of Mach 3 (2,193.27mph). No 'ordinary' plane has ever beaten this.

1965: Another world-shattering invention, the miniskirt, was created by London dress designer, Mary Quant. The French ripped it off (not literally) but called the new style haute couture ('high' fashion). Mary's clothes were worn by everyone (well, mostly women).

1967: Bad year for the insect community. The US Department of Agriculture started a test project that zapped insects while lunching on wheat or other crops.

R. M. Dolby starts taking the hiss. He developed a method of eliminating background sound in tape recording.

1968: The first power station to use the power of the tide was built at the estuary of the river Rance in the Gulf of St Malo. It now produces 544 million kilowatts of electricity every year.

1969: Stock Car Racing: The rather aesthetic sport of thrashing old cars round a track until they are smashed to bits, started in the United States. The object of the exercise is to be the last car still able to move. Sounds like Friday night on the M25.

1970: Flying elephants? The first 'jumbo jet', the Boeing 747 took many more happy punters across the Atlantic.

The fabulous floppy disc was introduced as a portable storage unit for computer data.

1972: American Howard Wilcox put forward the idea of using seaweed to produce methane. He reckoned that if a 'field' of seaweed 530 miles long could be cultivated in the ocean, the entire annual gas consumption of America could be produced. No one, unfortunately, took the idea up. The only other use for seaweed I ever see these days is as a rather whacky veg. in Chinese restaurants.

1975: Have you ever seen a Parisian homme's bathroom? There are usually enough creams and lotions to put Zsa Zsa Gabor to shame. Facial preparations for men were introduced by the Parisian Yves St Laurent in this year.

1976: Charles William Clark, an English eccentric inventor, patented a car powered by a giant elastic-band. I feel a Skoda joke coming on.

1977: If you thought that sounded daft, Paul McCready got people interested in his Gossamer Condor (I said condoR!) which was the first aircraft to fly by pedal power. Mind you, we all laughed on the other side of our face, when Paul's next pedal plane 'cycled' across the English Channel.

1979: The infuriating cube that drove everyone round the bend ten years ago was invented by the now extremely rich Hungarian, Erno Rubik. You don't get many millionaires up Hungary way, but flogging a hundred million of those stupid cubes sure did it for our Erno.

1981: The IBM personal computer, using DOS as its standard disk-operating-system, was introduced this year.
Name a game that has sold fifty million copies in nine years and made three young Canadians embarrassingly rich? Answer – Trivial Pursuit. What colour 'cheese' does that get you?

1983: A very special mouse was born. It was the one used first by Apple computers to chase a cursor around the screen and tell the machine what to do.

1983: Want to impress your chums? Borrow Henk Vink's rocket-powered motorbike one evening. It does 248mph, but has to be stopped by parachute, which might look a bit daft in the average street.

One of the most weird (but beautiful) pieces of machinery ever seen, is the 'Stealth' bomber, developed by Northrop for the US army. It looks like a huge flying wing and is called invisible. Not because it can't be seen, but because it's made of such strange materials that radar can't pick it up. Also it gives off no heat, which fools the infra-red detectors. If you want one, give me a ring. I can get it for $520 million (which just leaves $4 million for my trouble).

1984: You can at last buy a parasol that you can sunbathe under, safe from the harmful glare. It's made from Solmax which cuts out 90 per cent of the horrid rays, but lets through 75 per cent of the groovy ones that turn you brown. Thanks be to John Sear and J. A. Cuthbert.

The first parasite farm was started in 1984. A dear little insect, called Encarsia formosa, was reared. It loved eating the insects that loved eating the tomatoes and cucumbers which we loved eating.

H. S. Song, a Malaysian, invented talking bathroom scales. You'd have thought they could sing too.

YOU MUST BE JOKING !!!

1986: So you think you're pretty quick on a bike. Well, Fred Marckham rode his specially designed boneshaker at 65.48 miles per hour.

The latest burglar alarm was invented, based on the recording of a British Bulldog, which only went off when a human was nearby. Obviously, it didn't need much care and couldn't eat children when out for a walk. It was invented by Dutchman A. van de Haar.

Nicorette (which are not small undergarments) were invented to help smokers give up. They are a nicotine-based chewing gum, supposed to ease the craving for tobacco. Some people who tried Nicorette in order to stop smoking became addicted to them — AS WELL!

1987: Sometimes I think I'm a bit on the slow side. The New Numerical Aerodynamic Simulation Facility, a rather bright super-computer, used to simulate flight, managed 1,720,000,000 computations a second. Easy Peasy!

A surgical laser, which is as easy to use as a pencil, was invented by Professor Jean Lemaire in France. Just imagine what a nasty weapon that would make if it got into the wrong hands. I can almost see the movie now.

Massimo Osti created this rather fab jacket out of crystals which changed colour as the temperature dropped. White went to blue (I know the feeling), pink to khaki, and yellow to green, as soon as the leaves started to fall.

How could we ever have lived without an umbrella that has a light inside. It was invented in California (where else?) by Lawrence Lansing.

1988: An incredible helmet has been developed in France that actually electronically treats the noise coming to it. It can bring down noise levels by 20–40 decibels. Its future might well lie in silencing cars (and Cilla Black?).

Just as the American Strategic Defense Initiative have got to grips with their new killer laser, which can bring down enemy missiles at the press of a button, they begin working on the antidote. The California-based company Harlamor-Schadek are developing a material called laser shield.

The perfect crime. Some naughty American inventors came up with a cheque which self-destructs a short time after being cashed. They've cost banks $70,000 this year alone. No comment!

Having trouble feeding your koala bear? I've been told that

eucalyptus, their favourite food, is hard to find in the Australian winter. Worry no more – there's now a biscuit which the little dears love, developed by scientists after years of research.

Roland Winston tested a new mirror system that concentrated sunlight 60,000 times. It will be used to discover all sorts of new materials and a new breed of lasers. I don't think there's much future in the suntanning business.

Scott Shakespeare was born without a left arm (or hand!), so he developed, in California, the 'Simplistic Hand'. It not only looks like a real hand, with veins and finger-prints (whose, I wonder?), but can give a very realistic handshake too. Best of all, it's actually cheaper than the rather embarrassing electronic hands that went before.

1990: It all started with the video cat. Why have all the trouble of owning a moggie when 'Creative Programming' can offer you a video cat which you can watch for hours and then turn the damn thing off. I somehow think they might just be missing the point somewhat. Having said that, the idea's been a huge success and the company's now doing the same thing with babies. Now that's different!

1993: Stop Press! The Norwegian Tikkeo Cruise Line have ordered a liner from Harland and Wolff the British shipyard. The hugest cruiser ever seen, called the *Ultimate Dream*, it should carry 3,026 passengers, have 12 swimming pools and a 1,500-seat cinema. Afraid it's not that ultimate; even more spectacular is the Phoenix project, also Norwegian, which will be literally a floating island carrying 5,600 passengers. Based in Florida, it will bob around the Caribbean. If you can't take a boat to an island – take the island itself. Some people are never satisfied.

Which I suppose sums up the whole book . . .

Index

acetylene, 184
acupuncture, 8
adrenalin, 170
aeroplanes, 186, 189–90, 199, 237, 239, *see also* flying machines
aerosols, 196, 219, 230
agriculture, 2–3, 7–9, 13, 45, 203, 210
alchemy, 41–2, 43, 48, 56
alcohol, 8, 42, 43, 54, 78, 126, 170, 174, 214–15
alum, 56
aluminium, 134
ambulances, 110
amino acid, 170, 230
anaesthetic, 39, 126, 127, 132, 184
animals, 2, 6–7, 8, 153, 170, 171
anthropology, 115, 164–6, 204–8
antibiotics, 130, 181
antihistamine, 185
aqualung, 199
archaeology, 115, 164–6, 204–8
asbestos, 43
aspirin, 128
assembly line, 192–3
astigmatism, 130
astrology, 4, 9, 22, 39, 48
astronomy, 3–5, 21–4, 37–9, 49–53, 93–4, 118–21, 167–8, 222–8
Astroturf, 235
atmospheric pressure, 77
atomic bomb, 160, 177–8, 200–1, 221
atomic theory, 16, 22, 27, 89, 133, 174, 176

bacteria, 124, 125–6, 130, 131, 183
ball-bearings, 61
balloons, 108–9, 150, 151, 156, 178, 188, 224
barbed wire, 155
barbiturates, 137
barometer, 59
baths, 14
bathysphere, 180

bazooka, 199
beer, 8, 197
bicycles, 109–10, 187, 239
Big Bang theory, 167, 168, 222
biochemistry, 169–73
biology, 39, 54, 71–3, 121–6, 169–73, 208–13
black holes, 222
blood, 26, 54, 55, 89, 72, 74, 128, 182, 184, 185, 205, 217
boats, 13, 31, 77, 78, 151, 191–2
bombs, 46, 150, 160
boomerang, 12
botany, 39
bra, 193
Braille, 148
brain, 24, 74, 129–30, 183, 210, 218
breakfast cereal, 158–9
bricks, 12, 149
Brownian motion, 140
building techniques, 10, 12, 147, 149, 206
burglar alarm, 239–40
buttons, 14

Caesarean operation, 54
cake-mixes, 233
calculator, 63, 158
calculus, 69
calendar, development of, 3–4, 21, 22, 32, 37, 93
camera, 157, 233
camera obscura, 61
cancer, 74, 87, 182, 215, 216
candles, 13, 133
cannon, 47, *see also* guns
carbolic, 130
cars, 147, 152, 157, 186, 192–4, 197, 198, 231, 237, 238
cash register, 156
catapults, 30–1, 32
cathode ray tubes, 114–15, 139
cathode rays, 143, 176
cats' eyes, 197
cell biology, 115, 122
celluloid, 137
Chain of Being, 83
chain reactions, 137

Charles's Law, 101
chemistry, 41, 48, 56, 75–6, 89–92, 133–8, 174–5, 219–21
chemotherapy, 216
cheques, self-destructing, 240
chewing gum, 154
childbirth, 40, 54, 185
chinchona bark, 88, 127
chloroform, 127, 217
Christmas card, 151
chromosomes, 125, 127–8, 169, 170
cigarettes, 150, 215, 218, 240
cinema, 186
clocks, 10, 29, 31, 33, 36, 45, 57, 60, 78
clothing, 12, 13, 14, 133, 232
coaches, horse-drawn, 61
coal, 42, 43, 62, 77, 78, 84
Coca-Cola, 187
cocoa, 134
coelacanth, 173, 209, 213
coffee, 44, 198, 232
coke, 62
combustion, 89, 90
comets, 37, 51, 94, 121, 223, *see also* Halley's Comet
compass, 46
computers, 149, 186, 200, 210, 229, 231–2, 234, 235, 238–40
concrete, 32, 33
contact lenses, 132
continental drift, 178, 179
contraceptive pill, 215, 217
cortisone, 214
credit cards, 234
crisps, 193
croissants, 78
crossbow, 47
crosswords, 193
cyclamate, 220

DDT, 137, 202, 203, 212
Dead Sea Scrolls, 205
deep-freeze, 234
dentistry, 14, 42, 75, 86, 109, 126, 215
detergent, 194
diabetes, 39, 74, 181, 214
dictionaries, 29

245

ART:

A COMPLETE AND UTTER HISTORY
(without the bulls**t)

BY

JOHN FARMAN

If you're one of those people who think
Caravaggio is an Italian motor home, or
that **Botticelli** is some kind of pasta, that
Gilbert and George were a sixties' pop group,
and you're baffled by Art in general, then fear not! You too
can be an expert . . .
The author of A VERY BLOODY HISTORY OF BRITAIN
(without the boring bits) continues to debunk the
establishment: from the days before paint was invented,
the HISTORY OF ART makes it's doomed way towards
the present day and **a pile of bricks** in
the Tate Gallery . . .

£9.99
Macmillan